Hidden Pursuit

The Living Oracle

Book Three

Melissa McShane

CHAPTER ONE

When I was a little girl, I'd dreamed of living in a castle, and when Malcolm and I married, my dream came true. More or less. Our house wasn't a castle, but it was three stories tall, with a stone façade and pillared portico and rosebushes beneath all the ground floor windows, which to me was basically the same thing. It had been Malcolm's childhood home, restored and updated when we'd moved in more than eleven years ago, and now I felt I'd lived there forever. I'd had free access to Malcolm's fortune when I decorated it, so the interior was as beautiful as the exterior, but it still felt homey and comfortable. It was my refuge.

Which explained why I was throwing Alastair's ninth birthday party at Jungle Jack's Pizza Emporium.

From where I sat, in one of the many booths lining the walls of the arcade, the dimly-lit room boiled over with small running figures screaming in excitement above the tinny music. There couldn't possibly be as many kids as it appeared, though twenty-three was more than enough. Alastair had kept adding to the list of people he *had* to invite until it amounted to most of his third-grade class, and I, influenced by a barely remembered sense of duty regarding Valentine's cards and not leaving anyone out, had suggested making it a blanket invitation. And now I was supervising twenty-three children hopped up on pizza and soda and buckets of game tokens. The things I did to preserve the peace and quiet of my home.

Someone slid into the bench seat opposite me. "How badly are you regretting this right now?" Judy said. She took a slice of pizza from the open box on the table and bit into it. "Wow, this pizza is terrible."

"Kids don't have a refined enough palate to care." I sipped my Diet Coke and squeezed my eyes shut briefly. "Just half an hour more, and the ordeal is over. Though, honestly, I don't regret it. I like it when Alastair makes connections with his classmates. He has a tendency toward snobbishness—unintentional snobbishness, but even so, I want him not to think of himself as a superior person just because he's smarter than the other kids."

Judy nodded at where Alastair and a blonde girl with her hair in two low ponytails were playing a dual-person arcade game. "He seems to be getting along all right now."

"I don't recognize the girl. She must have been in a different class last year." The game was heavy on fighting, but it wasn't bloody or hyper-violent, so I chose not to make a fuss.

"I'm glad Duncan and Sophia are getting along," Judy said, taking another bite of pizza. "They were playing Skee-Ball and I think Sophia was letting Duncan give her tips. It's so much nicer when they don't fight."

"I agree." My son Duncan and Judy's daughter Sophia, born within weeks of each other, had turned that early commonality into a fierce rivalry that had them friends one day and enemies the next. I hoped they'd outgrow the need to outdo one another, but that wasn't going to happen any time soon.

On the wide game screen, one of the fighters knocked the other one unconscious, and a big "K.O.!" appeared in the middle of the display. Neither Alastair nor the girl looked disappointed, so I couldn't tell who'd won. Both of them patted pockets, apparently looking for tokens and not finding them. Then Alastair turned, searching the crowd, and his eye fell on me.

"Mom!" he shouted, racing toward me. "I need two tokens. Liv and I are out and we want just one more game, okay? But hurry before the timer runs out!"

Smiling, I plucked two tokens from my reserve and handed them over. Alastair darted away again. "Liv," I said. "That's the girl he and Kenny were talking about. A new student they did a project with."

"New student?" Judy asked with her mouth full.

"Wow, you're sure packing it away for someone who hates the pizza."

"It's something to do." Judy swallowed and sucked down Diet Dr. Pepper. "Didn't some of the parents stay to help supervise? Maybe Liv's mom or dad is here."

"I'll go take a look. I'm curious now. Alastair doesn't have a lot of friends who are girls." I left my drink and token cup at the table and circled the arcade, looking for parents. I hadn't paid attention when the kids arrived to whose parents stayed, so I might not have noticed a stranger.

But I came across her almost immediately, an unfamiliar woman with chin-length blonde hair standing where she could watch Alastair and Liv's game. My first impression was that she was too dressed up for Jungle Jack's, though I didn't know why; she wore jeans and a lightweight jacket just like everyone else. Then I caught sight of her necklace, an extra-long affair of chunky dough-nut-shaped amber rings and small dark faceted beads that caught the low light and let off occasional glints. It was pretty in a very elegant, expensive way and was far too opulent for the T-shirt she wore beneath her jacket, but she made it look chic instead of overdone.

I told myself to stop judging strangers on their accessory choices and approached her. "Hi! Are you Liv's mom?"

The woman jerked, startled, then laughed a little self-consciously. "I am. Are you Mrs. Campbell?"

"Please, call me Helena. Are you new to Talbott Academy?"

The woman nodded. "We moved here just at the start of the school year. I'm Maddy Hubbard."

"It's good to meet you. Alastair and Liv certainly seem to have hit it off." They'd finished another round, or so I assumed because I couldn't see the screen anymore, and had run off in search of something that didn't require tokens.

"Yes, Liv says Alastair is interested in science, particularly space exploration. It's all Liv ever talks about, space, I mean." Maddy pushed her hair behind her ear in a restless gesture. "I'm surprised. Don't kids usually separate their friendships by gender?"

"I was thinking exactly that. When I was their age, boys thought girls had cooties." We both laughed, and I added, "It's nice to see things have changed."

"I agree," Maddy said. "Is Alastair your only child?"

"He's my oldest, and then there's Duncan, who is running around here somewhere, and Jenny, who is with her father at a classic car show. They both love cars."

"Really?" Maddy perked up. "My husband Bronson is into classic cars. His Firebird is his pride and joy."

"I'd suggest getting Bronson and Malcolm together, but experience tells me we'd never see either of them again," I said with a laugh.

"That's probably true," Maddy said. Some of the animation had gone out of her, and she had stiffened, just enough for me to notice. She was scanning the crowd, searching for someone.

"I think Alastair and Liv are at Skee-Ball, watching Duncan," I offered.

Sure enough, she relaxed when she had eyes on Liv. "Is Duncan the little blond boy with the surprisingly high score?"

"Yes, that's him, and no, he didn't get that score by climbing on the machine and dropping balls by hand into the high point hole." I watched Duncan square up the way I'd taught him, but he didn't roll the ball immediately, just stood there staring into space. I froze. "I should just—"

Then Duncan shook himself and made his throw. It bounced awkwardly and sank into the gutter. Duncan shrugged and gathered up his pile of tickets while Sophia did the same with her smaller pile. But instead of running to redeem the tickets, Duncan came straight to me. "Mommy, I have to go to the bathroom," he announced. "Will you take me?"

I was aware of Maddy Hubbard staring at me and could practically hear her thinking about the weird little boy who was clearly old enough to go to the bathroom by himself. We were going to have to come up with a better code phrase. "Let's take these to Aunt Judy, and I'm sure you can go by yourself. Excuse me, Maddy."

I hustled Duncan to the table where the pizza was almost gone. "What did you see?" I murmured as we walked.

"Alastair," Duncan said. "He's going to have a prophecy and try to act on it, only he'll get himself in trouble. It's going to happen just before we leave."

I suppressed a profanity—Duncan already knew way too many swear words for a six-year-old—and gathered up the tickets to pile them on the table. "Thank you, Duncan. I'll talk to him."

"Talk to who?" Judy said as Duncan ran for the bathroom. He might really have needed to go.

"Duncan saw Alastair in trouble over a prophecy in a few minutes. Damn it, I thought we'd straightened things out. He's not supposed to play vigilante hero." I pinched the bridge of my nose. The headache forming there was only partly due to noise and flashing lights.

"Isn't it strange that Duncan would have a prophecy about someone else's prophecy?" Judy asked. "Like, you'd think the oracle could look out for itself."

"Not so strange if Alastair is in danger. The kids see things all the time that protect them from riding their bikes into traffic or minor threats like that. I have a feeling it looks out for their safety in other ways, too. But... yeah." I sighed. "The new girl is Liv Hubbard, and she's interested in space, so it makes sense she and Alastair might become friends. Her mom seems nice enough."

"I thought boys all thought girls had cooties," Judy said.

"Not these days, I guess. Or it could just be Alastair. Stop eating pizza, you'll get sick."

"I don't get sick over cheap pizza and too much Diet Dr. Pepper," Judy said with a smirk. "Jalapeño poppers are my downfall."

I checked my phone display for the time. "Fifteen minutes. I'll go start the parents rounding kids up."

Maddy Hubbard had moved again, following Liv like the two of them were tethered by an invisible rope. It seemed unnecessarily cautious to me, but I reminded myself not to judge. I had my own protections against kidnapping, and just because I felt safe in Jungle Jack's didn't mean everyone did. I stopped to talk to her again. "I hope Liv had a good time."

"She hasn't stopped running around this place since Alastair opened his presents," Maddy said with a smile. "Thank you for inviting her."

I felt stupid saying I'd invited everyone, like that would make Liv's invitation routine, when I was sure she'd been on Alastair's original list. "We should arrange a play date," I said, feeling inspired. "Do you think Liv would like to come to our house some afternoon?"

"Yes—or, actually, it's easier if Alastair comes to our place. If you don't mind," Maddy said. Again I saw that strange stiffness, as if despite her words she didn't want Alastair in her home.

"I don't mind at all. After school sometime next week? Alastair is free every day except Tuesday."

We settled on Wednesday just as Liv darted toward us. "I had fun," she declared.

"Say thank you to Mrs. Campbell," Maddy said.

Liv dutifully chanted the words, but her attention was on the other children. "Do we have to go now?"

"It's time. Thanks again, Helena, and I'll text you my address so you can pick up Alastair from our house Wednesday."

I almost asked how she had my phone number when I remembered the school had a student/parent directory. "Thanks for coming, Liv, and it was good to meet you both."

The kids were milling about now, some still clinging to the arcade games and begging a parent for just two more minutes, some picking up jackets—it was a clear but chilly Saturday. Parents were chatting in groups of two and three. I didn't see Alastair anywhere.

I moved through the crowd, searching, and found Alastair standing next to the fighting game he and Liv had been playing. One of his hands rested on the console, and the other was clenched into a fist. Just as I reached him, he blinked and started scanning the crowd as I had.

I grabbed him by the shoulder. "What did you see?"

"I didn't see anything," Alastair said. He didn't meet my eyes, which was his number one tell for when he was lying. "I was just going to say goodbye to Liv."

"Liv's gone," I said, "and I know you had a prophecy and you were about to do something about it. What have we discussed, Alastair?"

He wrenched away from my grip, but didn't go anywhere. "If I can stop a fight, shouldn't I?"

I bit my lip nervously. This was the sort of question I hated, because my own instincts were to intervene to prevent violence. But Alastair was nine, or would be on Monday, and *his* instincts weren't fully formed yet. I wanted him to understand the limits of his gift, and I wanted him to act responsibly within those limits.

I took his hand. "Alastair, take me to the fight."

Alastair didn't resist even though I would have guessed he wouldn't want his classmates see him hold his mother's hand. Maybe he was more mature than I thought.

He led me through the crowd and stopped some distance from a couple of boys in a heated argument. "Marcus is gonna punch Owen," he whispered. "They're going to hurt each other."

Insight, for once not prophetic, filled my head. I crouched to where I was closer to Alastair's level and said, "If you stop them, do you think that will make them like each other?"

Alastair gave me a skeptical look. "They're not going to be friends after they get in a fistfight, Mom."

"You and Kenny are friends now, and you started off fighting," I pointed out. "But it's not about what will make them friends. It's about them working out their problems without you short-circuiting the process. If you step in, they'll still resent each other, and they'll get in a fight some other time when you're not around. That's if they don't resent *you* for interfering like some snobby do-gooder."

"I'm not—!"

I shushed him. "You're not, but they might see it that way."

Owen flinched, and Marcus punched him in the nose. I continued to hold Alastair's hand as Owen's mother and Marcus's father hurried to separate the boys. "You can't prevent every pain, Alastair," I said quietly. "You can't save people from the consequences of their actions. I know you want to protect others, and that's good. But you need to think beyond stopping fights. Sometimes the fight is what will make them grow."

Alastair's jaw was clenched tight, but he nodded. He released my hand and walked away from me and from the two boys. I decided to let him go. Sometimes I needed to think beyond easing his immediate pain, too.

Finally, the last children left, and I corralled Duncan and Sophia, who didn't look even a little tired though they'd been racing a complicated pattern between the arcade machines. Alastair had his jacket on already and was slumped near the door. I felt guilty immediately. I'd used prophecies to stop violence or accidents so many times I wasn't sure I had a right to demand Alastair not do the same.

But when I approached him, he said, "You were right, Mom. Marcus's dad didn't know he'd been bullying Owen, and he's going to make sure it stops. If I'd gotten in the way of the fight, Marcus would go on being a bully, for a long time, maybe." He looked up at me, his eyes reddened. "But why would I see the fight if I wasn't supposed to stop it?"

"I don't know, Alastair. There's still a lot I don't know about this gift." I hugged him. "Maybe the oracle is training you. You're getting to be more grown up, and maybe the things you prophesy are more grown up, too. I wasn't an oracle when I was your age, so you're on a path no one's ever walked before. But I hope you know how proud I am that you want to use your gift to help people."

Alastair hugged me back. "I know. Aunt Viv says we're paladins."

"She told me that, too. I wonder what that makes Duncan and Jenny?"

Duncan ran up at that moment. "There's an accident on the Banfield, and we have to go a different way."

"Thank you, Duncan." I squeezed his shoulder.

"I think you're a rogue," Alastair told him. "Mom and I are paladins."

"I'm not a rogue, I'm a ranger," Duncan said.

"Why does everyone know about roleplaying game characters but me?" I exclaimed.

CHAPTER TWO

On the first Saturday of every month, Malcolm and I had dinner with our friends the Kellers, as well as Mike and Judy and Viv and Jeremiah. Harriet and Harry Keller were still going strong despite being in their eighties, and Harriet had responded to my gentle hinting that maybe one of us should make dinner sometimes with a laugh and a "The day I can't whip up lasagna with fresh pasta on an hour's notice, I'll let you take over gladly, dear."

Tonight's meal made me feel sorry for Judy, who'd filled up on awful pizza: peach-glazed ham dripping with juices, cheesy scalloped potatoes with a light crunchy topping, and fresh steamed carrots and green beans. That was a sign of times changing; ten years ago the vegetables would have come from the Kellers' garden, but it had been two years since Harry and Harriet had agreed garden maintenance was too much for them. I didn't think the vegetables tasted any worse, but it was a sign that our friends were slowing down.

"And the guy was exactly where Viv scried him out," Jeremiah was saying as he helped himself to more potatoes. "We laid an easy paper trail to the motel, like always, but the client didn't care how we found him so long as we did. Very grateful that client was, too."

"I'm sure the client would have cared if he'd known I used magic to find the man who owed him money," Viv said. "But it's true he didn't look too closely at our methods."

"Aren't you afraid of taking a job from someone criminal?" Harriet asked. "Suppose someone hired you to find someone they claimed was a debtor, but was actually a witness against them in a criminal trial?"

"We always check out the client first," Viv said. "Very few of them have ever lied to us about their motives, fortunately. If they do, we either refuse to take them on or report them to the authorities. Secretly, of course. Now that Greg Acosta is retired, and Lucia hasn't replaced him with another contact within the police, we can't just hand it to them and have them get probable cause or whatever."

"I think you both win points for coolest job," Judy said. "Sorry, Helena, oracles are passé."

I laughed. "That's not so much a job as it is a calling. And it's been almost boring this last week. Which is fortunate, given that I had to plan the party for today. I am so glad I had this to look forward to." I cut a piece of ham and scooped potatoes up with it. Heavenly.

"We did brush up against Witness Security once," Jeremiah said. "We were checking out someone we believed was our target—the clues all matched the woman's description—and ran up against evidence that someone had altered her background, professionally. So we backed out quickly. That's not something we want to do, out someone in that position, even accidentally."

"What I really wanted to do was make people disappear," Viv said dreamily. "I read a book once about a woman whose job was to help people start new lives away from the Mob or an abusive spouse or whatever, and it was so cool how she got them free of danger and invented new lives for them. But that's not something you can advertise as a business."

"And it would be extremely dangerous, which I notice you didn't mention," Jeremiah said with a smile.

Viv waved that away. "You're a badass fighter and I'm a glass magus. We'd make it work."

"I'm with Jeremiah. That sounds too dangerous," I said.

"It would be exciting, though. And you could help people," Judy said.

"Maybe you could work with Witness Protection," Harry said. "Or is it called Witness Security? Who runs that program, anyway?"

"The U.S. Marshals," Jeremiah said. "Which is way more regimented than I ever want to be, however good the work they do." He sipped from his wine glass and added, "They wouldn't be on board with a couple of magi carrying out policy, either."

"You *are* satisfied with private investigator work, though, right?" I asked Viv.

"Of course," Viv replied. "Talking about making people disappear is all just daydreaming. In practice, that would be so stressful. I like our job now—set our own hours, choose our own clients."

Harriet rose from her end of the table. "Time for dessert! Is everyone interested in strawberry shortcake?"

"I *love* your strawberry shortcake," Malcolm declared. "So much better than with storebought sponge cake."

"I'll help," Mike said. He was seated on Harriet's left side and got up when she did, though he moved heavily as if he'd overeaten.

"I felt that way about owning my own business, back in the day," Harry told Viv. "Though in practice, I had to keep regular hours with the barbershop if I wanted repeat customers. But I had all the control."

"I thought you worked for the Gunther Node as a glass magus," I said.

"I did that, too. But I needed a front to explain my income, since

I couldn't tell anyone I earned a living researching and building electromagical glass inventions." Harry winked at me. "Too bad, because we were years ahead of the mundane world in developing wireless earbuds."

Harriet and Mike returned, Mike with a tray full of cut glass plates heaped high with biscuits and strawberries and cream, Harriet with the coffee pot. I helped pass plates to the others while Harriet went around the table pouring coffee.

For a while, no one spoke. I was too busy devouring strawberries whose juice soaked into the light, flaky biscuits to make every bite sweet and delicious. From Harriet I'd learned to cook several recipes, from my mother a few more, but I didn't love cooking the way either of them did and I felt it showed. My cooking was good; theirs was phenomenal.

"Helena, you're humming," Viv said.

"I hum when I'm eating something I love," I replied, refusing to be embarrassed. "This is so good. Do you have a secret, Harriet? Because this doesn't taste the way mine does."

"You brush butter across the biscuits before baking, right?" Harriet said. "Heat up a tablespoonful of honey next time and mix it with the melted butter. It gives the biscuits shine and a hint of sweetness that blends with the strawberry juices."

"That is so clever! I'll do that." I scraped the last bit of strawberry-flavored whipped cream off my plate and sucked it off my fork. "And now I'm definitely full."

"I think someone will have to roll me out of here," Viv said. "Harriet, thank you again."

"It's my pleasure," Harriet said.

Harry pushed his chair back and put a hand on his aluminum walker. "Let's sit in the living room and digest, since I don't think anyone brought a dolly to wheel Viv home."

The Kellers' living room was by now as familiar to me as my own. Pale sofas and chairs flanked the giant prism pretending to be a coffee table, an element Harriet used in her glass magic. The fireplace had recently been cleaned in preparation for the cold months coming soon, but the framed family photos on the ash mantel hadn't changed. I passed the drinks cupboard, which was of dark oak and didn't match the rest of the Scandinavian-inspired furniture, and idly pushed one of the doors shut. I heard a clink as the door came up against one of the pieces of glassware inside, not wine glasses or brandy decanters, but more glass magic components in a variety of colors and shapes.

I sat with my coffee cup next to Malcolm and enjoyed how he put his arm around my shoulders. We'd been married for almost eleven years, and gestures like that still never failed to thrill me. Occasionally I thought back to how we'd met, and how our romance had progressed, and how we'd fallen in love despite the Accords prohibiting it, and the life I had now felt briefly like a dream.

"Harriet won't let me talk shop at the dinner table," Harry said, settling slowly into his recliner, "so I'll ask what I've been wondering all night—have any of you heard about Craig Jessop?"

"Didn't he go missing?" Mike asked. "I didn't know him well, but I have friends at the Gunther Node who did. Wood magus, I think."

"He's been found," Harry said, more grimly than I could remember him ever speaking before. "Murdered."

Viv gasped. "Murder? Not an accident?"

"Not unless someone accidentally made him kneel down to be shot execution-style," Harry said.

"Dear, is that detail really necessary?" Harriet was pale, and I knew it wasn't because she was squeamish; she'd fought in the Long War years ago, before I was born, and although she'd never said anything, I suspected she'd taken lives. If I was right about that, the experience had given her a deep respect for life and a complete lack of interest in violent movies.

"I could be less blunt, I suppose." Harry looked apologetic as he clasped his wife's hand. "The point is, no, it was definitely not an accident. What I heard from Marge Ferris was that he disappeared between his office in downtown Portland and his home in Beaverton three and a half weeks ago, and the highway patrol found his body outside Washougal yesterday around noon. Lucia's people have been paying attention to the local law enforcement chatter, so they were able to spirit the body away from the morgue."

Malcolm leaned forward, moving his arm from around my shoulders. "Did Jessop have any enemies?"

"He might have. He wasn't the friendliest fellow. But I doubt any of them felt more than minor dislike or irritation toward him." Harry leaned forward, mirroring Malcolm. "It's possible this was a random killing by some madman."

"But that's not what you think," Malcolm said.

Harry shook his head. "I think it was the Savants. And I'm not the only one."

That chilled me. The Savants were the Wardens' enemy, and not a minor one, either. A secret branch of the megacorporation Astraeus Resources, they were wealthy, well connected, and had extensive paramilitary resources, all of which they put toward their only goal: enter the world we called Faerie and drain it of its magic. Their leader, Michael Castellan, had kidnapped me only a little over a month ago, intent on forcing me to use my magic to open the way to Faerie. It didn't matter that I couldn't do that, since the magic of the oracle didn't work that way; he was the sort of obsessed akin to crazy, and I was sure he hadn't given up on his quest.

"If the Savants had him for three and a half weeks, they weren't throwing him a party," Mike said. "They wanted information. And with that kind of murder, they also wanted us to know about their involvement. Otherwise they'd have made it look like an accident."

"That's what worries me," Harry said. "Jessop wasn't a high-ranking Warden, and I doubt he knew the secrets of the Gunther Node. But the Savants are clever, not to mention convinced they're more powerful than we are. I hate to think of them knowing anything at all about the Wardens."

"I'm sure Lucia is handling it," I said.

"Between elves entering our world and the Jessop thing, I'm sure she's stretched thin," Jeremiah said.

"How many alarms have gone off now, does anyone know?" Judy asked.

"There have been twelve," Malcolm said, "mostly in Great Britain and Ireland, with a few in northern Europe and another handful here in North America. In every case, the alarm installed at the slip went off as designed, and for the three that weren't being directly monitored, we were able to get teams in place almost immediately. None of the elves who crossed over made it more than half a mile from the slip."

"Is that because they were killed?" Viv said.

Malcolm shot her a sharp look. "You sound as if you disapprove."

Viv shook her head. "Not really. I mean, I sort of wish we were in a position to negotiate with them, and us killing them immediately— if they weren't enemies, that is—that looks pretty bad. But I know we can't assume any of them are friendly. We did poison their world for a thousand years."

"Not *us*," I protested, though really, I understood her meaning. A millennium ago, humans using magic had erected a barrier that kept elves confined to their world, and that barrier had contaminated Faerie and corrupted its inhabitants. As far as elves were concerned, it didn't really matter which humans were directly to blame.

Viv waved a dismissive hand. "My point is, I think it's too bad our first contact with intelligent alien creatures has to be hostile, but I understand the necessity. I'm mostly asking if any of the elves retreated. It might be a good thing if some of them took news to their leaders that humans aren't defenseless."

"I agree," Malcolm said, "and yes, a few retreated. Some of them acted as if that was their intent all along—as if they entered our world for reconnaissance. But they continue to enter."

"I think that's strange," I said. "They have to know by now that we'll kill any of them that make it through the slips if they don't immediately turn and run. Why are they wasting their manpower?"

"They have backed off somewhat," Malcolm replied. "There were only two incursions this last week. But we know so little of our enemy we can't know if their behavior actually *is* strange. For elves, I mean. What matters is that if they were interested in spying out our resources, they haven't learned anything the elves have taken advantage of. They still simply try to evade our forces and escape into the world."

"And if they succeed, we'll have to change tactics," Mike said. "We can't let elves make themselves known to the world, or we'd have widespread panic. Alien creatures with magical abilities to deceive and manipulate humans—and that's before you consider they look like undead monsters from everyone's worst nightmares."

"What happens if the elves decide to attack in force? Not one at a time?" Judy asked. She looked pale, but I suspected that was discomfort from eating too much rather than fear, as in my experience Judy wasn't afraid of anything.

"The same thing that happened every time there was a major invader incursion during the Long War," Malcolm said. "We Wardens will set about containing it."

"But these aren't invaders," Judy persisted. "Most of those were unintelligent and weren't motivated by anything but hunger for magic. Elves are smarter than that. Isn't there a possibility that the Wardens will have to reveal themselves to the world?"

"That would be a nightmare," Harry said. "Convincing the government—all governments—that magic is real? I'm afraid it's going to take a real catastrophe for them to believe it."

"And we have no idea how the mundane population will react," Harriet said. "People tend to fear what they don't understand, and it's unlikely the revelation of a secret cabal of magic users spread throughout the world will be viewed with anything but suspicion."

"We don't know that," Judy said. "If we show how beneficial magic is, people are bound to respond to that."

"Or they'll see us as tools to be manipulated," I burst out. "Suppose some totalitarian government imprisons all its magic-using citizens and forces them to work magic on its behalf? Or worse, a government that's supposedly free and ruled by law?"

"That's not going to happen, Helena," Judy said.

"You don't know it's not," I shot back. "Look, I know I'm pessimistic about our chances when it comes to revealing the Wardens, but that's because the cost to me and my children is so potentially high. I don't want their identities known until there's no more way to conceal it."

"Helena," Malcolm said, and by the tone of his voice I'd been shriller than I realized. "Helena, when we discuss magic being practiced openly, that doesn't include the oracles. I am committed to giving our children as normal a childhood as I can, and to keeping them safe from anyone who would use them. You have to believe that."

I drew a deep breath. "I do. No, really I do. But I don't trust the average person not to freak out at the thought of magic, and freaking out could include violence. Just ten years ago, the Wardens were fractured along factional lines, and they all knew the capabilities of magic. That shows how counter to their best interests people can behave when they're caught up in their own problems."

"You know I disagree with you, Helena," Judy said, "but at least we're on the same side. I worry about what happens if the Savants think to approach the mundane authorities and reveal the existence of magic before we do."

"Savants can barely use magic," Jeremiah said.

"Enough that they can make their point." Judy's lips pinched tight together. "That could make the Wardens look really bad. At the very least, it would put us in the awkward position of following whatever the Savants do. Like raising your hand in class and having someone else give the same answer you were going to. We shouldn't be the ones to say 'oh, yeah, we're magical too.'"

That thought hadn't occurred to me, and a crack formed in my iron-clad belief. "I hope the Savants don't think of that."

"Your point about the Savants not having much magic is valid," Malcolm said to Jeremiah. "I think that scenario is unlikely. But I'll mention it to Lucia, just in case. She hasn't told me anything about how she's dealing with the Savant threat, since Campbell Security has been preoccupied with challenging incursions, but I'm sure she's not sitting idly by."

I leaned against Malcolm and stared into the depths of my coffee cup. All that was left were the dregs, and I recalled how some people read the future in tea leaves and idly considered what the bottom of the cup might tell me. How nice to be an actual oracle and not have to depend on tea leaves or coffee dregs. "And I might give her a call," I said. "I'm not sure what question I'd ask the oracle, but if Craig Jessop was interrogated by the Savants before they killed him, maybe we need to know what kind of a threat his information is to the Wardens."

Malcolm rested his arm around my shoulders again and squeezed gently. "I don't want you to be afraid."

"Neither do I," I said, but the thought of a mob coming after me and the children for prophecies was hard to shake.

CHAPTER THREE

Monday was my day for carpool, something I liked because it was a nice, definite start to the school week. Carpool, oracle business, errands, Jenny's nap, then carpool again—the schedule helped me reset after the chaos of the weekend.

This afternoon, I had to go to the school early to drop off some donations for the school's fundraiser dinner and silent auction. I'd served on the parents' committee last year, and I'd gone into that year curious about why Talbott Academy needed a fundraiser when tuition payments were already substantial. I hadn't known the fundraiser provided scholarship money for deserving students. That was a service I could enthusiastically get behind. I hadn't set up donations through my corporate giving program because that felt too much like benefiting personally, but as a parent, I supported the fundraiser as best I could.

Juggling two duffel bags and a cardboard box full of donations left me with no hands for Jenny, and I kept a close eye on her as we walked up the sidewalk to the school's front door. I mashed the door opener button with my elbow and said, "Stand back, Jenny, don't let the door hit you."

Jenny retreated behind me. "What's in the bags?"

"Things for the auction. Dresses from Aunt Judy's store, and some fancy jewelry, and glassware." I held the door open with my hip, and glass clinked inside the box, a muffled sound thanks to how well swaddled the vases were.

We passed through the security door, and I signed in at the office, where Clarice, one of the office staff, greeted me cheerfully as she always did. Clarice was the most upbeat person I knew, with a ready laugh and a sincere if intense interest in making people feel at home. When Alastair had started at Talbott Academy, I'd been suspicious of Clarice and her outgoing demeanor, wondering if it was fake enthusiasm. But careful observation had showed that no, she really was that friendly.

Clarice directed me to the auditorium stage, where the fundraiser committee was collecting and sorting donations. With Jenny tagging along, I strolled down the hall and turned left, away from the lunchroom, which still smelled of tomato soup.

The auditorium was bigger than I thought the school's population needed, almost as big as a high school auditorium. Rows of seats upholstered in gold-shot red nubby fabric made it look more like an upscale movie theater than any size school auditorium, but the aisles' carpet runners were more plush than a movie theater's and less worn. Ahead, where the seats ended, the curve of the stage filled the far end of the room. The red curtains were pulled back to reveal the entire stage, which was currently full of long folding tables, half of them piled with donations.

Two women and a man moved between the tables, with a third woman seated at a smaller table behind a laptop. As I approached, I recognized one of the women. "Maddy!" I said. "It's good to see you again. You got roped into helping, huh?"

Maddy, her arms full of colorful fabric, twitched at the sound of my voice and looked up. Her expression of confusion cleared. "Oh, hi, Helena," she said. "Yes, I volunteered. My daughters' old school in Denver did a similar fundraiser, though that one was a live auction." She set down the fabric pile, which I thought might be a tablecloth, and ran a hand over its smooth surface. "It's fun to see what people donate—and of course an early look at the goods never hurts, right?" She smiled, which gave her a more relaxed air.

"That's true. I love the interesting things available. Last year, I was in a bidding war with Rajesh Sodhi—actually, that's him with the tablet—over a set of wooden serving spoons from Nepal, and that was a blast. He won, unfortunately, but we both had fun." I put my burdens on one of the empty tables. "Here, let me show you this —I'm really pleased about it."

Maddy joined me at the table. Today, she wore khaki jeans and a plum-colored T-shirt with a multi-strand necklace of opals strung at intervals on nearly invisible wires, accented with gold beads. Thanks to Judy's boutique clothing store selling trendy jewelry, I could recognize most gemstones, and Maddy's necklace looked like actual opals and not imitation. It was pretty, but I still couldn't help thinking it was strange to pair such relatively expensive jewelry with an ordinary T-shirt.

I decided to let it go—Maddy's fashion sense wasn't my business —and carefully removed one of the wrapped bundles from the box. I unfolded the pillowcase I'd used to protect my treasure and revealed a blue glass vase webbed with silver-tinged black lines like a tree's bare branches. White ovals the size of thumbprints dotted the branches here and there, giving the impression of blossoms just blooming in spring.

Maddy gasped. "It's beautiful. Who made it?"

"An artist named Donald Griffith here in Portland. I discovered his work a few years ago and bought several of his vases for my bedroom and guest room. It didn't occur to me to ask if he was willing to donate for the fundraiser until last week. There are three of these." I removed another vase, this one squat and round made of luminous golden glass striped with dark green.

Maddy picked up the first vase and turned it around, examining all sides. "I may have to bid on this myself. It's extraordinary work."

I waved at Rajesh, who'd sauntered over to join us. "Those are great, Helena," he said. He scribbled a note on his tablet. "What's the retail price? We'll mark them down some to get the bidding going—unless you feel like arm wrestling me for them right now," he added with a smile.

I laughed. "You know I can take you."

"Uh-*huh*," Rajesh replied. "Seriously, I'm impressed."

"Well, I promised Donald we'd set out his business card with the display, so it wasn't a hard sell on my part." I dug in my purse for the little box and set it beside the vases.

"I'll unpack the rest of this, if you want to catalog it, Rajesh," Maddy said. "Do you need these bags back, Helena?"

"Eventually. They've got our name in them, so you can take them to the office and I'll pick them up later." I looked around. "Oops. I didn't keep an eye on Jenny."

"She's over there by that enormous dollhouse," Maddy said, pointing.

The Victorian-style dollhouse was easily five feet tall and fully furnished, so it was no wonder Jenny had been drawn to it. I hurried to corral her, but she hadn't handled any of the furniture, just stood staring at it. "Mrs. Anderson wants to live here," she told me. "Her and Jenny and Jenny and Jenny."

All Jenny's dolls were named Jenny except for one called Mrs. Anderson. "I'm sure she does," I said, looking over the extraordinary dollhouse and considering whether Jenny needed it, given that she already had a very nice dollhouse two-thirds the size of this one. "I'll think about it, all right?"

Jenny looked up at me. Her eyes flashed silver. For a moment, she was perfectly still. Then her face scrunched in fear, and she let out a terrified scream.

I swiftly knelt and pulled her into my arms, holding her tightly. "It's all right," I murmured. "It's just pictures. They can't hurt you."

"Bad men hurting her," Jenny said between sobs. "She's scared."

I silently cursed. Jenny wasn't just an oracle like the rest of us; she was an empath, capable of feeling others' emotions as if they were her own. We'd only discovered this a few weeks ago, and despite the help of Dr. Loretta Deveaux, an expert on empathy, Malcolm and I still had no solution for helping Jenny distinguish between her own emotions and the ones she perceived. We didn't even know if doing so would ease her fear and pain. Worst were the visions she had in which someone felt a traumatic negative emotion. I didn't care if people thought I was a terrible parent, or if they believed Jenny was one of those children who screamed those shrill, awful shrieks at random in public. I *did* care about the possibility that Jenny would associate the oracle with pain and terror.

I squeezed my eyes shut briefly, reaching for an answer. "Do you know any of the people you saw?"

Jenny shook her head. "It's gone now. I'm okay."

That made me feel worse, like the oracular gift expected Jenny to be more emotionally mature than a three-year-old ever was. Unless coping with her empathic power meant growing up fast... and that was worst of all. "I'm glad, Jenny. Remember what we said about screaming when you're afraid?"

Jenny swallowed and wiped her eyes. "It makes other people scared. I don't want that, Mommy."

"I know you don't. We'll get there, sweetie, I promise."

I rose with Jenny in my arms and carried her back to where Maddy stood, not even pretending she hadn't witnessed that little drama. "Is she all right?" she asked.

"She's fine. Just one of those things, right?" I hoped I didn't sound unnatural.

"My older daughter, Emma, used to shriek like that. It was so embarrassing." Maddy sounded understanding, and I didn't feel the need to elaborate on how that wasn't what Jenny had done.

"Well, Jenny will outgrow it like I assume Emma has." I shifted Jenny on my hip and awkwardly picked up my purse. "Alastair is looking forward to his play date at your house on Wednesday. What time should I drop him off?"

Maddy twitched, and her gaze shifted away from me. "Oh, he can ride with us, if you're all right with that," she said, sounding much too nonchalant. I had no idea what had made her suddenly nervous, and it made *me* nervous, like she meant something underhanded. But I'd asked for a prophecy Sunday night—*Is Maddy Hubbard a danger to Alastair?*—and gotten no reply, which was a reassurance. If Maddy was nervous, I couldn't figure out why.

"It's all right, I have an errand to run in that area," I lied. Trusting the oracle that Maddy wasn't a danger wasn't the same as being willing to let my child ride with someone whose driving habits I didn't know. Still, I wasn't going to offend Maddy by coming right out and saying that.

"If you're sure," Maddy said. "Liv's looking forward to it, too." With that, her demeanor relaxed, and she met my eyes again.

I decided against pursuing the issue. After all, what would I say— "why did you look at me in a funny way?" "That's great. Thanks again for inviting him."

The bell rang, startling both of us into nervous laughter. "I'll see you around," I said, and headed for the door, Jenny in tow.

I listened with half my attention to Duncan and Sophia's loud discussion about some television show they both liked. It didn't sound like an argument, so I let it go. Maddy's weird, nervous twitches made me anxious. Since the revelation that there was a whole other magical community in our world, complete with warring factions, I'd become more conscious of my family's potential vulnerability. I'd been kidnapped and I'd been threatened in my own home by a crazy adept. So far, my children hadn't been attacked, but maybe it was only a matter of time.

But Maddy didn't strike me as someone interested in hurting my family. If Castellan meant to attack my family by way of sending a secret agent, he was too competent to send any but the best, someone I would never suspect. Maddy acted more like someone afraid of being found out. Saturday's conversation about Witness Security came to mind. Suppose the Hubbards were on the run?

I shook my head and chuckled. Now my imagination was running away with me. Not about Maddy's behavior—she definitely had some weird quirks—but it was a bad idea to make assumptions about what that meant. Still, I might do some prophesying later, when I wasn't driving.

"Mom!"

I jerked. "Alastair, what?"

"I said, are we having cake tonight? It's my actual birthday." Alastair spoke with the impatient sound of someone who'd tried to get my attention several times.

"Strangely, I remember," I deadpanned. "And I'll tell the story of the day you were born."

"Aw, Mom," Alastair grumbled.

To my surprise, Malcolm's car was in the garage when we pulled in. Carrying Jenny, I followed the shouting children into the house and discovered Malcolm in his office, studying something on a tablet. He smiled when he saw me, with the look of someone who'd been doing an unpleasant task. "I'm so glad to see you. I take your arrival as a sign that I should stop battering at this problem and have a break." He kissed Jenny's cheek, then kissed me on the lips, long and sweet.

"Mmm," I said when I regained my breath. "What have you been doing that's so awful? Don't tell me if talking about it will drag you back in to whatever it was."

Jenny wriggled to get down. "I want to play cars with Daddy."

"Maybe in a little while," Malcolm said. "You go see what the boys are doing."

I heard the music of Duncan and Alastair's favorite racing game come on. "Hey, don't—" I shouted, then changed my mind. "They can play for a bit. You look like you need to unload."

"It's nothing serious. I've been reviewing the reports Renfro produced about the pattern of elven incursions. Or, rather, what we hope is a pattern. It looks random, actually. Nothing to say why they choose the slips they do for their infiltrations. The only thing we're sure of is they never use the same slip twice, which is sensible once they know a slip is guarded." Malcolm set the tablet on his desk and nudged it with one finger. "And yet I find it difficult to believe the elves don't have a plan."

"Maybe they're too alien for us to understand their plan. Though that's a depressing thought, that we'll end up unable to fight them properly because they don't think like we do."

"It is depressing, which is why for now we're acting as if they're rational the way we are. There's no other way to go about it. Gabriel Roarke says the elves of his time were as cunning as humans, but who knows what a thousand years of corruption might have done?"

"That's my fear." Gabriel Roarke, an elf from before the barrier was erected, could pass for human; modern elves could only pass as extras from a horror movie. I hated the idea that maybe more than their bodies had been corrupted. It made sense that elves wanted revenge for what they probably assumed had been an intentional attack by humans, but if they meant to get that revenge in a way even the oracle couldn't predict, humanity might be in serious trouble.

"At any rate, we have to act as if the elves have a plan we might be capable of predicting, because otherwise we fall into reacting rather than acting. I don't suppose you've had any luck with prophecy?"

"No, and I've stopped trying. I think the question of what the elves intend is too large, or possibly too far in the future. I just give myself a headache." I perched on the corner of his desk and chewed my lip in thought. "Maybe... no, even if I ask about which slip the elves will try next, that doesn't give us more of an edge than the alarms and the teams monitoring the slips. And you said the elves don't make it far even if it's a slip that isn't monitored in person."

"Yes, and that would be a waste of the oracle's gift," Malcolm said. "Someday, we will have better knowledge. Lucia wants us to try to capture an elf for questioning."

I sat upright. "Can you do that?"

"In theory, of course. But all the elves we've encountered fight to the death or suicide once they've been subdued. We're looking into other options." Malcolm drew me into his arms and held me close. "But I'm done thinking about this now. Shall we control our raging mob and start making dinner?"

"So anticlimactic."

"But relaxing, don't you agree?" Malcolm kissed me and helped me stand. "You should tell me how your day was. It can't have been as harrowing as mine."

I remembered Maddy Hubbard's weird tension and unnatural pauses. "Not harrowing," I said, "but certainly a puzzle."

CHAPTER FOUR

Wednesday evening, Lucia called unexpectedly. Malcolm had left to pick up Alastair from the Hubbards', and I was sautéing vegetables for stir fry when my phone rang. Seeing Lucia's name on the display reminded me that I'd wanted to call her to ask about Craig Jessop and see if there was anything I could do to help. This call worried me, though. Lucia wouldn't call at dinnertime unless something important had come up.

"Sorry about the interruption," Lucia said when I answered. "I'm taking advantage of knowing your dinner hour. Do you have a minute?"

"It's not quite time to eat. Is this urgent?"

"Not in the usual sense. Did you hear about Craig Jessop?" Now Lucia's voice was muffled, like she was eating.

"I heard. Was it the Savants?"

Lucia let out a low *hah* of mirthless laughter. "Even if it wasn't, we have to assume it was, since the consequences of not preparing to defend against them are worse than being vigilant against a threat that doesn't exist. Besides, he was worked over hard before being shot, and who else would do that?"

I shuddered at the thought. "All right. I assume you called for a prophecy."

"I called to see when you can come to the Gunther Node, but if you're in a position to prophesy now, it would help me and save you a trip."

I gave the vegetables a stir, turned down the heat, and stepped back from the wok. "All right."

Lucia paused before saying, "Did Jessop reveal anything about the Wardens that will endanger us?"

The swooping sensation of a prophecy unfolding swept over me, and I set the phone on the counter before my vision clouded. I saw bright lights in a harsh, unforgiving concrete room with pale green-tiled walls, and people of indeterminate gender dressed in all-enveloping jumpsuits and goggles that made them look like malicious insects. It all looked so much like a scene from a horror movie about medical torture I felt sick. Then the vision swooped again, and the concrete room had a higher ceiling, and I recognized it as the Gunther Node transit hub. Another shift, and I saw the transit hub from above, like I was clinging to the ceiling, and anonymous men and women thronged the room, some of them surrounded by flickering red haloes.

Then the vision ended, and I blinked and took a steadying breath. Automatically I stirred the vegetables again and picked up the phone. "I think he might have given the Savants names of Wardens," I told Lucia. "I don't know whose, but people at the Gunther Node. Which means it might have been other Wardens as well."

Lucia swore, making me glad she wasn't on speaker because Duncan had passed through the kitchen just then. "You didn't see which Wardens?"

"No, but that's why I think the vision was more symbolic. Like those people represented a general threat to the Wardens, and we all need to be careful." The rice cooker beeped, but I ignored it. "Could Mr. Jessop have revealed people's addresses?"

"I doubt it. But a good web search will pull that up. Damn it. We might be looking for assassins."

"You don't sound certain."

Lucia sighed. "Davies, taking out the Wardens by way of murdering individuals is impractical. The Savants would need a direct strike that kills many, and no one knows the location of the Gunther Node, including me. Not to mention that as important as this place is, it's not the only node, and destroying it wouldn't eliminate the Wardens as a threat. But I can't imagine what other use the Savants would make of Jessop's information." She paused again. "Did you think to ask if Jessop outed you?"

A chill passed through me. "I didn't know him."

"No, but he sure as hell knew who you are. And he might have known details that would bypass your protections."

The beeping sounded again. "I—right. I have to get to dinner now, but I'll ask for a prophecy later. Thanks, Lucia."

"Good luck." The connection cut as abruptly as it always did when I talked to Lucia.

I scooped rice into a serving dish and shouted for Duncan to set the table, then returned the strips of cooked beef to the wok and finished heating it all together. When the meal was ready, Malcolm and Alastair still hadn't returned. I checked Malcolm's location on my phone app and discovered he was just turning into our neighborhood.

Minutes later, the garage door banged open, and Alastair ran inside, with Malcolm following more sedately. "Sorry, Mom, there was construction and we had to go around," Alastair said. He shed his coat and shoes in the mud room and hurried to the table. "I'm starving."

Malcolm removed his own jacket and kissed me. "That smells divine."

Once we were all sitting down, I confirmed that it tasted divine, too. I diced the meat and vegetables small for Jenny, who scooped the pieces up as fast as I could cut them. "Did you and Liv have a good time?" I asked Alastair.

Alastair, his mouth full, only nodded. He swallowed and said, "Yeah. Liv has even more space books than I do, but some of them are about old space missions. She's building a Saturn V rocket and we did that for a while. Then we watched space launch videos online."

"That does sound like fun," I said.

"But we're late because Dad and Mr. Hubbard were talking about his car," Alastair said.

I raised my eyebrows at Malcolm. "Maddy said her husband is into classic cars, but I didn't think you'd actually get so involved in talking to Bronson you'd forget the time."

Malcolm smiled wryly. "Well, his Firebird is impressive. He rebuilt it himself. I don't think I've seen a '71 Firebird in such good condition as that."

"So, you made a friend!" I teased.

Malcolm's smile deepened. "You're so funny. Actually, I got the feeling Bronson Hubbard is the kind of man who has only a few interests and is bad at making conversation about anything else. I learned that he's a dentist and that they moved here so he could take over a friend's practice when the friend retired."

"Liv said they used to live in Denver," Alastair volunteered.

"Where's Denver?" Duncan asked.

"In Colorado. You should look at the puzzle map and see if you can find it." The kids had a much-loved puzzle of a map of the United States that I encouraged playing with, hoping they'd absorb some geographical knowledge.

"I was thinking," Malcolm went on, "that we should invite them over for dinner sometime. They don't live too far away, and maybe they'd like to get to know the neighbors."

"That sounds great. I'll give Maddy a call." I remembered her odd reluctance to let Liv come to our house, and wondered if that would extend to a dinner invitation. Well, I'd make the overture, and she could decide what to do about it.

Dinner over, I retreated to my office while Malcolm and the children cleared the table and washed the dishes. I sat in my office chair and spun back and forth in a semicircle a few times, letting my mind drift. Then I stilled my movement, gripped the chair arms lightly, and let a question settle into my bones: *Did Craig Jessop reveal my location?*

Nothing happened. I saw no images, felt no impressions. Relief surged through me, but it didn't last long. Jessop might not have told the Savants where I lived, but that didn't mean he hadn't given them other information that endangered me and the children.

I sorted through possible questions for a minute or two and settled on *Did Craig Jessop tell the Savants about my children?*

Instantly I was caught up in vision, but a fragmented one: the same horrible concrete room I'd seen when talking to Lucia, then flashes of green like looking up through a tree's branches at the sun, then, one by one, Alastair and Duncan and Jenny's faces.

The prophecy faded, leaving me cold and stiff and aching as if I'd sat rigid with all my muscles tensed for an hour. My breathing was ragged, and my eyes ached like the rest of me. I closed my eyes and focused on calming my breathing, but fear still made my heart race. Michael Castellan now knew I had children. And although my prophecy hadn't said so, I had to assume he knew they were oracles, too. Keeping them safe had just become a thousand times harder.

"You think somebody might try to kidnap us?" Duncan said. His eyes were wide with astonishment, but he didn't sound scared, which reassured me.

"We don't want you to be afraid," Malcolm said, "but it's important you be aware of the potential danger."

"Even though it's unlikely," I added, seeing Alastair's face pale and his hands clench into fists. "We told you because not knowing could put you in more danger, like if you thought you could go off by yourselves without telling anyone."

"We know not to talk to strangers already, Mom," Alastair said. "What else could happen?"

"I'd rather not go into details that will frighten you," Malcolm said, "because if you're afraid of possibilities, you'll start jumping at shadows. Just be sensible. Pretend it's a game like *Legend of Kerigon*."

"Except we don't fight the bad guys, we stay hidden from them," Duncan said, his eyes lighting up.

"That's right. Definitely don't attack anyone." I fixed first Duncan, then Alastair with my gaze. "I think your prophecies will protect you like they do from physical danger, but there's no sense not being cautious."

"We will," Duncan said.

Alastair looked away briefly. "Is it bad?" he asked. "I feel like there's more you didn't tell us."

We hadn't explained the details about Craig Jessop's torture and death, just that someone had accidentally revealed our identities. "There is," I said, "but it's nothing that will help you protect yourself more. You know there are things we believe children don't need to hear—well, this is one of those things. But we haven't concealed anything that could endanger you." I hoped that was true.

Alastair nodded. "I get it," he said, and the way he squared his shoulders, like he anticipated taking a blow, made my heart ache.

I hugged Alastair and then Duncan, who wriggled away after a second. "Bedtime," I said. "Daddy will read us all a story."

I settled in Alastair's room with Jenny on my lap as Malcolm read a chapter of *Binny for Short*, their current bedtime story, but as good as the book was, it didn't keep my attention tonight. I'd been reluctant to tell the kids about the Savant threat despite my conviction that Michael Castellan would have no doubts about acting on his knowledge of them. Given that I didn't know for sure what he would do, I'd worried that telling Alastair and Duncan the chance of an attack was a greater possibility than before would just frighten them. I didn't want them too scared to go to school or to a friend's house— though I'd already decided I would carefully control visits to friends' houses until we knew for sure what the threat was.

But Malcolm had pointed out that even as young as they were, the boys were old enough to understand watching out for their own safety. "It's like teaching them about busy streets so they won't ride their bikes into traffic," he'd said, and I'd seen the wisdom of that.

Now I watched them, both lying on their stomachs where they could see the illustrations, both with their chins propped on their hands, and felt calmer. In those poses, they looked more alike than usual, though Alastair had his father's dark hair and Duncan's was blond like mine, and Alastair was thinner in the face than Duncan. Both their brows furrowed in a short line above the bridge of their noses when they were intent on something, and both of them had Malcolm's dimple that was going to break hearts someday, if my experience was anything to go by. They were smart, and strong, and yes, maybe they were growing up a little too fast, but that wasn't something I could control. All I could do was love them and guide them in their oracular gifts.

Jenny was drooping by the time the chapter was over, so I carried her to her bed and tucked her in, then returned to say goodnight to the boys. When I'd closed their doors, Malcolm took me in his arms and said, "You know, I love you more every day."

I blushed and smiled. "What brought that on?"

"You do what's best for the children even when your instincts are to wrap them in cotton wool and put them where nothing can harm them." Malcolm kissed me lightly, and added, "Because you know they'll never grow up if you shelter them completely."

"Even though it's tempting," I sighed. "I know I can't protect them from everything, but it hurts to see them suffer, even a little."

"Which is what makes you remarkable, that you don't let that influence you." He kissed me again, more deeply this time, then drew me closer. "Tomorrow I'll set Campbell Security to monitoring all of you. If the Savants make a move, we'll be there to stop them."

"I know. I love you, too." I rested my cheek against his shoulder and let myself relax. Our children were as safe as we could make them, between Malcolm's fighting abilities, the defenses of Campbell Security, and my own prophetic gift. There was no reason to fear.

After a while, I released him and said, "I'm going to find out if Maddy and her family can come to dinner next week, and I ought to do that before it's too late to call. Then afterward..."

"Afterward," Malcolm agreed, kissing me once more.

I found Maddy's contact, debated texting her, and decided for this, I should make a phone call. "Hi, Maddy, it's Helena," I said when she answered. "Thank you again for having Alastair over. He had a really good time."

"I'm glad. Liv hasn't made a lot of friends yet, and finding someone who can keep up with her enthusiasms was wonderful," Maddy said. "And I know Bronson enjoyed showing off his car to Malcolm."

"Malcolm doesn't have many people he can talk cars with, either. Mostly Jenny, and she's three and not a great conversationalist." We laughed, and I continued, "I was thinking it would be nice to get together as families, say for dinner? We'd love to have you over."

Maddy was silent long enough that I got nervous. I couldn't imagine why a dinner invitation would be something to ponder, and again I remembered Maddy's odd silences and stillnesses. Finally, she said, "All right. Sure. That would be fun. Did you have a date in mind?"

"Is next Wednesday too soon? I mean, probably you have things planned—"

"No, Wednesday is good, since Saturday night is the school gala and auction, and we're busy most nights this week." Maddy was back to sounding normal.

"That's great! How about six-thirty? And don't worry about bringing anything, I don't know what I'm making yet."

We chatted a bit more, working out details, and then said good-bye. I set my phone on my desk and stared at it as if it could reveal the reason for Maddy's odd behavior. She certainly seemed worried about letting Liv out of her sight—I was sure if I'd asked for Liv to come to dinner alone, Maddy would have refused. But then she'd hesitated for so long over my invitation I'd almost thought she was searching for a good excuse to refuse, like she didn't feel safe outside her home. Like she was hiding from something.

I shook my head and collected my phone. My imagination was running away with me, that was all. Probably Maddy, like Bronson, was one of those people who was socially awkward, and I was making up stories that had no basis in fact. I ignored the little voice that reminded me Maddy had not behaved perfectly normally when I encountered her at school. That little voice needed to stop reading so many suspense novels.

CHAPTER FIVE

Saturday morning at ten sharp I opened the door to a tall, slim woman with short fair hair and bold features. "Dr. Deveaux, welcome."

"Good morning," Loretta Deveaux said. She carried a clipboard in a leatherette cover, giving her a professorial look despite her ordinary jeans and sweater. "How have things been with Jenny?"

It had only been a few weeks since Deveaux's visits had started, but I was accustomed to her lack of interest in small talk. It reassured me, actually; I didn't want to be friends, I wanted her to help Jenny cope with her empathic power. "Good—well, no different than usual. We've made sure to point out when she experiences an emotion that isn't hers, but the episodes aren't more or fewer than before."

"That's good. This isn't something that will change overnight, but if she suddenly started feeling others' emotions more frequently, that might be cause for concern." Deveaux smiled. "It would also give me more material to work with, so it's not all bad. But that's nothing to worry about now. Let's go into the great room, and I'll take a look at her."

Duncan and Alastair were playing a video game in the great room, but they shut it off and ran upstairs without being prompted when they saw Deveaux. They knew why she was here. Malcolm, who'd been reading on his tablet, set it aside and stood to greet Deveaux. "I'll go get Jenny," he said, and followed the boys upstairs.

"Remarkable," Deveaux said. "I've never seen such obedient children. What do you do, drug their milk?"

"You caught them on a good day," I said. "Though the oracular gift has done a lot to make them appreciate when a situation is serious. And they love their sister and are worried about her."

"Still," Deveaux said with a shrug. "They know about her empathy?"

"Jenny used to have an emotional breakdown when they fought. I thought it was reasonable to tell them why that was. They felt guilty, and since then they've tried not to fight where she can pick up on their anger."

"I still can't tell you how unusual that is in children of that age." Deveaux shook her head slowly. "Mostly they're self-centered little brats who have all the empathy of a rattlesnake."

"That's harsh," I said, taken aback.

"You know I'm not sentimental, and I certainly don't have any illusions about the sweet tenderness of childhood," Deveaux replied. "We studied children—oh, don't look at me that way, Ms. Campbell, it was a non-invasive survey. I wanted a baseline for the development of human empathy. Children's self-centeredness is a survival trait. They're fragile and weak by comparison to adults, and they have to use whatever resources they can to ensure they'll live to grow up. It's up to adults to teach them to look beyond themselves for the traits that will let them survive in society—compassion, understanding, and a sense of community."

I gaped. "I hadn't thought of it that way."

"And yet I'm sure you teach your children to share with others and to consider how their actions will affect the people they encounter. Civilizing them." Deveaux settled into the seat she usually took and crossed her legs, looking as relaxed as a cat. Coincidentally, our elven caracal Night-Noon chose that moment to saunter into the great room and butt her head against Deveaux's hand for scritches. Deveaux petted her idly, and Night-Noon's powerful purr filled the air like a distant buzzsaw.

Malcolm returned with Jenny in his arms and settled next to me on the couch. "Thank you for coming, Dr. Deveaux," he said.

Deveaux waved that away. "How are you, Jenny?"

Jenny stared at Deveaux with wide eyes. "Night-Noon likes you."

"Most cats do. I think they sense a kindred spirit."

"What's 'kindred'?" Jenny asked.

Deveaux ran a hand down the cat's back. "It means being related in some way. Usually your kindred are your family, but it can also mean people you have things in common with. Someone else who likes cars might be a kindred spirit to you."

One of the things I liked best about Deveaux was how she didn't talk down to Jenny. Jenny nodded. "I saw the elves again."

"That's good. Did they scare you?"

"They only are scary when they fight, because they're angry and afraid and it hurts."

I shifted uncomfortably in my seat. This was the first I'd heard of Jenny feeling pain in others' emotions. But Deveaux merely said, "You feel both angry and scared, is that it?"

Jenny nodded again. She tapped her chest. "It gets mixed up inside me and I don't know what to do."

"You're already doing what you should by knowing those feelings are theirs and not yours." Deveaux folded open her clipboard and removed a pen from within the case. "Do you remember what I said about holding on to your own feelings?"

"You said, think about being happy and sad and angry," Jenny said.

This had been something Deveaux had told Jenny last week, and

I wasn't sure she understood, because *I* barely understood. "And you wanted us to point out when she feels a strong emotion, whether it's her own or an empathic feeling," I said. "How does that help?"

"What little research on empathy we accomplished before shutting down indicated that the empaths perceived a difference between natural emotion and induced or external emotion," Deveaux said. She clicked the pen a couple of times. "It was something that they became aware of over time as their empathic powers grew. Unfortunately, their grip on sanity declined as that happened, and we never did clarify whether the difference was something real or part of their madness. I'm hoping Jenny can answer that question."

"You're not talking about experimentation, are you?" Malcolm said. He sounded neutral in the way he did when he was deciding how angry to be about something.

"No, Mr. Campbell, but we will be gathering information based on Jenny's experiences." Deveaux didn't seem at all fazed by Malcolm's ill-concealed hostility. "Jenny, this week I have a game for you to play with your parents. You're going to tell them when you feel happy or sad or angry or afraid, all right? And they will let you color in a square every time." She displayed the page topmost on her clipboard, which was a grid of large squares drawn in black Sharpie. "But the game part is that you will have to tell them whether the feeling is yours or someone else's. And they will make a check mark in each box you get right."

"But—wait. What if she doesn't know?" I said. "She might say what we want to hear."

Deveaux pursed her lips. "Come here a second, Jenny."

Jenny hopped off Malcolm's lap and stood in front of Deveaux, who took her hand. "This is just a physical, don't worry," she said, though Malcolm and I hadn't reacted. We sat in silence for nearly a minute until Jenny started to fidget and Deveaux released her. "All right, Jenny, that's fine," she finally said. "Why don't you and Night-Noon play upstairs for a while, and I'll talk to your parents."

Jenny hugged Night-Noon, who endured the embrace with her usual placidity, and then ran away with the elven caracal at her heels. When she'd disappeared upstairs, Deveaux said, "These first few weeks I've been developing a baseline for Jenny's emotions and her behavior. She's a smart kid, and she likes praise as much as anyone. But when it comes to her empathic talent, she doesn't lie. It doesn't even seem to occur to her. So I have no doubt that anything she tells you about her feelings is the truth, not something manufactured to get your approval or win a reward."

"How can you be sure of that?" Malcolm said.

Deveaux frowned. "She's had many opportunities to tell me what she thinks I want to hear, and she hasn't used any of them. My guess is that on some deep level, she wants to reconcile both kinds of emotions she feels, and on that same level, she knows she can't do that if she's dishonest about them. Like I said, she's a smart kid. She's articulate beyond her years, and she has that tremendous memory for car makes and models, and both those things will benefit her in resolving her empathy problem. Just go on being matter-of-fact about her emotional outbursts, and I think we'll continue to see progress."

She handed me the grid paper, then made a few notes on a different page. "What I expect to see," she said, rising from her seat, "is an increasing number of check marks in the grid. Assign a different color to each of the four emotions we're tracking—the colors don't matter, they're to keep Jenny's interest. Make a note in the square as to date and time of an emotional episode, and of course check the box when she accurately distinguishes which emotions are hers and which are someone else's. I'll be back again next Saturday to go over the results." She smiled archly at Malcolm. "Not too invasive an experiment for you?"

"Don't think I've forgotten you were censured for unethical conduct," Malcolm shot back. "I'm not going to take your word for anything without considering it thoroughly."

"Which I respect in a parent," Deveaux replied. "And I admit it's refreshing to be part of this project—no, you wouldn't believe me if I called it anything else," she added as Malcolm opened his mouth to object. "A sane empath. I have no idea what Jenny will turn out to be, Mr. and Mrs. Campbell, but it's going to be something remarkable, I'm sure."

We accompanied her to the door and said goodbye. When the door shut behind her, Malcolm said, "I don't know if she's winding me up on purpose or if that's just who she is."

"I like her. I feel confident that she cares about understanding Jenny's problem."

Malcolm put his arms around my waist. "Not the same as caring about Jenny, love."

"I know. But in a way, that's comforting, too. Like she's not going to hold back if something she wants to do will help us figure this out. Maybe she only doesn't want to hurt Jenny because that would ruin the experiment, but it still means Jenny doesn't get hurt."

"Since when did you become so pragmatic?"

I cast a glance at the staircase. "Since I had children."

SINCE ALASTAIR HAD ENROLLED AT TALBOTT ACADEMY for kindergarten four years ago, the school's annual fundraiser gala had been held at the Marriott on the waterfront. This year, the gala date had been changed, and the Marriott was unavailable. Undaunted, the committee had chosen the Arbor Hotel and Conference Center, farther from downtown and slightly smaller than the Marriott, but still big enough for the gala. I liked the height of the rooms and the light fixtures like giant tiered cartwheels flat against the ceiling. There were no windows in the banquet hall, but floor-to-ceiling panels of rippling glass illuminated by pale blue lights gave the room the feeling of being underwater, also a pleasant touch.

Surrounded by men and women dressed in the same semi-formal style we were, we crossed the hotel lobby and entered the banquet hall. "You know," Malcolm said as he guided me past the many round tables set to seat six each, "we could break with tradition and skip the auction entirely."

"You'd better laugh when you say that," I said. "I love a silent auction. It's so much less stressful than a live auction, and worrying about if you accidentally bid on something by scratching your nose at the wrong time."

"That only happens in movies," Malcolm said. "And I'll have you know Kaira Sodhi and I have an agreement to intervene if you and Rajesh get into a bidding war again."

"That won't happen," I scoffed. "Rajesh and I already compared notes. We're not interested in the same things this year. Come on, you have to see this dollhouse."

I tugged Malcolm through the banquet hall to the smaller breakout room adjacent to it. The lighting here was brighter, less watery blue, so the many donations available for bidding were clearly visible. The enormous dollhouse stood on a low plinth that nevertheless put the peak of its roof higher than my head. We paused before it. Malcolm let out a low whistle. "We could practically live in that thing ourselves."

"Right? I've never seen another dollhouse this big. I wonder where it came from."

Malcolm circled the dollhouse. "I'm sure that information is in the auction app. You're not thinking of bidding on it, are you?"

"Jenny already has a very nice dollhouse—oh, wait, this one has electric lights..."

Malcolm chuckled and took my hand. "You were right the first time. Jenny doesn't need it. Come, let's get signed in so you can spend a lot of money."

I mock-scowled at him. "I'm very frugal. I just like helping others and incidentally getting nice things."

Some of the parents were seated at the registration table, where they were taking payments for supper tickets for those who hadn't bought them in advance. Since we had, I just greeted Erica and Jim Bryson and scanned the code to download the silent auction app. It was so much more convenient than the handwritten list method they'd used two years ago. Get the app, sign in—I used "Campbell" as my name, since Malcolm had no interest in bidding for himself and would have me bid for him on the rare occasions he wanted something—and a screen with all the items popped up.

I scrolled through the list, idly tapping the ones I'd had an interest in to see what the bidding looked like. We had arrived half an hour after the event began, so there was already some action. The dollhouse had five people bidding on it, some of whose names I recognized, though two of them had funny handles like "mkymaus" and "PRINCESS42" who could be anyone.

I wandered the room, looking at things, and bid on a set of Caldecott-winning picture books and a landscape painting that would look good on the wall at the top of the stairs where they came out on the second floor. I stood next to that for a while after entering my bid. It was an abstract painting in oils of a lake, with bright colors and bold strokes that despite its not very representational style made me feel like I was standing on the lakeshore, breathing in the cool wetness of lake and trees.

"It's beautiful," Maddy Hubbard said from beside me. "Did you bid on it?"

"I did." I angled my phone in her direction, showing the three bids with mine at the top. "What about you?"

"It wouldn't match my décor, unfortunately." Maddy wore a black strappy dress that shimmered in the clear light and had paired a strand of black pearls accented with sapphires with it. I didn't think the ensemble exactly matched, but the necklace was pretty enough I sympathized with her desire to wear it regardless.

"Yes, it is sort of a specialized taste. Which I hope will work in my favor. It's good to see you again. Are you having fun?"

"I like the system, and the hotel is beautiful." Maddy glanced around. "Though I appear to have lost my husband—no, there he is, talking to Malcolm by the television. Bronson might bid on that. He was saying ours seems to have been damaged in the move."

It was a perfectly normal thing to say, but I thought of our previous interactions, how banal they'd been, and felt this, too, was Maddy not giving anything away. I thought about challenging her, making it a joke but still meaning it, and decided there was no point. Maybe this was who Maddy was, or maybe it meant we couldn't be anything but superficial acquaintances, but bringing her weird behavior up in public wouldn't change that. I'd wait to see if she was different at dinner on Wednesday.

We strolled over to where Malcolm was having an animated conversation with a man with sandy blond hair who looked the way I imagined Duncan would as an adult, solid without being fat and not quite as tall as Malcolm. "And I did make a claim, but who knows if anything will come of it," the man was saying. "It's minor enough damage the moving company will say it was like that before."

"You'd think they'd care more about their reputation than that," Malcolm said. "Helena, this is Bronson Hubbard."

I shook Bronson's hand. "It's nice to meet you."

"So, have you blown through the children's college funds yet?" Malcolm said with an arch smile.

"Very funny," I said. "Just for that, I'm bidding on that antique jade and silver necklace."

"Oh, I love that," Maddy said, finally sounding genuinely enthusiastic. "We'll have to see which of us gets it."

"It might end up being Gabrielle Dunst," I said. "I saw her eyeing it."

"Helena, you don't even like jade," Malcolm protested.

"I do so! Not as much as turquoise... actually, I ought to bid on the turquoise earrings instead. My sister always says it's not my color, but I love the way it looks." I entered my bid, then on a whim looked at the listing for the jade necklace. Sure enough, Maddy's name was at the top again.

"Well, that's a relief," Maddy said. "I'd hate there to be bad feelings between us over who won."

"Oh, I never resent anyone for outbidding me." I paused, then added, "Maybe Rajesh. He's so smug about winning. Though that could just be my interpretation."

Malcolm checked his watch. "It's almost time for dinner. Would you care to join us?"

"Sure, that would be fun," Maddy said.

"I'm going to take another look at the earrings," I said. "You go ahead. I'll just be a minute."

Malcolm and the Hubbards left the room, and I circled around to the far side where the jewelry was displayed. The earrings I'd bid on were sterling silver with two turquoise ovals dangling from each fishhook ear wire. I leaned over and thought about trying them on— there was a mirror so bidders could see how the jewelry looked—but that would have meant removing my own earrings, so I just admired.

Someone bumped into me, hard enough to make me stagger. "Excuse me," I said, trying to stay polite though the collision had hurt. I stepped away, but the person continued to lean on me. "Hey—"

I turned to tell the person to back off and stopped with my mouth open. The woman standing next to me, dressed in black workout clothes rather than a dress, arched one thin, flexible eyebrow and smiled a nasty smile. I knew her, and not because she was a Talbott Academy parent; I'd met her under far more horrible circumstances. In seconds, memory dredged up her name: Eris Reichert. Michael Castellan's right-hand woman.

Eris was a Savant.

CHAPTER SIX

"Hello again, Helena," Eris said.

I didn't move. "What do you think you're doing?"

"I just want a little chat. Somewhere private." She drew a small but deadly-looking gun from her waistband. "Start walking."

"You have *got* to be kidding. I'm not going anywhere with you." To my surprise, I wasn't scared, I was angry. How dare this woman harass me?

Eris shrugged. "Tell me something," she said. "Do you see the gun?"

"Of course."

"And what am I wearing?"

I rolled my eyes. "What is this, some porn call line? 'What am I wearing,' really—"

"You see through illusions," Eris said.

I froze. "Illusions? I don't know what you're talking about."

"Right," Eris said. "We know more about you than I'm sure you like. Illusions are just one part of your magic, aren't they? So, *you* see the gun, but everyone else thinks I'm holding a phone—one that's nowhere near your body, too. I can shoot you and be gone before anyone thinks to look for me. You can either come with me now, or I'll shoot you here."

"How do I know you won't shoot me if we go somewhere else?"

Eris smiled again. "You don't. But I promise you Mr. Castellan doesn't want you dead, so long as you cooperate."

I stared her down. "No. Not a chance. And *you* might be willing to shoot me. You'd probably enjoy it. But I'm certain Castellan would disapprove, and he still pays your salary. Or whatever it is you get out of following him. So you go back to him and tell him I'm not interested in a conversation, polite or otherwise."

Eris's smile widened. "I thought you'd say that. How sure are you I won't shoot someone else? The way I did that friend of yours?" She ostentatiously looked around, too fast for me to kick the gun out of her hand. "Hmm, not a lot of people left in here. I guess that will make my decision for me."

"Don't you dare."

"You said it yourself, Helena. I'd do it, and I'd enjoy it." Eris's smile was a smirk now. "Your choice. Come with me, or be responsible for someone else being injured or even dying."

My hands were shaking as my anger turned into fear, and I had a feeling Eris knew it despite her eyes never leaving my face. There was no time for a prophecy. I frantically reviewed the few things I'd learned in my recent martial arts training and couldn't come up with anything that didn't result in someone, probably me, being shot. "I don't—"

"Last chance, Helena," Eris said.

I glanced down involuntarily and saw her finger move to rest on the trigger. "Fine," I said, resolving to turn on her the instant we were alone. "Where to?"

"Out the door to the hallway, then away from the foyer. I'll show you which door to take." Eris's grip on the gun shifted minutely, pressing it into my side. Grinding my teeth, I walked in the direction she indicated.

My phone vibrated, and I clutched it tighter. I didn't want Eris noticing and taking it from me, though I couldn't imagine how I would make use of it with her right there. I mentally went over my options. Once we were in the hallway, which I guessed was empty now dinner was being served, I would run for the banquet hall. The doors weren't far from here. Eris was evil, but she wasn't the kind of crazy that would shoot someone solely for fun. If I could get to the banquet hall, I'd be safe and Eris would leave. I hated letting her get away, but apprehending a Savant agent wasn't something even Malcolm could manage in a ballroom full of ordinary people.

Eris and I neared the hall door, with me scanning the hallway ahead, what little I could see, hoping no one was there. We had almost reached the dollhouse, and I sized it up, madly looking for a way to turn it into a weapon. As we passed it, I realized someone was standing on its far side, hidden behind its bulk. In the next moment, I recognized Maddy Hubbard.

"Oh, Helena," she said. "Did you decide to bid on this?"

I stopped, ignoring the pressure of the gun. "No, Jenny already has a nice one," I said. "You?"

Maddy let out a low chuckle. "Neither of my daughters are really dollhouse types. But I would have died to have this when I was Liv's age. I've been trying to convince myself I'm too young to buy a giant dollhouse for my midlife crisis." She glanced over her shoulder. "We should go in, unless..." She nodded at Eris, who stood behind me.

I made a decision. "No, we were done talking. I'll see you around," I said, stepping away from Eris and half-turning to wave. Eris looked like she was about to erupt. I hurried to the banquet hall, not waiting for Maddy. My palms were sweating and I felt if I stopped moving I would fall over. Any minute now, Eris would decide she was the kind of evil that killed for fun and would shoot me and Maddy both.

But the shot never came. I slowed when I reached the first of the round tables. Maddy stopped beside me. "I don't see—there they are," she said, pointing. Across the room, on the far side of center, Malcolm was waving at me. I risked turning around. Eris was gone.

I threaded my way between the tables and dropped a little too heavily into my seat. In addition to Malcolm and Bronson, Judy and Mike had joined us.

"We only just got here. Traffic was terrible," Judy said. "And Father was late for the same reason. Hi, I'm Judy, and this is my husband Mike," she said to Maddy. "I don't think we've met."

"Maddy and Bronson Hubbard," Maddy said, shaking hands. "It sounds like you and Helena know each other well already."

"We've been friends forever," I said, "and our children Sophia and Duncan are practically the same age. Judy, does that mean your father is babysitting tonight?" I hoped my voice sounded steady. I could not afford to have a nervous breakdown in public. That would have to wait until I got home.

I dropped my unfolded napkin into my lap and wiped my sweaty hands on it, then casually unlocked my phone and texted a swift message. A second later, Malcolm's phone buzzed. He didn't look at it. I felt like screaming. If Malcolm would just check his phone, he might be able to catch Eris before she fled.

"Will jumped at the chance to spoil his only grandchild," Mike said with a grin. "And eat at McDonald's. He pretends his palate is too refined for fast food, but I think he likes the fries."

"Viv and Jeremiah are watching the kids for us," I said. "They brought pizza, much to Jenny's disgust." Normally our next-door neighbor Ysabel would have babysat, but with the increased possibility of a Savant threat, we wanted protections a little more robust than Ysabel's knowledge of judo. I felt so stupid. I'd only thought of the children's protection, not of my own. And now the Savants had come after me in public.

Quickly, I texted Malcolm again. This time, Malcolm patted his suit coat pocket and said, "Excuse me." He looked at the message. Though his eyes widened fractionally, he made no other movement to indicate he was upset. He rose from the table. "I beg your pardon, I need to make a call. Some work emergency, but that never ends, does it?"

I caught the edge of the glance he sent Mike. It didn't look like anything to me, but as Malcolm walked away, Mike stood, saying, "I'll be back in a bit."

"I thought it was only girls who all went to the bathroom at once," I joked, trying to make this exodus look less weird than it was.

"Once a Marine, always a Marine. Semper fi," Mike said with a laugh, and followed Malcolm through the door.

"They were both Marines? How interesting. Is that how they met?" Maddy asked.

"They've known each other since high school," Judy replied. "High school, college, the Marines, Campbell Security—Mike used to work for Malcolm until he quit to focus on tool and machine restorations."

"Like on YouTube?" Bronson said. "I've seen some of those. It's miraculous how they take those ruined things and make them like new. Reminds me of restoring my Firebird."

I let Judy handle the conversation and made myself stop dwelling on Eris and the feel of a gun in my side. Thinking about it wouldn't change the past, and it wouldn't make me safer. I hoped Malcolm and Mike caught her, even if it meant I had to make up excuses for why they didn't come back.

My phone buzzed. I surreptitiously looked at the message.

<She's gone. Was she under an illusion at all?>

I typed back <clothes and gun>. I hoped Malcolm wouldn't overreact to the news that Eris had held me at gunpoint. I needed him to focus.

Malcolm didn't respond right away. I said a few meaningless things so Maddy and Bronson wouldn't be suspicious—or maybe so they wouldn't be more suspicious, since this hadn't exactly been a normal interaction so far. But they seemed engrossed in whatever Judy was saying.

My phone buzzed again. <Mike traced illusions to back of hotel. Found a transit square drawn on pavement. No idea where she went. We're coming back, more later>

A transit square was how adepts, including Savants, were able to teleport between places. It surprised me that Eris was capable of such magic. Adepts who took lives gradually became incapable of working magic, and I had no illusions that Eris was all talk when it came to violence. Still, she was gone. If we couldn't capture her, at least she wasn't an immediate threat anymore.

Malcolm reappeared just as the appetizers and salads were being served, and Mike showed up about a minute later. I ate, but I barely tasted the food. That Eris Reichert, and by extension Castellan, had approached me in public terrified me now that the immediate threat had passed. They knew I had children, and they knew where my children went to school. I'd warned Castellan of the consequences if he made this personal by going after my family, but I wasn't sure he cared.

Maddy and Bronson were more animated than I'd seen them before, laughing at Mike's jokes and telling stories of their own. I was beyond grateful that Maddy had been there to give me an out, but I still wondered about her and her husband. Going from bland and uninteresting to clever and funny... all right, maybe it was us, not them.

I only sipped my wine, wanting to keep a clear head, and nibbled my dessert because my stomach felt full of lead from nerves. Judy noticed and teased me— "saving room for after-party dessert, Helena?" and I made myself laugh with the others, though it hadn't been a very funny joke. By the time we all rose to return to the breakout room, I felt shaky and tired and not even a little bit interested in seeing if I'd won anything I'd bid on.

Maddy had successfully bid on one of Donald's glass vases as well as the jade necklace. I'd been outbid on the earrings, but I'd won both the set of picture books and the painting. Malcolm didn't joke about my extravagance or about how we were going to get the painting home. I said goodbye to the Hubbards and Judy and Mike and then sat in the Camaro while Malcolm put the painting in the trunk and the box of books in the back seat. As he pulled away from beneath the hotel's portico, Malcolm said, "Are you all right? Eris didn't hurt you?"

"I'm fine. I'm angry. I hate that she's so good at finding ways to force me to obey her. She threatened to shoot someone else if I didn't come with her to talk to Castellan. And I didn't have an opening— damn it, Malcolm, why can't life be like *The Matrix* where I could download kung fu into my head and be an instant expert?"

"You're not learning kung fu," Malcolm said.

"You know what I mean. I feel so helpless still."

"You're not helpless. You set me and Mike on her trail. I took a picture of the transit square and sent it to Cassie Leighton to see if she and her friends can make anything of it. Now, what exactly did Reichert tell you?"

"She said she wanted to talk. Who knows if that was true? And I found out—well, I don't know this for sure, but I think Craig Jessop might have told the Savants I can see through illusions. She knew about it, at any rate."

"He couldn't have told them much more, or Castellan would be interested in more than talking to you." Malcolm's jaw was set tight. "But I'm more concerned that the Savants knew to approach you at the gala. That means they know where the children go to school."

"I know. I thought of that. What do we do? We can't keep them out of school forever!"

"We don't keep them out of school at all," Malcolm said grimly. "We maintain vigilance, we walk them to and from the car, we warn their teachers to pay attention at recess, and we remind the boys that they need to be mindful of their own safety. I refuse to let those bastards control our lives."

"Haven't they already done that in making us take those precautions?" I demanded. "We have to do something to convince the Savants to leave us alone. I don't want the kids to live in fear."

Malcolm said nothing. I sat with my hands closed tightly on my clutch purse, feeling drained. That outburst had left me with nothing else to say, either. It was one thing to make dramatic declarations and something else entirely to know how to act on them.

We were nearly home when Malcolm said, "You're right."

"Right about what?"

"That we shouldn't let them control us. Tomorrow morning I'll set Campbell Security looking for a way to go on the attack. I don't care how big Astraeus Resources is, it's not invulnerable. The Savants are weak on magic, from everything we've learned, and we have magic they can't defend against no matter what Jessop told them. I will convince Michael Castellan that coming after us is a mistake."

His mention of Astraeus Resources, the giant corporation Castellan headed, made me shiver. I'd been thinking in terms of Castellan himself being a threat and had forgotten just how powerful his corporation was. Castellan had the rare ability to hold multiple beliefs, multiple possible actions, in his mind at once, which thwarted the oracle's ability to prophesy directly about him. It was something usually only seen in sociopaths, which told me everything I needed to know about my enemy.

"I guess we have the advantage in one way," I said. "Castellan can't send teams of paramilitary thugs to attack the school openly, and I'm willing to bet Eris's illusions tonight represent the limits of what the Savants are capable of, so they can't send thugs concealed by illusions. And I think Castellan might be afraid of what power I might possess."

Malcolm pulled into our driveway and waited for the garage door to open. "So you think Jessop didn't give everything away."

"I don't know. It's just a feeling, really. I didn't have time or focus to prophesy about what Eris wanted, and of course I can't find out what he knows himself. But my instinct is that if Castellan knew the truth about the oracle, he'd be more direct in his approach. This feels more like he thinks I have a weapon I could use against him." I waited for the car to come to a halt before opening the door. "I mean, the oracle is a weapon, sort of, but it's not a machine gun."

"I understand. I can use that fear against him." Malcolm retrieved the box of books from behind his seat and handed it to me. "Are you sure you're all right?"

I nodded. "I felt strong, facing her. Not like a victim. I think the fighting lessons are helping in more than just teaching me how to hit someone."

Malcolm popped the trunk and hauled the big painting, well wrapped as protection, out to lean against the rear bumper. "That's what I want to hear. So Sibby Gonzalez is working out?"

"She's wonderful. I feel like I'm getting lessons tailored just for me. Which is true." Sibby was no taller than I was, but she was muscled like a bodybuilder and had an air about her that made her seem six feet tall. Malcolm had chosen her in part because she had years of experience in instruction and in part because she was a bone magus, not a front-line fighter. He'd said a wood or steel magus would depend too much on his or her aegis-granted skills, something I lacked. I liked her because she was as totally committed to teaching me to incapacitate an attacker as if her own life depended on my skills. That reminded me I was learning these skills as much for my children's defense as my own.

Jeremiah and Viv were watching a movie in the great room when we entered, Night-Noon sprawled across both their laps. Viv turned around. "How was—wow, you look beat. Auction too much for you this time?"

I smiled halfheartedly. "I assume everything here was quiet?"

"There was some fuss over bedtime, but nothing serious." Viv's eyes narrowed. "What happened?"

"That Savant woman, Eris Reichert, tried to kidnap me," I said, not feeling like sugar-coating the news.

Viv hissed in shock. Jeremiah paused the movie. "At the gala?" he said. "Then they know where the boys go to school."

"Unfortunately, yes," Malcolm said. He put the box of books on the big square ottoman. "I intend to go on the attack tomorrow. This is too serious to wait on office hours."

"You'll need better security at the school," Jeremiah said. "I can keep an eye on them."

"We can't ask you to do that," I protested.

"I didn't wait for you to ask," Jeremiah said with his familiar brilliant smile. "With all the trees surrounding the property, I can be invisible, and I'd bet my staff against anything Astraeus fields against me. If Castellan is going to send someone after the boys, it will be while you're still off-balance from the attack on Helena."

"True," Malcolm said. "Thank you."

"Yes, thank you, Jeremiah," I said. Jeremiah was a wood magus, attuned to the natural world, and a master staff fighter easily Malcolm's equal. The thought of him watching over Alastair and Duncan eased my mind.

Viv hugged me. "This can't go on forever. Even Castellan's resources aren't infinite."

"I know," I said, and blinked away tears prompted by her compassion. "I wish we knew what else he was up to."

"Entering Faerie, probably," Malcolm said. "Looking for weak points in the elves' defenses. We can thank his obsession for not having had to deal with attacks on the Wardens."

"Maybe they'll destroy each other," I said. "All right, no, I'm not in favor of genocide," I added when Viv made a noise of protest. "But it would be convenient if both our enemies fought each other to the point that they're no longer a threat to humanity."

"That's more luck than even I want to count on," Viv said.

CHAPTER SEVEN

The doorbell rang at 6:32 Wednesday evening, and Malcolm left the kitchen to answer it. I continued tossing the salad and listened to the distant sound of voices and then footsteps. I was about to leave the salad to greet our guests when the oven timer beeped. Swiftly, I removed the lasagna from the lower oven and set it on the trivet I'd put on the stove top. I was good at lasagna after all these years, and it was the kind of comfort food I hoped would encourage the Hubbards to relax.

The bread still had a couple of minutes to go, so I set aside the oven mitts and hurried past the dining room into the great room. "Hi! Thanks for coming. I'm afraid I'm running about five minutes behind."

"It's no problem," Maddy said. Tonight she wore strands of freshwater pearls interspersed with faceted dark red gems, possibly garnets, and matching dangly earrings. The jewelry looked less overdone now that she was wearing a silk blouse and skirt instead of jeans and a T-shirt. Bronson looked more casual, in slacks and an olive-green polo shirt. Liv and another little girl, this one with darker blonde hair than Liv's, hovered beside them. "This is our oldest daughter, Emma, and of course you know Liv."

"It's good to see you again," I said. "Hi, Emma. Hi, Liv. Excuse me—oh, how nice!" Malcolm had handed me a bottle of very good wine. "Thank you—this will go perfectly with dinner. And that's the timer. Please, sit, and we'll eat soon."

I hurried back to the kitchen and removed the loaf of garlic bread to the cutting board, then set the timer for five minutes and leaned against the counter to cool off. With both ovens running, the kitchen became the warmest room in the house. But the smells were incredible, the zesty smell of tomato sauce, the sharp salty tang of garlic, the warm yeastiness of the bread. I breathed in the aromas for a few seconds, then took the wine into the dining room and checked to make sure the glasses I'd set out were appropriate. I wasn't much of a wine drinker, but Harry Keller had made me competent in pairing wine with the right food and the right glasses.

I went into the great room and perched on the arm of the couch next to Malcolm. Malcolm was saying "—long way to go, but I assume the opportunity was worth it."

"Absolutely," Bronson said. "It's hard to build up a practice from the ground floor, and Darrell is someone I'd worked with when I was just starting out in dentistry. He wanted someone he knew and trusted to take over when he retired."

"It's been hard on the girls, I admit," Maddy said. "But better now than when they're teenagers, I think."

"Yes, that's sensible," Malcolm said. "Helena, is the food ready?"

"Just giving the lasagna a chance to cool off to below the temperature of molten lava," I said.

"Oh, I love lasagna," Maddy exclaimed.

"It's my favorite," I said. "Um, where are all the children?"

"Upstairs," Malcolm said. "Alastair wanted to show Liv something, and I'm afraid Jenny claimed Emma."

Maddy laughed. "Emma loves little children. She won't see it as a hardship if she plays with Jenny all night."

"Well, then—" The timer beeped. "Excuse me. I'll cut the bread, and then we can eat."

Years of entertaining hadn't broken me of the fear of a meal turning out badly. I still had memories of inviting Judy and Mike over for dinner once, a long time ago, where the potatoes had been hard and I'd misjudged the amount of broccoli cheese casserole needed, and we'd ended up going out to eat instead. But this time, everything was perfect. The lasagna wasn't too hot, the salad was crisp and delicious, the garlic bread was just the right amount of garlicky, and as I'd thought, the wine was the perfect complement.

"I hope it's not rude to compliment you on Jenny's behavior," Maddy said as I was cutting up lasagna into small bites. "She's young to be so well-behaved at the dinner table."

"Thank you," I said, "but you might want to hold off on compliments until you've seen how she looks at the end of a meal. She's a little too fond of messes."

Jenny responded by scooping up lasagna and steering it to her mouth without smearing it on her cheek, just as if she wanted to prove me wrong. Well, that was a behavior I wanted to encourage, no matter how it made me look.

"Emma was a real terror at restaurants when she was little," Bronson said with a wink at his daughter.

"Daaaad," Emma said. "That was a long time ago. I'm ten now."

"I'm just saying you liked making a scene—"

"Daaaad."

"She's right, Bronson, that was a long time ago," Maddy said with a smile. "And it was a stage that didn't last long."

"Duncan was like that," I said, ignoring Duncan's glare. "Only his preferred place to make a scene was the grocery store. And that didn't last long, either, did it, Duncan?"

"Can I have more bread?" Duncan asked.

I handed him the bread basket. "Emma, how do you like Talbott Academy?"

Emma shrugged. "It's fine. I liked my old school better."

"But that will change. You've only been at Talbott for a few weeks," Maddy said, rather hastily. "Mr. Reese is a good teacher."

"Not as good as Miss Schwartz," Emma said. "She—"

"Oh, let's not be critical, all right?" Bronson said. "Liv likes Ms. Torres, right?"

"Yeah," Liv said. "She lets us choose our project partners. I hated group projects in my old school because I always ended up doing all the work. This way is better."

Maribel Torres was a Warden, and while she was an excellent teacher, her secondary goal was to help Alastair when he had a spontaneous prophecy. It wasn't at all unlikely that she'd arranged things so Alastair ended up in a group with kids nearly as smart as he was. "Alastair likes Ms. Torres too," I said. "So, what is this project you're working on?"

"It's spaceship design from years ago to now," Liv said, sitting up straighter in her enthusiasm. "And we're building our own spaceship."

"To show how the design might look in the next generation," Alastair added, equally enthusiastic. "Liv and Kenny and I."

"That sounds complex," Malcolm said. "Maybe you can sell your design to the space program."

Liv and Alastair both gave him the same look, the one kids give adults who might or might not be condescending to them. "We tried, but they said it was nice work and to come back in ten years," Alastair said. "We're going to show them by building a small-scale prototype that proves our design works, and then we're going to sell it to a private company."

"That's a great idea," Bronson said. "Make sure you don't reveal your design to anyone else. Technological espionage is a possibility."

"We know," Alastair said, sounding as if he really was ten years older. "Can I be excused, Mom? I'm full."

"Me too, Mrs. Campbell," Liv said.

"Sure, you can be done," I said. "Alastair, why don't you show Liv where to put her dishes—if that's all right," I added to Maddy. Maddy nodded. "And later I have brownies and ice cream."

Alastair was already halfway out the room with Liv following him. Duncan stuffed the last of his bread into his mouth and said, almost incomprehensibly, "I'm done too."

I nodded at him and set about cleaning Jenny up with a napkin. After that first tidy bite, she'd been her usual messy self. "I hope she outgrows this phase," I said to Maddy. "She just seems to enjoy the feeling of sauce on her face."

"At least she doesn't throw food on the floor," Malcolm said, rising. "I'll get a washcloth."

"She doesn't demand attention or shriek," Maddy said. "I'm so glad my children outgrew that phase quickly, shrieking for no reason in the middle of a store."

"She doesn't do that often," I began as Malcolm handed me a damp cloth. "Mostly—"

Jenny's eyes flashed silver. I sucked in a breath. "I think I need the sink," I babbled, and snatched Jenny out of her booster seat and ran with her into the kitchen.

"It's all right, it's all right, don't cry," I whispered. I turned the faucet to full and held Jenny's hands beneath the water. Jenny protested and tried to get her hands free of my grasp.

"Mommy, no water," she said.

"Sorry." I left the water running to mask any sound we might make, but Jenny didn't look frightened. "What did you see?"

"A house with lights on," Jenny said, "and people dancing inside."

That seemed both innocuous and irrelevant. "Nothing scary?"

"No. I felt happy. They had on pretty sparkly clothes and they twirled. Can I color a square?" Jenny grabbed the washcloth from my hand and rubbed it all over her face.

"You can definitely color a square." I took the washcloth back, rinsed it, and washed her face and hands more expertly. "That was a good prophecy, then."

"I like watching elves more," Jenny said, perfectly calmly.

I was so relieved she hadn't said that in front of the Hubbards. "I don't like it when the elves scare you," I said.

"It's only sometimes. The elves look funny, like they were sick and didn't get better. But they only scare me when they fight."

I hugged Jenny. "That's right. They can't hurt you."

Jenny wiggled to get down. "Can I have ice cream now?"

"We'll do that later. Why don't you see if Emma is finished eating, and maybe she will play with you some more." I felt only moderately guilty at sticking Emma with Jenny-watching duties, but I wanted some grown-up conversation, and Maddy had said Emma liked little kids.

With the meal over and the table cleared, the four of us adults returned to the great room while the children ran upstairs to play. I settled on the couch beside Malcolm and took in the room at a glance. The wall of windows overlooking the backyard was a dark mirror now that night had fallen, and the great room felt twice as big as it usually did. It was cold enough I'd started a fire in the big river stone fireplace, which to me made the room a perfect refuge from the world.

"That was an excellent meal," Maddy said. "Thank you for inviting us."

"It was our pleasure," I said.

"Malcolm was explaining about Campbell Security being an old family company," Bronson said. "How old, exactly?"

"It was founded by my great-grandfather Niall Campbell in 1939," Malcolm said. "He'd left Scotland after some trouble with the law—my grandfather always swore it was just that he liked a good fight, but I think it might have been more serious than that. At any rate, Niall hired out as protection for some of the lumber barons, and he got a reputation for honesty and competence, so his employers started giving him bigger jobs that required more than one man. That led to him expanding his business from bodyguarding to site security at the lumber mills and so forth. And then his children got involved, and..." Malcolm spread his hands as if to indicate an unstoppable force.

"How interesting," Maddy said. "And you know so much about your family. I don't even know my great-grandfather's name."

I knew there was a part of the story Malcolm hadn't mentioned: that Niall Campbell had accompanied Silas Abernathy to Portland when the oracular bookstore had moved there from England, and that his primary security job had been installing the wards that protected the store from invader attacks. "I don't either," I said. "But I'm not sure many people do. My great-grandmother died when I was two, so of course I don't remember her, but how many people live to see their great-grandchildren at all?"

"Right," Maddy said, nodding.

"And what is it you do, Helena?" Bronson asked.

"I manage a corporate giving fund affiliated with Campbell Security," I said smoothly. This wasn't the first time I'd answered this question. "I handle applications for grants, disburse the funds, that sort of thing."

"That sounds so rewarding," Maddy said. "It's as much as I can do to keep up with the children, let alone hold a job. I've put my career on hold for now."

She didn't sound defensive the way a lot of stay-at-home moms did, so I asked, "What did you do before?"

"Chemistry. I was a researcher for a company in Denver, developing synthetics."

"You can see where Liv gets her brains," Bronson joked.

Maddy shrugged. "It was engaging work, but I'd rather be there for my daughters while they're young. So I'm grateful we're financially in a position for me to do so."

"That's how we feel," Malcolm said, putting his arm around my shoulders. "So, how are you liking Portland?"

"It's very wet," Maddy said with a smile. "I don't know that I'll miss the snow. Were you both born here?"

"Yes, and I at least haven't traveled many other places, so I don't have anything to compare it to," I said.

"Really? I'd think you'd have gone all over the world, talking to donors or grant recipients," Bronson said. "Unless your corporate giving is mostly local."

"It is. And I didn't travel much when I was young. Are you two big on travel?"

Maddy stiffened, briefly enough I almost thought I'd imagined it. "Oh, no, not us," she said, recovering quickly. "We're real homebodies."

"I like going to new places," Bronson said at the same time. He shot a glance at his wife and added, "But I'm always happier when I return home."

"My mother is a real world traveler," Malcolm said. "I don't think I could pick up and leave the country at a moment's notice even if I didn't have a young family. But I've been to Denver a couple of times—I really liked that restaurant, Gillespie's, downtown."

"Gillespie's closed last year," Bronson said. "Such a shame, but I heard they couldn't compete with the new establishments outside the city center."

"That is too bad." Malcolm nodded in agreement. "If you liked Gillespie's, you might try Marco Polo's, over in the Pearl District."

"We'll do that."

The somewhat stilted conversation was starting to get to me. It felt like the Hubbards were doing their best to divert attention from themselves or anything personal about them. "I think we can do better than this," I burst out. "Bronson, tell me about your car. You didn't say anything about it at the gala, but I'm guessing you can talk about it for hours."

Both Maddy and Bronson laughed, I thought a little abashedly. "I don't want to bore anyone," Bronson said.

"And believe me, hours of car talk is enough to bore even hard-liners like Bronson," Maddy said, poking her husband in the ribs with a teasing finger.

"All right, then fifteen minutes. My daughter loves cars, and she's been carrying her model Firebird around like a baby ever since Malcolm told her about yours."

"*Jenny* likes cars?" Bronson said. "Isn't she a little young?"

"It was a game we played," Malcolm said, "one night when I was putting Jenny to bed and she just would not go to sleep. Duncan and Alastair had some diecast cars they rarely played with, and I used them instead of counting sheep—'this is a Mustang, this is a Volkswagen Beetle,' that sort of thing. And then the next night, she demanded the 'car game' again. Then I thought to play cars with her during the day, and before I knew it she'd appropriated all her brothers' cars and knew most of their makes and models."

"That's adorable," Maddy said. "And remarkable. She must be very smart."

"Don't think I've been distracted," I told Bronson. "You rebuilt the Firebird? I didn't realize that was a thing people did—I mean, I thought only garages had the equipment for that."

"I've always loved working on cars, and the Firebird Trans-Am was a dream of mine." Bronson leaned forward with his hands clasped, intent on me. "It didn't run when I bought it, but after a lot of work—"

"And a lot of money," Maddy interrupted.

"I restored everything but the paint job. That, I hired out. Speaking of things only garages can do. That is, individuals can, but I didn't have the right equipment, and bodywork doesn't interest me like engines."

"And it's an excellent restoration," Malcolm said. "How did you get it to Portland from Denver? Did you drive?"

This time, it was Bronson who twitched. "No, I had it shipped. I thought about driving, but that would have left Maddy alone with the girls."

"Of course," I said. "That makes sense."

Bronson went off on something to do with cars, but I listened with only half my attention. I couldn't understand why the mention of driving his car cross-country to Portland would make Bronson uncomfortable, any more than Maddy's talk of travel had made her tense. I told myself not to let my imagination run wild, but I couldn't help thinking that the Hubbards were hiding something. Mob connections, or Witness Protection, or...

I bit back a laugh. *Not* Savants. I'd asked the question about whether Maddy was a Savant and gotten a prophetic response that was the equivalent of a Magic 8-Ball saying "cannot predict now," which essentially meant I needed more information. The oracular gift had the strangest limits: it wouldn't tell someone how to commit a crime, it wouldn't give out lottery numbers, and it wouldn't spy on people except under exceptional circumstances. And it seemed to function better the more I knew about a topic. Maddy might still be a Savant, but I couldn't confirm it prophetically any more than I could rule it out.

But the longer I knew Maddy, the less inclined I was to believe it. Her nervousness about ordinary things, her occasional fearfulness, the way she never asked leading questions—and then there was the fact that they had two children. Surely even Castellan wouldn't enlist a couple of suburban parents as secret agents. That thought was courtesy of that anime Viv had showed me about the spy who got married and adopted a child so he could get close to his target. I'd continue to get to know Maddy, and eventually the oracle would be more specific.

We talked for another half hour before I got up to serve dessert.

Maddy offered to help, and I accepted, thinking I might grill her for more details that would explain her strange behavior. In the kitchen, serving out brownies, I asked, "Did you find it difficult to leave your job behind?"

Sure enough, Maddy twitched. But she sounded calm enough when she said, "Not really. My department's budget had been cut, and I was given a good severance package in exchange for not hanging around until they redacted my position. So the decision was half made for me. These are really good brownies."

"Thanks." I took the ice cream tub out of the freezer.

"Do you feel like your job gives you enough time with your children?" Maddy asked.

Again, she didn't sound accusatory, so I said, "Malcolm rearranged his work responsibilities so the two of us work together to raise the kids. I still do more of the errand-running and school-related responsibilities, because my job isn't terribly demanding, but I feel like we can both be there for them when they need us."

"That's really fortunate. Bronson's job takes up much of his time, since he's just starting out in this practice, but he does his best to stay connected. Here, I'll take some of those." Maddy picked up several small bowls filled with brownies topped with ice cream and carried them through to the dining room. I put the ice cream away before collecting the rest of the bowls. Maddy was nice, but there was an unnatural distance there that didn't fit with how open she was about her life. One more weird thing I couldn't explain away.

Liv and Alastair were quiet as they ate their dessert, not chattering about space as I'd expected. I decided not to interrogate Alastair about it. Quiet probably meant they were tired, and there was nothing strange about that.

Finally, the last bowls were scraped clean, the dishes returned to the sink, and Bronson said, "We should be going. It was really great getting to know you better."

"I hope that vase looks as good in your house as it did in the auction room," I told Maddy.

"As good as your painting does upstairs," Maddy replied.

"I guess we both won," I said with a smile.

When the door shut behind our guests, I said, "Bedtime, everyone. Don't forget to brush your teeth."

Duncan and Jenny ran for the stairs. Alastair followed more slowly. Impulsively, I said, "Alastair, are you all right?"

"Fine, Mom. Just tired." He slouched up the stairs and disappeared around the corner.

Malcolm took me in his arms and kissed me. "That was interesting," he said.

"It was nice," I said, "but I felt..."

"Felt like they were holding back? So did I."

I nodded. "I'm glad it wasn't just me. It was like we could be friends if they weren't so closed off. And they got tense any time anyone mentioned travel, did you notice?"

"I didn't. I was too busy testing them."

My brow furrowed. "Testing them, how?"

"Well, you know how I brought up that restaurant? I was thinking, if they'd lied about being from Denver, they wouldn't know Gillespie's had closed. But now I'm just not sure if they really are from Denver or they've just been coached really well. And I'm not at all sure Bronson restored that car by himself. He didn't know some of the details he would have been familiar with if he'd done the hands-on work."

"They're definitely hiding something. They didn't want us to pry into their pasts at all, and they deflected any questions we had about their family. The most Maddy would say about her job was that she left before she was let go." I snuggled into Malcolm's embrace. "Should we worry about them?"

"Meaning, are they a threat?" Malcolm shook his head slowly as if in thought. "I don't think they are, not directly. I doubt they're Savants, if that's what worries you."

"I couldn't confirm if they were or weren't, but I feel the same. It's so frustrating. I wanted them to be friends."

"They might still become friends. We could be wrong, and they're just not good with strangers." Malcolm released me to take my hand and lead me to the stairs.

"If they're not a threat, they might need our help," I said.

Malcolm looked skeptical. "I don't think we should interfere in the affairs of people we hardly know."

"It wouldn't be interference. I'm not saying swoop in and solve their problems, I'm saying if there's something we can do, we should consider it. For Alastair's sake if nothing else. He has so few close friends."

"I'll keep it in mind," Malcolm said. "But I have a feeling the Hubbards are going to remain a mystery."

I sighed. "I hope that's not true."

Chapter Eight

Friday morning, Jeremiah stopped by before I left for carpool. "It's been a quiet week," he said. "Nothing suspicious, no cars parked all week in the same place or along the main road where the driver can see the school doors. I've been paying attention to recess time in particular. I look for Savant agents regardless, but if a Savant knows when the kids are outside and presumably vulnerable, that would be a time when they're not watching their own surroundings so attentively."

"Jeremiah, thank you," I said.

"It's no trouble. I would hate to see anything happen to these rug rats." He aimed the last words at Duncan, who grinned. Jeremiah didn't like children as a whole, had no interest in being a father, but he had an attachment to my children I appreciated.

"Are you going to school with us?" Duncan asked. "Like a bodyguard?"

"No, I'll be watching for Savant agents," Jeremiah said. "You won't see me, but I'll be there."

"What if I do see you? Because I'm really good at spotting things. I'm a ranger." Duncan swiped the air with an invisible staff.

"If you see me, you have to pretend I'm not there. You know how it works—if they're watching you, they could figure out things you don't mean to give away." Jeremiah crouched to put himself on Duncan's level. "Time for you to be a ranger, right?"

Duncan nodded and ran for the land yacht. One of the things I loved about Jeremiah was how he treated the boys like they were as smart as adults. "Thank you for not saying he wouldn't see you," I said. "Or pointing out that he hasn't seen you all week."

"I wouldn't do that." Jeremiah went back to his car, a nice but unmemorable Honda Accord, and drove away.

As if the universe had heard Jeremiah's statement about a quiet week, my day was peaceful to match, more peaceful than I'd had in weeks. Between worries over the elves, being threatened by Savants, and the weirdness that was the Hubbards, I felt I'd been on edge ever since Alastair's birthday party. But the morning was calm. Jenny played quietly in her room while I did some tidying up of my office and the great room. I didn't have any spontaneous prophecies about horrible disasters. I listened to music and felt the tension drain away with Idina Menzel's voice. I suspected life wouldn't stay this peaceful, so I intended to appreciate it while it was.

Malcolm called just after lunch, when Jenny had gone down for her nap. "This is not entirely a personal call," he said after I exclaimed in delight upon hearing his voice. "Though I do love talking to you during the day. It cheers me considerably."

"What makes it not entirely personal? Do you need something?"

"A prophecy, though I'm not sure what to ask for. Is Jenny asleep? This may take a few minutes."

"I think she's lying in bed playing with her dolls. She's getting old enough she might not need naps anymore. But I figure as long as she's quiet, that's enough." I hurried downstairs and settled on the couch in the great room. "Tell me what's going on."

"Nothing. Literally nothing. The elves haven't made any incursions since last Tuesday." Malcolm's calm words were at odds with his tone of voice, which suggested he was frustrated. "It would be too much to expect this means they have given up on entering our world, but if they have changed tactics, it's in a way we haven't been able to pinpoint. They may be preparing for a bigger assault, an attack in force instead of one or two elves at a time. And *that* is something we can't depend on quick responses to counter. We need to know in advance where that will be, because getting our people there only after it's happened could be catastrophic."

"I see." I thought about it for a moment. "Hang on."

I lowered my phone and leaned back against the cushions. Then I let the question *Where will the elves strike next?* sink deep within me.

Immediately I was caught up in the whirling, dizzying sensation of a prophecy. Images flew past, scenes of a moonless night, of dark shapes that might be trees, of long grasses moving in an intangible wind. If this was the answer, it was useless without context. I told Malcolm about it anyway. "Let me try again."

A second prophecy wasn't much clearer than the first. I wished I could see the location on a map, which I knew was possible because I'd had such prophecies before. Before replying to Malcolm, I tried something different: *Are the elves still trying to enter our world?* Yes/no questions were harder, as I'd proved in trying to determine if Maddy was a Savant, but it was worth the attempt.

The prophecy swept me up, higher and higher, and then I plummeted like I was on the biggest roller coaster ever. When my vision settled, I was at the base of a tall mountain range, as tall as Everest, with snowy peaks and bare stone foundations. Nestled into the foot of the nearest mountain was a city like nothing I'd ever seen outside fantasy illustrations. I wasn't sure what made it seem so alien, aside from how its many spires and towers seemed to emerge from the stone as if it was a carving of a city and the artist was only half done.

I had just enough time to absorb this when the vision caught me up again and flew me hummingbird-fast toward the city, stopping me so abruptly if I'd been physically there, my neck would have snapped. Enormous copper doors as bright as a new penny loomed over me, gaping open, and beyond them I saw hundreds of elves—

—and I gasped as if I'd been holding my breath and blinked my dry eyes. Then I said, "Malcolm, I don't think the elves have given up. I think they're waiting for something."

"Something like what?"

"I don't know." A final image returned to mind, the figure of a pasty-skinned elf with stringy white hair, and I knew I'd seen him before. Not physically, not like the dark-haired muscular elf I'd seen snap the neck of one of his comrades outside Seattle. Him, I sometimes had nightmares about. No, this one I'd seen in front of those same rose-copper gates, but in vision, not in real life. At that time, he'd seen me as well, and I thought that might have been the case this time. He hadn't looked threatening, but I wasn't going to make assumptions. "I think it might be safest to increase monitoring of the slips. Whatever the elves have in mind, they intend to strike hard."

"Understood. Thank you. I'll be back at five tonight."

"Wait, Malcolm! I keep forgetting to ask—what have you learned about the Savants? You said you wanted to go on the attack, but you haven't said anything about it all week."

"There isn't much to say yet. The Campbell Security investigation is twofold. On the one hand, we're watching you and the children—"

"I suspected you had someone following me."

"I hope that doesn't disturb you."

I sighed. "Mostly it makes me angry for the necessity, but I'm grateful not to be alone. Marlin Dunfee's attacks are still too recent. Anyway, you were saying?"

"You and the children are under surveillance, particularly when any of you are at the school. That's the only place we know for sure

Castellan can link to you. Then I have people investigating Astraeus Resources, searching for weaknesses. We won't attack preemptively, but the minute it looks like the Savants are ready to move against us, we will be prepared to strike."

"Thank you. That's comforting."

"You have nothing to fear. I love you."

"Love you, too."

I let my phone fall into my lap and took a deep, calming breath. It *was* comforting to know there were plans in place to protect me and the children, though I was also comforted by my growing skills with martial arts. Even so, I hoped Castellan had given up on attacking my family. It was unlikely, but I could dream.

And then there were my visions. All those elves... it really had felt as if they were waiting for something, but the oracle didn't give me any hints as to what that was. I felt too unsettled to prophecy again, not right away. Once Malcolm knew more, he could ask directed questions, but until then, I would be grateful the terrifying elf only showed up in my dreams.

That afternoon I took advantage of having carpool to volunteer in Duncan's classroom after school. Halloween was fast approaching, and I liked decorating for holidays, especially when I wouldn't have to take down and put away the decorations. And after my unsettling visions, I found myself craving something normal and harmless. So, with Jenny in tow, I entered the school and found all three children waiting where I'd told them to meet me. It struck me as semi-miraculous that they'd obeyed, let alone that Duncan and Sophia weren't sniping at each other.

"Thank you for obeying," I told them, not caring that I sounded slightly condescending. "Now, you can either help me decorate Ms. Gorham's room, or you can wait in the library. Which will it be?"

"Library," Alastair replied promptly.

Duncan and Sophia exchanged glances. "*Not* running around," I reminded them. "You have to sit still and look at books. Mrs. Vance won't put up with rowdiness in her library." Mrs. Vance was about five hundred years old and had singlehandedly catalogued every book in the school library when they switched from the card catalog to computers. She was friendly and outgoing except when she was talking about books, and then you'd have thought she was a Marine drill sergeant, laying down the law about appropriate library behavior. Not even parents were exempt.

Duncan scowled. "Mrs. Vance is scary. I think she's a vampire."

"Vampires don't come out in daylight," I pointed out, playing along.

"I want to decorate, then," Sophia said. "I'm good at that."

"I'm better," Duncan said.

"Are not!"

"Am so!"

"*Enough*," I said forcefully. "You can help so long as you aren't disruptive. Alastair, would you be willing to take Jenny with you? I'm sure she'll be bored in the classroom."

Alastair shrugged. "I guess. I don't want to read to her."

"That's up to you, but I'm sure if you picked a book about animals, that would interest both of you." I didn't like putting Alastair in charge of Jenny often, not because he wasn't responsible but because I felt it was an unfair burden. "Mrs. Vance will keep an eye on both of you, and if Jenny gets restless, you can bring her to me, all right?"

"All right." Alastair shrugged again.

"Are you feeling well? You seem a little down."

Alastair straightened. "I'm fine. I just—I was going to read something else. But it's okay, I can check the book out for later. Don't worry about me."

His sudden rapid-fire response worried me more than his seeming despondency. Alastair wasn't a good liar, and I suspected he was concealing something. But now wasn't the time to challenge him on it, not in public where he might be embarrassed. "Okay. Thank you for taking care of your sister."

We all walked to the library, which was a high-ceilinged room near the center of the old building—the one forming the nucleus of the current campus—and I asked Mrs. Vance if Alastair and Jenny could read there for half an hour. Mrs. Vance cast an eye over both of them and said, "I hope they can behave themselves. You know I'm not a babysitting service."

"I know, and Alastair is aware of what to do if Jenny becomes disruptive. They just need a responsible adult present in case of an emergency. You don't mind that, right?" Mrs. Vance's steely glare unsettled me, coming as it did from eyes mostly buried in a topographical map of wrinkles.

"If it were anyone else, Mrs. Campbell..." Mrs. Vance smiled unexpectedly. "Alastair loves reading more than I do, and that's saying something. Perhaps I will have them help me shelve books."

"Oh, but Jenny can't read—"

"No one is ever too young to learn how to handle a book properly," Mrs. Vance said in her familiar lecturing tone. "Don't worry. I'll keep an eye on them."

Cautiously relieved, I took Duncan and Sophia to their classroom, where Sabina Gorham was busy sorting through decorations, discarding ones too worn or damaged to use. "Helena," she said in some relief, "I'm so glad. Brent Decker called and said he forgot he had an appointment, so it's just you and me." She laid down a string of dancing skeletons and freed her masses of thin black braids from the headwrap confining them, gathered them in one hand, and rewrapped her hair so it wasn't coming down in back anymore.

"Brent always seems to forget appointments," I said. "His wife Sally tells me he is genuinely forgetful and not making things up to get out of tasks when he changes his mind. How can we help? I figure Duncan and Sophia can hand us things."

Sabina smiled at the children. "Bet you didn't think you'd be staying late in class, did you? How about you pick which monsters we put on the back wall?"

Between the four of us, it took only twenty minutes to hang all the decorations, an assortment of paper cutouts of monsters, plastic skeletons, and orange and black crepe paper ribbons. Duncan and Sophia kept up a running commentary as we worked, all about the Halloween costumes they wanted to wear, the details of which changed by the minute. When we were finished, and Duncan and Sophia were chasing each other around the room. I leaned against Sabina's desk and said, "How has Duncan been about prophecies?"

Sabina settled her brightly colored gown around her ample form and leaned beside me. "I haven't seen any reluctance to speak up if he sees something important. I don't think he asks for prophecies at all. I assume he has more spontaneous prophecies than he tells me about, though I don't know how many is common. We haven't had any problems."

I watched Duncan and Sophia dart between the desks. "He used to feel pressured to act on what he saw. Now that he knows it's not his responsibility, he's been so much more open about his prophecies."

"That must be a relief for all of you. Really, I don't know how you manage it." Sabina straightened and said, "Parent-teacher conferences are coming up. You want to sign up now?"

"Sure."

I set a reminder in my calendar for the meeting and rounded up the kids. On a whim, I said, "Ms. Torres might be decorating her classroom today. You want to see if we can help her, too?"

"Yes, yes!" Duncan and Sophia chanted.

They ran ahead of me down the hall, shouting over my repeated requests for quiet. Well, it wasn't as if there were many people around to be disturbed, and I could remember wanting to do the same thing when I was in elementary school. The two passed Alastair's third grade classroom, ran to the end of the hall and the closed double doors leading to the lunchroom, turned around, and sped back in my direction. "Duncan, Sophia!" I exclaimed. "Stop running... oh, never mind." Parenting was sometimes about knowing what futility looked like.

The racing children passed me again, heading for the front hall. Shaking my head, I kept walking. They'd eventually turn around and run back, and if someone in the office chastised them, maybe that would stick better than my own gentle reprimands.

The door to Maribel Torres's classroom was open, and I entered to find Maddy Hubbard there, standing on a stepstool and cradling a fake bat with a furry body and paper wings in both hands, staring down at it. "Oh, hi, Maddy!"

Maddy jerked in surprise and stepped abruptly off the ladder. "Helena," she said. "You're so quiet, you startled me." She clasped one of the wedge-shaped rose tourmaline beads strung on her long necklace exactly like a Victorian dowager clutching her pearls.

"I'm sorry." I saw the box of thumbtacks on a desk some distance from the stepstool. "You want some help with that?"

Maddy glanced at the decoration in her hand, then at the row of identical bats lining the wall just below the ceiling. "I guess I forgot I needed a thumbtack," she said with a laugh. "Yes, if you'd hand it over?"

I brought her the box, and she attached the bat and stepped down again. "I didn't know you'd volunteered for this," she said.

"I didn't. I was helping in Ms. Gorham's class with Duncan and Sophia—and there they are now." The sound of shouting children grew louder as I spoke. "Hang on a sec."

I stepped out into the hallway and glared at the oncoming racers. "That's enough," I said, putting enough force into my words that it brought Duncan and Sophia to a halt. "Time to calm down. Come in here and sit for a minute, and then we'll go back to the library."

When I returned, all the bat decorations were up, and Maddy was putting away tacks and tape. "All done," she said, in a tone of voice so cheerful I was instantly suspicious, though I didn't know of what. It was just that most people didn't sound like that unless they were Clarice the office worker or on drugs.

"Fast work," I said. "Where is Ms. Torres?"

"Taking a call in the office." Maddy smiled. "Teachers' work is never done, right?"

"...Right," I said. "Is Liv with you?"

"Bathroom." Maddy gathered up her purse. "I guess I'll see you around, huh?"

"Sure." I eyed her skeptically.

Maddy waved at Duncan and Sophia and hurried away before I could say anything more. I stared at the empty doorway. That had been the behavior of someone intent on hiding something—the kind of behavior Alastair exhibited when he was lying. But I couldn't imagine what Maddy could have lied about. There hadn't been anything *to* lie about, as brief an interaction as that had been.

We returned to the library to find Alastair sorting books on a cart and Jenny looking at *Skippyjon Jones*. "Mom, this is fun!" Alastair said. "It's like a puzzle. Mrs. Vance says if I beat her time, she'll let me choose a book from the discards!"

My genius child was seriously weird. "That does sound fun," I said.

Mrs. Vance emerged from between the bookcases with an armload of books. "Alastair's memory is prodigious," she said approvingly. "I'm sure he'll make a fine librarian one day."

"I think he wants to design rocket ships," I said.

Mrs. Vance waved that away with a frown. "There's no reason he can't do anything he sets his mind to. Alastair, I found the book on Go strategy I mentioned."

Alastair left his sorting and accepted the book. "Thanks, Mrs. Vance. I like Go, but I'm not good at it yet."

"What a relief," Mrs. Vance said cryptically.

As I herded the children outside, I watched my surroundings carefully. Jeremiah hadn't reported any suspicious activity, and I hadn't seen any villainous strangers, but I wasn't taking chances. The children chattered, oblivious to my wariness. Jenny held Alastair's hand so I could have both hands free to defend us all. I didn't kid myself that I was great at martial arts yet. But I'd do whatever it took to protect my children.

On the drive home, after dropping off Sophia, my thoughts turned to Maddy, and I mentally ran over the list of weirdnesses she'd exhibited. Her unnatural worry over Liv's location at the birthday party. How she'd insisted Alastair come to their house—even after they'd had dinner with us, which I'd hoped would loosen her up, she still wouldn't let Liv come over. How distant she and Bronson had been at dinner, and how outgoing at the gala. Her swift departure from the classroom just now. Taken individually, they were nothing, but as a whole, they painted a picture of a woman—a family—afraid of something.

My first instinct was to help. I liked the Hubbards and, as I'd told Malcolm, I wanted to see them secure if only for the sake of Alastair and Liv's friendship. But immediately I slapped that instinct down. I had enough problems without adding the Hubbards' security to the list. Besides, Maddy and Bronson were grown adults who could handle their own affairs without my interference. And, as if that wasn't enough reason, they hadn't asked for help. I needed to stay out of this.

I glanced back at Alastair in the rearview mirror. He was staring out the window instead of reading. "You all right?" I asked.

He nodded without tearing his gaze from the window where rain pattered lightly. "I'm fine."

"Should we arrange another play date with Liv?"

Alastair shrugged. "I guess. I'm tired right now."

That was enough of a rebuff to shut me up. Rather than feeling hurt, I was worried, this time for Alastair. He wasn't as exuberant as

Duncan, but usually he was a cheerful boy, and I didn't like how withdrawn he'd become. "Alastair," I said.

"What?"

"...Nothing. Never mind." Alastair, when pressured to talk, always turtled up. As worried and frustrated as I was, I had no option but to wait for him to decide to tell me what was wrong—and keep a close eye on him in case more was wrong than I believed.

CHAPTER NINE

Tuesday night was girls' night out, and Judy, Viv and I took turns choosing where we went for dinner. We each had our favorites. I alternated between Giuseppe's, my favorite Italian restaurant, and a diner called Frank's that served the best cheesesteak sandwiches in Portland. Judy liked more upscale restaurants like Marco Polo's, fancy without being so elite we couldn't go there in jeans. And Viv tried something new every time.

Tonight it was Viv's turn to pick. She'd opted for the incongruously named Lobster Shack, a seafood place she'd heard served authentic Basque dishes "like Anthony Bourdain wrote about," she'd told us, selling us on its virtues. I didn't love seafood the way I did lasagna, but it sounded appealing.

The restaurant itself wasn't Basque themed, but had an almost cheesy décor centered on pirates. A tiny brass cannon filled the center of the foyer, whose walls were draped with pirate flags. More nautical paraphernalia decorated the walls above the booths, and the napkin holders looked like old-style sailing ships. It was a weird mix of kitschy and cool, and I said so once the greeter, who fortunately was not dressed like a pirate, seated us and was gone.

"It's not about the ambience, we're here for the food," Viv declared airily. "Besides, look at these salt and pepper shakers. Tiny lighthouses!"

"Those are cute," Judy admitted. "And the place smells great."

"See? Trying something new is fun," Viv said.

Our server, also not dressed as a pirate, brought us menus, and we studied them in silence. I knew nothing about Basque cuisine, but fortunately the restaurant's offerings were grouped by origin. I settled on Basque seafood stew, which at least had ingredients I recognized. The restaurant did smell good, and maybe this would become my new favorite dish.

Having ordered, we settled in to talk. Usually it was about our children or our jobs, with Viv always having funny stories to tell about her work as a private investigator. Tonight, though, Judy abruptly said, "I think something strange is going on."

"Stranger than our lives usually are?" I said.

"Strange in a different way." Judy leaned forward and lowered her voice. "You know I have web alerts set for mention of aliens?"

"Your unlikely obsession, yes," Viv said.

"It's not an obsession, it's an interest," Judy replied with a friendly scowl. "I don't believe in aliens, given that other realities are a thing. But the psychology of alien enthusiasts intrigues me. The desire for there to be more to life than the mundane. So I have alerts set for key words. And there's been a dramatic increase in reports of alien sightings in the past week, maybe week and a half."

"Does that mean something?" I asked. "Maybe it's UFO season."

"They're called UAPs now, unidentified anomalous phenomena," Judy said, "and there is a time of year when sightings increase, but it's not this time. And I don't know if it means anything. But it occurred to me this afternoon that it's a weird coincidence that alien activity—reported alien activity—shot up just as the elves have slowed their advance across the slips."

"I don't think—" Viv's mouth abruptly closed. "What kind of activity?"

Judy pulled out her phone. "People claiming to have seen mysterious figures, mostly. Always in remote areas, hikers or campers. They're reported as being tall and thin, not your gray alien type. That's what clicked for me this afternoon. What if the elves are sneaking in somewhere else?"

"Did you tell anyone else? Campbell Security?" I demanded.

"What, that I have a hunch about a bunch of UAP nuts? I wanted to talk to you to see if I'd turned into a conspiracy nut myself." Judy gestured with her phone. "There should be some way to confirm my suspicion and save the Wardens some legwork."

"All right," Viv said. "If it is elves, there ought to be other evidence. I think the biggest objection to your theory is that no one has showed up dead. Because why would the elves let anyone get a good look at them and not kill the person?"

"Good point," Judy said, and began typing on her phone. "Though I'm not sure how likely it is that I'll find many results on —whoa."

"What?" I said.

"I searched on 'mysterious deaths remote locations' and it actually returned something. A lot of somethings." She scrolled down her screen. "Some of these are old. Let me narrow this search. Huh." She handed her phone to me. "I limited the search to the last week, and that's the second hit I got."

I scanned the article, which came from some news organization in Australia, and felt cold. "Knife wounds. And the victim was out in the middle of nowhere."

"Listen to this," Viv said. "This woman in England says she saw angels in her vegetable garden."

Judy and I stared at her. "What does that have to do with aliens?" I asked.

"Elves look tall and thin and pale. Not everyone will assume they're aliens. Why not angels instead?" Viv was already typing on her phone. "I bet some of those sightings didn't show up on your alien search because people thought the elves were something else."

"I can't do a full search and compare on my phone—"

We were interrupted by our server bringing our meals. I tasted my seafood stew, which was delicious, but my anxiety over elf incursions we didn't know anything about had killed my appetite. "I have to call Malcolm. I think you've hit on something, Judy. Somehow the elves have found slips we don't know about. They could be gathering for an attack right now."

Viv and Judy waited while I called. "Malcolm, this is urgent," I said when he answered. I explained Judy's theory and what we'd found, ending with, "I know it sounds ridiculous—"

"It doesn't," Malcolm said. "We assumed the lack of elf incursions recently did not mean they've given up on entering our world. Unfortunately, we don't yet have a way of discovering an elf incursion that happens somewhere other than a slip we're monitoring. Judy's insight is valuable."

"But not a solution," I said, feeling disappointed.

"It's a partial solution only because mundane sources can be unreliable and erratic. It's more than we had before. I have to make some calls as soon as the children are in bed, but if you are willing to interrupt your dinner further, you might let Lucia know."

"I will. Thank you."

"Thank Judy for me," Malcolm said.

I disconnected and called Lucia. It took her a while to answer, but finally I heard her say, "Davies? Don't you have things to do?"

"Judy and Viv and I came up with something. Well, mostly Judy." I repeated what I'd told Malcolm and waited for her to stop cursing.

Finally, Lucia said, "That's the kind of clever thinking I need more of. We can see about tracing those elves and maybe identifying how they're getting in."

"I thought it was impossible to cross between worlds except at a slip."

"That's true. But do you remember Jeong's device for identifying thin places between the worlds? It was designed to look for where slips might be encouraged to form, at places that are too... his word was 'thick', but I think of it as using a machete rather than a butter knife to open a slip. If we can do it, maybe the elves can, too."

"Malcolm says it's a partial solution."

Lucia snorted. "I'll take even a partial solution to this problem. But in a few days, we'll have a better one. Jeong and his people are repurposing the Pattern to identify elves anywhere in our world."

"That sounds like a real solution!"

"Should be. And I want you there in case we turn it on and I need a prophecy to best use the information. I'll be in touch." She hung up without another word.

I lowered my phone. "They'll act on it. And they're working on something that will tell the Wardens whenever an elf enters our world, something beyond the monitors at the slips, which it sounds like aren't effective anymore."

"Pattern 2.0," Viv said. "It's not my kind of glass magic, but from what Harriet said, it's going to revolutionize scrying, even the kind I do."

"I can't wait to see how it works," I said.

I PARKED THE LAND YACHT IN THE SCHOOL PARKING LOT the following afternoon and turned off the engine. The car would hold onto its warmth for the short time it took for the kids to leave class. Behind me, Jenny sang a wordless song with a tune I almost recognized. It had been a peaceful day despite my low-grade anxieties about elves and Savants. When I wasn't fretting about whether the Savants might try something, I was fretting over what use Campbell

Security or Lucia had made of Judy's discovery. I wanted Malcolm to come home with the news that they'd eradicated the elf threat and closed all the slips—no, that was unreasonable, but even a little good news would be welcome.

Someone waved at me from the driver's seat of a pearl-gray Honda CR-V across the way. I squinted through the raindrops on my windshield and recognized Maddy Hubbard. I waved back, and Maddy got out of her car and ran over to me, shielding her head from the light rain with the hood of her coat.

I rolled down my window and said, "Hi, Maddy. How are you?"

"Fine, thanks. I was wondering if Alastair would like to come over tomorrow after school." She met my gaze directly, showing no unease.

I didn't know why her directness irritated me, given that I'd previously disliked how furtive she was. "Maybe Liv should come to our house instead. You know, take turns."

"I'd agree, except she and Alastair have been working on this enormous model rocket, and I don't think it would survive a trip in my car." Maddy gestured back at her CR-V. She still sounded perfectly calm.

I didn't know how to counter her. Pushing harder would make *me* sound suspicious, like I didn't trust her home to be a safe environment. "I'll see what Alastair says and have him call you, all right? Thanks for the invitation."

"I'm happy to have him over. Maybe Liv can take a turn when this model is built." Maddy nodded and hurried back to her car just as the bell rang.

I turned on my engine and watched the school doors for Alastair and Duncan and Sophia. That had been a perfectly normal interaction, not at all suspicious, but that in itself made me suspicious, given Maddy's previous behavior. And yet I was still sure they weren't so much a threat to us as they were hiding something that might be a danger to them.

"Alastair, Mrs. Hubbard has invited you over again," I told him as we got on the road. "Do you want to go?"

"Maybe," Alastair said.

"That's not very enthusiastic," I said. "Aren't you and Liv building a model?"

"Yeah. I don't know."

I came to a stop at a red light and turned in my seat to look at him. He was staring out the window, obviously avoiding my gaze. "Is something wrong? You and Liv aren't fighting, are you?"

"No."

"Alastair—"

Someone honked, and I turned my attention back to the road. "You know you can tell me if something's bothering you," I said.

"Nothing's bothering me. I guess I want to go to Liv's house."

I ground my teeth in frustration. Maybe Malcolm needed to try talking to our son. Alastair rarely kept secrets, especially about things he'd done wrong, because eventually the guilt got to be too much. Unfortunately, the longer he waited before that happened, the bigger the emotional crisis. But I still knew no way to coerce the truth out of him.

"You can call Mrs. Hubbard when we get home," I said. "Be sure to thank her for the invitation. I'll drive you there after school."

"I could ride with Liv."

"I'd rather take you." If Maddy could be weird about her daughter coming to my house, I could be strict about not letting him ride with... well, I knew Maddy, but not well, and she was as strange as they came.

Back at home, I settled the kids in at the table for a snack, then reclined on the couch and enjoyed the quiet for a moment. Maddy's face came to mind, and I considered how calm she'd been so long as I wasn't pushing her out of her comfort zone. She was afraid, and she was protecting her family. I knew what I was capable of if my children were threatened.

I closed my eyes and let the question sink into the heart of me: *What is Maddy Hubbard afraid of?*

The images that filled me didn't make sense at first. I saw nothing familiar, not even the Hubbards' faces. Then, to my surprise, I saw a scene from a movie. *Jurassic Park*, the original, a movie that had scared me silly because I was a total chicken when it came to horror even as mild as that. It was a scene with two children cowering in an industrial kitchen as vicious predator dinosaurs searched for them.

As if the oracle knew when I'd absorbed the image, the scene shifted, and I saw more movies, scene after scene of people hiding from danger. Then the vision ended, and I drew in a breath. Hiding. Danger. Fear of discovery. That explained a lot, but didn't give me any direction or reveal what or who the Hubbards were afraid of being found out by.

I thought for a moment, then reached out for an answer again: *Did the Hubbards come here to hide from what's pursuing them?*

My vision whirled, and the sensation of being lifted filled me. I saw a moving truck, a big one, and some cars, and realized I was looking at a freeway. The vision shifted, and I saw mountains, higher than the ones in the Cascades, that I thought might be the Rockies, and a house in a suburban neighborhood, and a couple of kids' bikes. I couldn't understand what it meant. My vision shifted again, and I saw Mount Hood, and another house, and then the prophecy faded.

I blinked rapidly to clear my eyes, which felt gritty. That had been inconclusive, and it frustrated me because I couldn't tell if it was the vision or its interpreter that was at fault. I settled in for another question, but before I could ask *Who is the Hubbards' enemy?* I heard a cry from the kitchen. "Mom! Jenny's making a mess!"

"Am not! You took my cookie!" Jenny shouted.

I heaved myself up from the couch with a heavy sigh. And just like that, I was back in the real world. Good thing in the real world, there were cookies as well as arguments.

CHAPTER TEN

I'd forgotten I'd said Alastair could go to Liv's house until the following morning, when Alastair said, "What time will you pick me up from the Hubbards'?"

"Oh," I said. "Actually, Alastair, maybe that's not a good idea."

"Why not?"

I hesitated, torn between wanting him to be safe and not wanting him to be afraid. "Maybe I was too quick to agree. I don't know if we can protect you at the Hubbards'. Are you sure you can't get Liv to come here?"

"Mom, I'll be fine," Alastair said, in a tone of voice that said I was being unreasonable. "The Savants aren't going to follow me around, are they?" His earlier reluctance about the play date had vanished entirely.

"They might. Alastair, we shouldn't take chances."

Malcolm entered the kitchen where we were having this discussion, and Alastair immediately seized on the opportunity to pit his parents against each other. "Dad, it's okay if I go to Liv's house today, right?"

"What did your mother say?" Malcolm said.

Alastair's head drooped. "She said 'no'."

"You know better than to try to get us to override each other." Malcolm turned to me. "But if you're worried about a Savant attack, I can make sure someone watches him secretly at the Hubbards'."

I considered this. The last thing I wanted was for my children to have to give up things they loved out of fear. "All right. But you won't do anything foolish, right?"

"I won't. Thanks, Mom!" Alastair shouted, and dashed off to get his backpack. He seemed back to his usual cheerful self, but I was sure he was still hiding things.

I sighed. "I need this to be over soon."

"It will be," Malcolm said. "Do you want me to drop him off or pick him up from his play date?"

"I'll pick him up. I want to talk to Maddy again. She's behaved so strangely before this, I want to see her on her home turf." I collected dishes from breakfast and set them in the sink. "I wish I knew what bothered her. Her and her family. They're definitely afraid of something."

"How afraid? Or maybe I mean, in what way?"

"My visions say they're afraid of discovery, but I don't want to draw conclusions on no more evidence than that. But it is tempting to imagine them hiding from the Mob because Bronson is a material witness against them."

The morning was so uneventful Malcolm decided to go into the office for a few hours. I played games with Jenny and managed to forget for a while that the Savants were out there somewhere. Of course, actually forgetting about them was dangerous, because that was when they would strike, but I could stop dwelling on what I didn't know.

Lucia called around noon. "Got any plans for this afternoon?"

"Um..." I didn't trust Lucia when she sounded that enthusiastic. "The boys come home from school around three."

"Perfect. How would you like to see Jeong's experiment put into action?"

"The Pattern? That was quick. Is Rick ready?"

"He says he is. Like I said, I want to be able to follow up on whatever he finds, plus I thought you might want to be present for history being made."

I made a face. "The last time that happened, I nearly lost a hand."

"You're not in any danger this time. I anticipate needing some guidance about which of those probes to take seriously."

I grimaced again. "Probes. That sounds so alien abductiony."

"It fits the nature of the incursions to date—swift entrances and retreats, for specific purposes. Like reconnaissance."

I shushed Jenny, who'd started to get loud in an effort to be heard over my conversation. "Just a minute, Jenny. When should I be there?"

"We can afford to wait on your schedule, but sooner is better. It shouldn't take long. I appreciate the sacrifice of your quiet afternoon." Lucia laughed again. "And Jenny can nap here as well as anywhere."

"Good point."

I said goodbye and disconnected, then clamped down on a sharp reprimand, saying instead, "You know it's not polite to shout over Mommy's phone conversation unless there's a real problem, and no, wanting me to answer your question about lunch for the tenth time doesn't count as a real problem. Come on, let's put away your toys and have sandwiches, and then we're going to the Gunther Node."

The promise of day care and seeing Lucia motivated Jenny to tidy up faster than usual, and it wasn't long before we were on our way north. I'd called Malcolm to let him know where I was going, and he was so calm about it I was surprised, until I remembered he had Wardens following me. The idea that Savants might know how to follow me filled me with anger again rather than dread. Castellan had no right to interfere in my life, and I wished I knew how to scare him off.

Lucia met us in the transit hub and walked with us to the day care, where Jenny abandoned me without a second thought. "I'm glad she still sees it as a treat," I said. "Day care here has been a marvelous help, and I'd hate for her to resent it."

"She's got too easygoing a personality for that," Lucia said. "How are things going with treating her empathy?"

"It's not treating it so much as understanding it," I said. "Dr. Deveaux says there's no way to cure her—that 'cure' is entirely the wrong word, even. It's something she'll have to learn to live with. And it's getting better. Well, not exactly getting better, but Jenny is learning to distinguish between her own emotions and other people's, and that seems to ease how those episodes affect her."

"So, she's still afraid." Lucia gestured to me to turn, and we followed the red line where it paralleled a white line that wobbled slightly, as if it had been painted by someone with a trembling hand.

"Yes. And she still sees visions that frighten her. But she's learning not to react so violently." I sighed. "I'm not sure suppressing her emotions is the right approach, either. But for now, it's what we have."

"I hope Deveaux's solution is a practical one. Jenny needs to grow up into a normal person. Don't think I didn't do my research. Deveaux is the sort of person who'd transplant a kitten's head onto a fish and then wonder why you objected."

"Oh, I don't think..." My voice trailed off. Lucia's example might be an exaggeration, but it wasn't much of one.

We'd reached the point where the only line on the floor was the white one. This part of the node was even more depressingly sterile than the rest of it, with cinder block walls painted institutional gray and pairs of buzzing fluorescent bulbs making a double line along the ceiling, illuminating the hall. Our footsteps echoed down the empty hall, making a light clapping noise that, since Lucia's strides were longer than mine, sounded like someone far away applauding a performance. I was grateful to reach the door, even though it wasn't a normal door, but an aluminum screen door with a small floodlight perched over it.

The room beyond didn't look anything like the gray concrete hallway; it was more like a tunnel, with a ribbed roof of olive-painted steel, and it had impossible skylights of yellowed Plexiglas, impossible because I was sure we were still deep underground. The men and women bending over computer consoles or walking briskly from one set of monitors to another looked in the yellow light either sallow or sepia or, in the case of some very dark-skinned Wardens, plum.

But I noticed this only in passing, because my attention was immediately drawn to the Pattern.

The tunnel walls to a height of about six feet were an extraordinary mosaic of square glass tiles about two inches on a side in every conceivable color. Even the weird yellow light couldn't do more than dull their brilliance. The original Pattern, I'd been told, was a masterpiece of glass magic devised to track the presence of monstrous alien invaders in our world. Back before the invaders were destroyed, the Pattern had been in constant motion as magi moved and reorganized the tiles to follow the paths the invaders took to reach us. Now, it gleamed in a beautiful wave of color, predominantly blue-green, untouched by anyone.

I'd only been in this room a few times, but until now, it had always felt like walking into a wind chime factory from all the glass clinking together, either being moved or being used in other glass magic. Now, it wasn't silent except by comparison to my memories. Men and women carried on murmured conversations, and I occasionally heard the chime of a mobile phone alert or someone's cheerful ringtone. But the sound of tinkling glass was gone. The only other difference was the presence of an enormous display screen, like a computer monitor the size of a theater screen, bolted to the wall above the Pattern. It was currently switched off.

Lucia made straight for the central bank of computers, which to me looked like a heap of discarded electronics. "You're still ready?" she asked Rick Jeong. "Don't make me a liar. Davies has stuff to do."

"I don't, actually," I reassured Rick, who looked just as he always did, disheveled and with a serious case of bed head. "But this is exciting."

"Not *that* exciting," Rick said. His youthful face was intent on something he was typing into a cracked beige keyboard. "That is, the results won't be dramatic. The exciting part is if it works at all."

"He's being pessimistic," an older woman who stood nearby said. "There's no reason to believe it won't work. We had Gabriel Roarke to use as a baseline, and honestly, this is far less complex than tracking invaders."

"I don't feel pessimistic," Rick said. "Just practical. I should have said, making it work is the exciting part. It's not like there are a lot of elves in our world for it to find, is all. Even if there are twice as many undiscovered slips as we suspect, that's still a number in double digits."

"Which is why I want Davies here to narrow down the best approach to the ones it does find," Lucia said. "I assume there are many more elves in the world than we're aware of, and I want them caught."

"Now who's being pessimistic?" Rick said with a smile.

"Pessimistic is in my job description," Lucia retorted. "But don't let us rush you, Jeong. There's no hurry."

Rick nodded. "Let's turn on the display, Meredith," he said to the older woman, who left us to walk over to the wall and flip a very large switch. The giant monitor hummed to life—literally hummed, like a choir of medieval monks all tuning up together—and its surface took on a grayish sheen. Then it flickered a couple of times, and suddenly an outline map of the world appeared, drawn simply in colored lines of light, centered on the Atlantic Ocean like every world map I'd ever seen in school. But it was more familiar than that—and in a flash, I recalled why I knew it. *"WarGames,"* I exclaimed.

Rick grinned. "Someone appreciates the classics."

"Jeremiah showed it to me. And it's hardly a classic, it came out in 1983," I replied.

"We can agree to disagree about how the '80s were the pinnacle of filmmaking," Rick said. "Anyway, yes. In terms of the effectiveness of Pattern 2.0, there's an inverse correlation between its ability to detect elves and the accuracy of its display. So I'm afraid the GUI isn't very refined. It will still show us—here."

He moved to a second computer, one that looked marginally newer than the one with the beige keyboard, and put his hand on a mouse. Immediately, a slim arrowhead appeared on the outline map. Rick moved it around in a swoop, then clicked on a part of the map over Australia's northern coast. Instantly, the display expanded, or shrank in closer, I wasn't sure how to describe it, except that the screen now focused on a square surrounding that point.

"It only looks archaic," Rick explained to Lucia. "We'll be able to focus in on any individuals Pattern 2.0 identifies."

"Looks good," Lucia said.

"Give me a few minutes, and we're good to go," Rick said. He clicked again, and the map went back to being the familiar one of the world. I wasn't sure I liked Rick's choice. After all, *WarGames* had been about the threat of nuclear war, and suppose there was some horrible coincidence arising from the use of that same map?

I silently chided myself for being superstitious and watched Rick walk between stacks of antiquated computers. My first impression, that they were junk, faded when I noticed how regularly they were laid out, all in geometric lines, and how the cables running between them were taped down to resemble a circuit board rather than taking the shortest route between two places.

After only about a minute, Rick said, "All right. Let's light this thing up."

People scurried to get into position, and for a few seconds, the tunnel echoed with the sounds of movement. Then everything was still. Rick stood before a laptop perched on a couple of old desktop towers. I couldn't see the laptop screen past his body, but I was more interested in the giant map anyway.

Rick clicked his mouse a few times, making the map tremble and then come back into better focus. I didn't remember *WarGames* all that well, but I was sure that despite the similarities, Rick's display was a thousand times more refined than the movie's had been. The red and green and blue lines didn't look pixelated, more like someone had drawn them with neon ink on a velvety black background.

"Count off," Rick said.

Someone to my left said, "Peg one is a go." Another voice, farther away, said, "Peg two, go."

The list went on: "Peg three"—"Peg four"—"Peg five," bouncing around the room until someone said, "Peg eleven is a go," and Rick said, "Thank you. On my mark—"

Nothing had changed as far as I could tell, but almost everyone around me tensed—everyone except Lucia, whose eyes were intent on the screen, and Rick, who still stared at the laptop monitor.

Rick said, "On three... two... one... *mark.*" He clicked the mouse like the snap of a finger.

The entire map blazed with points of light.

I gasped, but the sound was swallowed up by the shouts and cries of everyone around me. Hundreds, maybe thousands—no, *tens* of thousands of pinpricks of white light covered the map, rendering it too bright to look at directly without my eyes watering. I stepped forward, my heart pounding, but Lucia beat me to Rick's side. "That's impossible," she said. "Thousands of elves—"

"Hundreds of thousands," Rick said grimly. "I'll have a count in a minute."

"What's that?" I asked, pointing. Two of the pinpricks fluttered, flicking on and off so rapidly they seemed to tremble.

Rick stilled. "No," he said, and moved the mouse. The map shrank down to display the Pacific Northwest. "*No.* That's the Gunther Node—I set it to flag any elves near a Neutrality. The elves are here."

That sent my heart into overdrive. "I thought they couldn't get into a Neutrality."

"They can't open a portal here," Lucia said. "But we already know the node isn't completely invulnerable. Take a closer look, Jeong. Tell me where they are."

Rick clicked again. The display rippled, and a tangle of straight and curved lines appeared. I didn't recognize it, but I guessed it was the Gunther Node's floor plan. "One's just outside Green sector."

Jenny. The day care was right at the mouth of the green door.

I turned and bolted for the door, ignoring Lucia's shouts for me to return. I had no idea what I was going to do, but I wasn't going to wait here and leave Jenny unprotected. Then Lucia was in front of me, barring the door. "Listen to him, Davies," she said. "He says the other elf is in here with us."

I spun on my heel, scanning the room. That was ridiculous. Elves didn't look like humans, and there was no way one had gotten in here without anyone noticing. Then I saw Rick's expression. He looked stunned, but it was the kind of stunned that said he'd just discovered cold nuclear fusion going on in his kitchen sink. "Helena," he said. "I think you're the elf."

CHAPTER ELEVEN

I was too startled to say anything but a garbled, "Huh?" that sounded more like "hnugh."

Rick stepped away from his laptop. "There's no way there are 1,010,451 elves in this world," he said. "And no way Pattern 2.0 is throwing up false positives—except it is, so that's not what I mean. More accurately, it either works or it doesn't."

I pointed a shaking hand at the giant screen. "So what do you call that?"

"We used Gabriel Roarke as the baseline for the new Pattern," Rick said. "Except Gabriel alone wouldn't work, because he hasn't been corrupted by a thousand years of poison. So we had to guess based on what we learned from autopsying the elves killed in their incursions. Ultimately, we came up with a fairly broad definition of 'elf' that we fed into the Pattern. One I was certain would tag any other elves."

He drew in a breath and released it. "Only it looks like it was too broad, and it picked up something else as well."

A scream was building in my throat. I clenched my fists to hold it back. "I'm not an elf."

"You have a genetic difference," Rick said. "You and all the other sports. It looks like we just figured out what that is."

I turned on Lucia, who was watching me warily as if she expected me to explode, a reasonable fear. "How is that even likely? Doesn't it make more sense that Pattern 2.0 is broken?"

Lucia glanced past me at Rick, who said, "We never did figure out exactly how many genetic sports there are in the world, but estimates put the number at somewhere between 900,000 and 1.1 million. Just what this number says."

"Roarke and Leighton both said elves and humans used to interbreed all the time," Lucia said in a low voice. "It's not that farfetched to think some of those descendants are still around."

Now my head had started to throb. "I'm *not* an *elf*," I snarled.

"Helena," Rick said.

"No!" I shouted. "This is insane. Wouldn't I have known it if I was an elf? And shouldn't all my children be the same, not just Jenny? Fix your stupid program and try again!"

"Stop it, Davies," Lucia said in that same low voice. "Use your head. This explains everything we know about the genetic sports—the fact that you all crop up very irregularly, but you all have the same basic abilities and a shared immunity to being drained of your magic. Roarke has that immunity—"

"How do you know that?"

"Irrelevant. Look at the map—no, *look at it*." Lucia grabbed my chin and forced me to look at the giant display. It had focused even more closely and now showed the outline of the tunnel containing the Pattern and, right by the door, a flickering pinprick of light. I wrenched away from Lucia's grip and then, keeping my eyes on the display, walked toward Rick. With only a slight delay, the pinprick followed my path. I stopped, reversed, walked in a circle. The light did the same.

I stopped and closed my eyes, feeling lightheaded. "It's ridiculous," I said. "I'm starting to feel like the main character in a magical girl anime."

"It's not like that," Rick said.

I turned on him. "I'm an oracle. I'm an elf. I see through illusions. I even have strange-colored eyes. How is it *not* like that!"

"Because you don't get any benefits from elf genetics the way Gabriel Roarke does," Rick said patiently. "You were able to touch the barrier with no consequences, right? And you age normally, and I'm sure if you could absorb language through your skin, you'd have noticed by now. All that's happened is that we now know specifically what the genetic difference is that makes you see through illusions." He hugged me. "You're still you. Don't be afraid of that."

"I'm not—" He was right. I was afraid. I hugged him back, not gently, but he didn't seem to mind. "What does this mean? For the Pattern, that is. We still need to be able to find the actual elves—can you, I don't know, tune the rest of us out?" It took everything I had to sound casual, as if I'd come to terms with the news.

"Sure. It won't even take more than half an hour." Rick pounded me lightly on the back and released me. "But we'll need a full-body scan and some blood from you, if you don't mind."

I became aware that everyone in the tunnel was staring at me. Refusing to blush with self-consciousness, I said, "Of course."

Twenty minutes later, I sat beside Lucia and watched as Rick's associates bustled about, moving computers and changing how the power cords were laid out. Lucia said abruptly, "That was fortunate."

"Fortunate, how?"

"If you hadn't been here, we might have seen two 'elves' in your house and drawn the worst conclusions." She stretched her legs and popped her neck like we'd been waiting for hours. "And I'm not sorry we learned what we did. It's never sat well with me that there was a genetic difference we couldn't predict and yet was incredibly consistent in its effect."

"I guess it's good that the new Pattern can identify all the genetic sports, or whatever we're called now. Though it would have been more useful ten years ago." Another thought occurred to me. "You don't think this second attempt will override the first? I mean, erase the record of all those elf descendants?"

"I doubt it. Jeong is too practical. He'll save the information somewhere." Lucia looked up. "Is that it?" she asked Rick.

"Yes, though I'm sure this will be anticlimactic," Rick said. "We've set it to exclude anyone with your genetic difference, Helena, so what's left will be actual elves."

Once more, Rick led his people through a recitation of different "pegs" being ready, once more he called out a count of three. I held my breath, waiting for another blaze of light.

Instead, the map stayed mostly dark except for a handful of bright points scattered across North America and the British Isles and Ireland, with two points in South America and three in Australia. "Back out," Lucia demanded. She examined the big map for a minute, texting rapidly, then said, "Davies, can you tell me which of these are the most immediate threat?"

I hadn't left my seat because I still felt wobbly from the non-oracular revelations. I closed my eyes and didn't even put my request into words, just let myself feel the fear and uncertainty that centered on the presence of elves in our world. The swooping sensation of a prophecy calmed me. I might be descended from elves, but that didn't matter nearly so much as my oracular gift did.

The prophecy guided me in what felt like a tour of several locations before returning me to myself. I blinked at the map. "The ones in South America will be gone before your people get there," I told Lucia. "Three elves entered Western Australia at a remote location and are working their way toward civilization, possibly Alice Springs. The slips the elves created in North America were at the limit of what they can manage—the membrane between worlds is too thick. So they're not as great a danger. But you should watch out for elves appearing in the United Kingdom and Ireland. They see those places as their rightful homelands."

"Thanks," Lucia said, and turned away, tapping madly at her phone's keyboard.

"I'm sorry," Rick said.

"Sorry for what?" I asked.

"I could have been more understanding. I know this was a shock." He did look penitent, and it made me feel guilty remembering how I'd yelled at him.

"You were understanding," I said, "but I don't think any response would have made it better. I just needed time—Rick, this is crazy! How can *I* be descended from elves, but not all of my children are? Because we tested Alastair and Duncan after we found out about Jenny, and they're definitely not sports."

Rick dragged a folding chair next to mine and sat. "I'm not an expert on genetics, but I am a bone magus, so I know something of how genetic inheritance works," he said. "My guess—and keep in mind this *is* just a guess, subject to confirmation—is that the 'elfness' you and Jenny have, in the form of your alteration, is passed on the way something like eye color is. If you had blue eyes, for example, you'd pass that on to all your children, but those children would only have blue eyes themselves if they got the right gene from their father. However it works, you and Jenny were handed the right combination of factors for that 'elfness' to show up. That means you might end up with grandchildren with the same genetic difference even though Alastair and Duncan seem perfectly normal."

"That sounds like something you could research," I said with a weak smile.

"You'd better believe it. I wish I could clone me. So many projects, so little time..."

That made me laugh, a real laugh. "I should call Gabriel. I wonder if he knows anything about elven half-breeds?"

"He could at least tell you how they fit into elven society. What if you're an elf princess? Lost daughter of a forgotten house?" Rick's grin was contagious.

"I'd rather be a magical girl anime character," I said.

WITH JENNY SETTLED IN HER CAR SEAT, I DROVE HOME, but the anxieties and confusion I'd been suppressing soon drowned out the sound of the *Newsies* soundtrack until I couldn't enjoy it. Finally, I gave up and called Gabriel. I'd wanted to wait until I was in my reassuring haven, but this was going to drive me crazy otherwise.

I'd expected the call to go to voicemail, but to my surprise Gabriel picked up on the second ring. "Helena. Is something wrong?"

"It's something... unexpected," I said. "Do you have a minute?"

"Of course. What is this unexpected thing? You sound shaken."

I hadn't realized my inner turmoil was noticeable. "Well, you know how you said humans and elves used to interbreed? Rick Jeong accidentally discovered how to identify some of those descendants."

"Really? Why only some?"

"It's a genetic trait that marks someone as an elf descendant, but based on the math, there have to be more people who have elf ancestors than manifest this trait. And... actually, it turns out it's the genetic trait I have. The one that lets me see through illusions. We thought it was an anomaly, but it's more specific than that."

Gabriel was silent long enough that I started to fidget, but I couldn't think of anything else to say that wouldn't be babbling. Finally, he said, "Sun and Moon. How did he discover that? He can't possibly have been looking for it."

I explained what had happened with Pattern 2.0 and what we knew based on myself and my children. "That's how we know it only identifies some of us, because my other children could still trace their lineage back to an elf even if they don't have this difference. Assuming records went back that far."

"Astonishing," Gabriel said. "Though I doubt it makes a difference. The human genome is more robust than elves', and even the direct offspring of a human and an elf has more in common with their human parent than their elven one."

"So half-elves—is that what they're called?"

"They could be. Elves called them 'the riven,' because they were torn between two natures. Very few of them ever embraced their elven heritage, between being physically more human in appearance and not having elven longevity. But all the riven were magically inclined, and now I wonder if that wasn't a result of the genetics you share."

"Rick says it's possible, now that we have this information, to figure out how it gets passed on as well as identify what small magic it gives a person. Are you really immune to having your magic drained?"

"What? Oh. That's what Rick told me. I didn't think it mattered now that there aren't any invaders in your world." Gabriel chuckled. "So you and I are cousins of a sort. How strange."

"Don't take this the wrong way, but I'm not thrilled about it. It's frightening to think of having anything in common with people who are currently my enemy."

"Understandable. Are you worried about how they might use that commonality against you?"

"If there's some kind of correspondence magic, yes."

"Don't worry about it. It is possible to work a kind of sympathetic magic, where one thing stands for many, that would affect a group of people with certain characteristics. But any such magic that draws on the similarities between elves and their half-breed descendants would kill everyone involved. There's no way to isolate you and your kind and still work that sort of magic."

"Are you sure?"

"Very sure. Someone tried it about—sorry, I forget sometimes that I've lost a thousand years. It was roughly a hundred years before the barrier was erected, so before my time, but the story was told often." Gabriel cleared his throat. "Excuse me. There was a clan leader who tried to eliminate an enemy leader through sympathetic magic based on a particular elven trait. He thought he'd isolated the target, but instead the magic worked on every elf with that trait. It killed nearly a thousand men and women. He was executed for it. Gruesomely, though the stories all vary as to how it was done."

I shuddered. "That's horrible. And reassuring."

Gabriel laughed. "Is there anything else I can tell you? You wouldn't be able to claim kinship with an elf clan even if we could figure out who your ancestor was. And if you haven't manifested other elf magics by now, you won't spontaneously do so just because you found out the truth."

"*Are* there other elf magics? I mean, I didn't think seeing through illusions or empathy were things you could do."

"They aren't. Those must arise out of a combination of elf and human traits. Let's see. Elves are good at *making* illusions—we do that as easily as breathing in Faerie, and almost as easily in Tempus, which is what elves call your world. We're capable of shadowstepping, which is teleportation between areas of shadow. It's short-range transportation, and it's very hard to take another person along, worse physically than your ward-stepping. We can put ourselves into stasis for indefinite periods of time—"

"That's what brought you here, right?"

"Yes. I put myself into stasis for protection, and then I was trapped here where no one could free me. A thousand years later... anyway, that's an elf magic. Some elves can take memories away from humans, but that's a skill we have to develop, just like the ability to put others to sleep. And, of course, we can absorb language through the skin."

I looked at the backs of my hands gripping the steering wheel.

The skin looked as normal as ever. "That's an elf ability I'd love to have."

"It's very useful. I can speak—wait a moment." I heard muffled conversation, like Gabriel had covered the speaker. A few seconds later, he said, "I'm sorry, Helena, I have to go—unless there was anything else?"

"No. You've relieved my mind. Thanks."

"I'm still astonished. Knowing that there are humans living now who are descended from elves is different from finding out you're one. I—well, I was always interested in lineages, so it's true I really am curious about your ancestor, but that's because if it were me, I'd want to know those stories. That elf is as much family to you as your great-grandparents."

"That's true. Now you've given me something to think about. Thank you."

I ended the call and, after a moment, turned the music back up. I'd been so caught up in my fears and my confusion it hadn't occurred to me there was a person responsible for my being born with this genetic difference. Somewhere way back in my family tree was an elf. And now I wondered about that person. She, or he, linked me to another world, and Faerie before its corruption had been beautiful. I was part of that, though in a tiny way.

"Mommy," Jenny sang, "mommy, can I have cookies when we get home?"

"One cookie," I said absently. My mind was still caught up in imagination. How terrible that elves had persecuted those long-ago humans to the point the humans built the barrier to protect themselves. How awful that those humans hadn't known, or possibly hadn't cared, about what the barrier did to elves and Faerie. For the first time, I pictured elves and humans living together peacefully. How marvelous if we could help each other!

Jenny fell silent. A few seconds later, she said in a trembling voice, "I was scared but I didn't scream."

It was a good thing I was a careful driver, because I nearly slammed on the brakes, which might have caused an accident even on the quiet suburban street we were on. Instead, I eased to the side of the road and turned. "I'm sorry, sweetie. I don't want you to be scared. Can you tell me what you saw?"

Jenny's eyes were shiny with tears, but she nodded. "It was the scary elf. He has a big sword and he hurt someone with it. He's always angry and I don't want him to see me."

"We won't let him hurt you, you know that," I reminded her. Then a chill ran through me. "Jenny, did he hurt an elf or a human?"

"It wasn't an elf, it was a short man." The tears that had been threatening spilled over. "There was blood."

I closed my eyes and held back my anger. Jenny shouldn't have to see violence. She was only three, damn it, and she ought to be protected from such things. I only let her see the boys play *Legend of Kerigon* because the violence was cartoonish and no one ever died.

But that wasn't the only issue. I knew elves were loose in our world—that had been the point of today's activity. But I'd imagined them far from civilization, since slips couldn't form in cities. If Jenny's vision was right, some elves had already killed humans, and they'd go on killing humans until they were stopped. I hoped Pattern 2.0 was as effective as it seemed.

CHAPTER TWELVE

At five o'clock I drove to the Hubbards' house, which was about four miles from ours. I'd seen it in vision once, so I had no trouble identifying it, but when I arrived, I pulled up to the curb and sat with the land yacht idling in front of the house. The memory of Malcolm saying I was being watched over infuriated me even as it was a comfort. Stupid Savants and stupid Michael Castellan. Probably Malcolm wouldn't let me leave our house without that surveillance. That made me even madder.

I drew in a breath and made myself relax. I didn't want to encounter Maddy when I was in a hostile mood, not if she was as skittish here as she had been at school. Eventually I felt calm enough to walk at a sedate pace through the drizzling mist and knock on the door.

Emma opened it a moment later. "Oh, hi, Mrs. Campbell. Come in. Alastair and Liv are upstairs."

I waited in the entrance, feeling uncomfortable about going upstairs uninvited, until Maddy appeared and said, "They'll be done in a minute. Do you want to come in to the kitchen?"

The kitchen smelled deliciously of pot roast, which I usually associated with big family Sunday dinners and therefore found incongruous but appetizing. Maddy returned to mashing potatoes. "Thanks for letting Alastair come over," she said. "They've been working on that model all afternoon."

"I appreciate the invitation. Liv really is welcome to come to our house sometime." I hoped that didn't come out as too antagonistic, since I wasn't quite as calm as I'd believed.

"Oh, it's no trouble. And of course Liv couldn't pack up the model and transport it without damaging it. It's quite large." Maddy's attention was on the potatoes, but that had sounded a little too glib, like she had worked out a reasonable objection in advance.

"I... guess that's true." I leaned casually on the counter, hoping Maddy would relax in turn. "It's so wet out there. I guess Portland is a lot different from Denver."

Sure enough, Maddy twitched, just like she always did when I mentioned her previous home. "More snow," she agreed. "I think I like the change. I'm not much of a skier."

And now she was back to being bland and boring. I cast about for a different topic. "Liv must be very intelligent. Alastair doesn't have many friends who can keep up with him."

"Liv feels the same." Maddy set aside the potato masher and added butter to the steaming dish. "You never wanted him to skip grades?"

"No, we wanted him to have a normal social development. Genius is great, but he needs to be human, too."

"I agree," Maddy said. "He's a very polite boy. We enjoy having him here."

The way Maddy still wouldn't meet my eyes set my nerves on edge. "That's good," I said, wishing this inane conversation was over.

Maddy nodded. "I can see how you'd be concerned about his development. It's so easy for smart children to start thinking they're superior to their classmates."

And *that* felt like an insult, and I couldn't tell why. I was by now thoroughly confused by Maddy's manner, how she seemed perfectly calm and yet had an edge to her words, like she really meant to say something else. I controlled my annoyed reaction and said, "That's so true. We hope we've done right by Alastair."

"I'm sure you have," Maddy said.

At that moment, Liv and Alastair entered the kitchen, and Liv said, "Can we have cookies?"

"It's too close to dinnertime," Maddy said, "and besides, I'm sure Mrs. Campbell needs to get home to her own dinner."

"Thanks for letting me come over, Mrs. Hubbard," Alastair said.

"It was a pleasure," Maddy said. "I'll see you later, Helena. Have a safe drive."

Alastair was quiet the whole way back, but I was still stewing over Maddy's strange behavior, going back and forth about whether I was overreacting and had read too much into her words, and I didn't register his silence until we pulled into our neighborhood. Finally, I said, "Did you have a good time?"

"Sure."

"That doesn't sound very enthusiastic. You and Liv didn't have a fight, did you?"

He shook his head. "No. It was fine. The model rocket is almost done."

I contemplated his half-shadowed face in my rear view mirror. "Alastair, what's bothering you?"

"Nothing."

It was so obviously a lie I almost leaped on it, challenging him. In time, I remembered that Alastair only became more closed off if he was badgered, and went for a different tactic. "Well, you're always welcome to tell me anything, even if it's not something that's wrong. I want to hear about your problems so I can help. But if it's nothing, then I won't worry." Suggesting that my worrying was a possibility was calculated to start Alastair's strong desire not to upset others going. I wasn't above a little manipulation to prime the pump.

"Okay." Alastair rode in silence until we reached our driveway. Then he said, "Mom?"

"Yes?"

There was a long pause. "What's for dinner?" he finally said.

I was pretty sure that was not what he'd intended to say. "Dad made tacos. I have my martial arts lesson tonight, so I asked for something easy to clean up."

"I love tacos," Alastair said with some of his usual enthusiasm.

He raced ahead of me into the house. I followed, considering his silence. Something was wrong, but it couldn't have been serious or I'd have had a prophecy about it. Which meant I just needed to wait, and hope eventually Alastair would confide in me or Malcolm. Alastair hiding something, Maddy hiding something... and of course I was hiding something, though I didn't feel the knowledge of the oracle was in the same category. Even so, I felt I was drowning in secrets.

"YOU CAN'T BE SERIOUS," VIV SAID. SHE PUSHED HER TRAY with its chicken sandwich to one side so she could put her elbows on the table. "That's impossible."

"Not impossible," I replied. The smell of my own meal of chicken fingers wasn't so appetizing in the face of Viv's disbelief. "It's true." I couldn't bear to wait until Tuesday to tell my best friends what I'd learned, so I'd asked to meet for lunch the following day. Now, with the way they were staring at me, I almost wished I'd found a different way to tell them.

Judy held a chicken finger in one hand as if she'd forgotten it was there. "You'd think you'd sparkle or something," she said.

"Judy!"

"I'm only half joking. If I didn't know that elves are vicious and cruel and look like undead monsters, I'd say this was romantic." She set the chicken finger down and wiped her hands on a paper napkin. "But it's not."

"No." I shook my head. Around us, the noise of dozens of conversations filled Impeckables' dining room. We'd come here because of the noise and the crowds; I'd wanted to go somewhere no one would be able to listen in, though I couldn't imagine anyone would believe anything they heard me say about elves and Faerie. I dipped a chicken finger in the fast food restaurant's famous sauce and ate, though my appetite had disappeared.

"In fact," Judy said, her eyes narrowing, "what if the elves can do something about it?"

"Like what?" Viv asked.

"Like use kinship magic to track you down," Judy said. "Or whatever it is elf magic is capable of. It's similar to adept magic, right? Since adepts a thousand years ago learned to use magic based on what they saw elves do. And adept magic is all about connections and correspondences. If Rick Jeong could use elves to identify all the ones who are in our world now, why couldn't elves do the same, but in reverse? Or even track them all down and kill them?"

"Gabriel Roarke said that was impossible. That it would kill everyone involved, not just the riven. That's what he said elves called the half-elf children." I propped my elbows on the table and put my face in my hands. "Even so, suppose they wanted something from us other than death?"

"It's not likely," Viv said. "Why would elves care about their half-breed descendants? We already know they despise humans, so they'd probably think you're tainted or whatever."

"I didn't say it to worry you," Judy said. "My point is that there's no reason to think this makes you any more special than seeing through illusions does. It's more like having heterochromia."

"What *is* heterochromia, anyway?" I asked, raising my head.

"Having different-colored eyes, like one brown and one blue. It looks interesting, but it generally doesn't change how good your vision is. If anything, it can make it worse." Judy took a long drink of her Diet Dr. Pepper.

I made myself take another bite before pushing my food away. "And as if that weren't enough, I have to worry about what the Savants are doing. I don't know what to make of the fact that they haven't approached or attacked since the night of the gala."

"I don't blame you for being anxious. I don't know why the Wardens don't go after the Savants directly. Personally, I'd love for Michael Castellan to get a serious poke in the eye." Judy smiled evilly. "Serve him right for having me shot."

"That would waste Warden resources that ought to be spent on the elf threat," Viv said. She bit into her sandwich and chewed blissfully. "This is the best chicken ever."

"You don't want this knowledge about your heritage spread around, do you?" Judy said.

"No. It's weird, and it's not like most Wardens even know about the sports. But I should—oh, I'd better let Greg and Victor and Ines and Mangesh know." I grimaced. "Greg's going to be hard to convince." My friends, the only other genetic sports I knew personally, deserved the truth. But Greg Acosta, former police detective and professional hardass, still tended not to believe anything he couldn't see for himself despite his more than ten years' association with the Wardens.

"He's the sort of person who hears 'elf' and thinks 'Tinker Bell,' too," Viv said with a grin.

"Anyway, tell Jeremiah and Mike if you want, but... no, I really would rather not deal with this becoming public knowledge, not now. I wish I could go back to last week, when all I had to worry about was Maddy Hubbard being weird."

"I thought she seemed normal at the gala," Judy said.

"That's part of the weird. Every time I'm alone with her, she starts acting funny, like she's afraid of something."

"Afraid of you?" Viv asked.

I started to shake my head, then said, "I hadn't considered that. I mean—my first instinct is to say it's not that, because why would I be a threat to her? But I guess it's possible."

"Well, you *are* an elven half-breed," Judy said, straight-faced. "Maybe she can tell."

I mock-scowled at her. "I thought you were going with the 'not special' theory."

"I stand by my words. Seriously, though, is there a way you might pose a threat to her?"

"How? She'd have to know about the oracle, or Wardens, and that would have made her act funny at the gala regardless of who else was there. And my prophecies all say she's afraid of being discovered, like there's someone hunting her." I sat upright. "Viv, why don't you investigate her?"

"Investigate?" Viv's eyes narrowed in thought. "You think it's that serious?"

"Maybe not serious, but it's more than idle curiosity. I like her, I like her family, and if there's something I can do to help them, I'd like to."

"Typical paladin," Viv joked. "Isn't the oracle a better investigator than I am?"

"It gives prophecies on its own time, and filtered through my understanding. It almost never gives me a glimpse of things like credit card statements or Social Security numbers. I think your skill set is more suited to this than mine. Will you do it? I can pay."

"As if I'd let you pay me," Viv scoffed. "Sure, I can do it. Jeremiah and I just submitted our invoice to our current client, so I have a day or two. It shouldn't take long."

"Unless there really is something, and you have to dig," Judy pointed out.

"Is pessimism a rogue class trait?"

"We prefer to call it 'planning for the worst,'" Judy said airily.

TELLING VIV AND JUDY ABOUT MY WEIRD REVELATION HAD reassured me, and I returned home feeling calmer. They were right; being descended from an elf wasn't a big deal, because it wasn't as if it gave me superpowers. All right, yes, I could see through illusions, but except with the recent incident with a crazy adept stalker, seeing through illusions never benefited me. I made myself stop thinking about it. There was no point fretting over something I couldn't change.

After dinner, Malcolm went into his office and I cleared the table with help from Alastair and Duncan. Alastair had been unusually quiet—or, rather, he'd been quiet in the way he'd been all week, which wasn't like him but was starting to seem like a new and disquieting behavior. After the dishes were done, I followed him to his room. "Alastair, is something wrong?"

"Nothing's wrong." He wouldn't meet my eyes.

I considered my options for a moment, decided not to reveal that I knew his tell, and said, "You've been so quiet lately, and I've barely heard you talk about spaceships all week. If there's something bothering you—"

"There isn't. And nothing exciting is happening with the spaceship model, so there's nothing to talk about. Can I read now?"

I couldn't think of a single thing that would break through Alastair's obstinate refusal to communicate. "Sure. But you know you can tell me anything, right? Even if you think it's no big deal."

"I know." He was already nose-deep in a book.

I left his room and closed the door behind me. It hurt that Alastair wouldn't confide in me. I'd gotten used in the last year or so to feeling that we had a connection based on our mutual desire to use our oracular gifts to help others, and while I loved all my children equally, I loved them in different ways, and this was part of how I loved Alastair. And now in addition to feeling hurt, I was worried.

I returned downstairs and settled on the couch. After listening to the noises of the house and determining that no one was getting into trouble or in need of Mom, I embraced the question *What is Alastair hiding?*

The prophecy was slow to appear, literally slow as the feeling of being caught up in vision was more like a languid ballet of leaps and turns than the whirling, swooping ride it usually was. I saw Alastair, and then Duncan, and then Jenny, their images fading in and out like slides under a microscope, first fuzzy, then clear, then fuzzy again. Then my own image appeared, not like I saw myself in a mirror but a photograph I recognized from a family vacation to Maine. It hovered behind the children's faces, staying clear while theirs shifted. Then the vision was gone, popped like a soap bubble, and I rubbed my eyes and stretched.

I wasn't sure what it meant. Alastair was hiding something about us, but not about his father—that suggested it had something to do with the oracle. Something to do with a prophecy he'd seen, perhaps? Or something that was going to happen related to the oracle? I felt suddenly impatient with my oracular gift, and as suddenly felt embarrassed about my reaction. If I couldn't interpret the visions my own self produced, whose fault was that?

Night-Noon padded into the room and nudged my hand for pettings. I scritched behind her ears as she leaned into me, putting more and more of her weight behind her leaning until finally she jumped onto the couch and settled on my lap, or half on my lap—she was too big to fit entirely. I groaned, mostly for show—I liked how affectionate she was—and shifted my legs into a more comfortable position.

"That cat thinks she's still a kitten," Malcolm said.

I squeaked. "You could make a little more noise. You startled me."

Malcolm chuckled. "I think we've established I'm naturally stealthy. Move over, Night-Noon." He gave the elven caracal a push, then a firmer push when she ignored the first one. Finally, she gave up and leaped off my lap to wander away. Malcolm sat in her abandoned place beside me. "I thought you'd like to know that we've cracked the Savant defenses."

"Oh!" Then I said, "What does that mean, exactly?"

"It means we have access to their personnel and military installation records. We know many of the clandestine sites Astraeus uses to conceal their Faerie-related activities, and we know who the important people are associated with those sites." Malcolm put an arm around my shoulders and hugged me. "It's the first step in being able to strike at them once they make a move against us."

"I know this is bloodthirsty, but should we maybe go after them first? I can't help thinking that a move they make against us might involve the children."

"I know." Malcolm squeezed my shoulder. "At the moment, we don't know what they intend. It's possible—unlikely, but possible—the Savants have given up on attacking you or the children directly. If we strike at them, that could prompt them to retaliate when they otherwise had no intention of doing so. The best outcome is no fight. Something I know you appreciate."

"I do." I leaned my head against his shoulder. "Knowing we have the ability to hurt Castellan if he makes it necessary cheers me up. Thank you."

"I won't let anything happen to you or the children," Malcolm said, and kissed me, his lips exploring mine, his hands caressing my waist. I kissed him back, enjoying the feel of his powerful body against mine.

When we broke apart finally, I said, "Maybe you should talk to Alastair."

Malcolm blinked. "I must be losing my touch if you can think of anything but sex after that kiss."

I laughed. "It was something that was on my mind. But now you mention it..."

"Alastair's asleep by now," Malcolm murmured, sliding his hands around my waist and pulling me close. His lips found mine again, and this time I fell deeply into his embrace. "Any other unromantic non sequiturs, love?" he murmured.

I smiled. "I can't think of anything now but you."

CHAPTER THIRTEEN

After learning Campbell Security's progress against the Savants, I spent the weekend expecting an attack every moment, as if the Savants knew they'd been found out even though I was sure that was impossible. By Sunday night I was so keyed up Malcolm insisted I go to bed early. "And stop fretting," he added. "You're being superstitious. We weren't detected."

"You know that because the Savants didn't attack?" I said.

"I know that because no one on the team wants to face the oracle and tell her they failed." Malcolm kissed me on the forehead. "Go to sleep. You'll feel better when you're rested."

He was right. A peaceful night's sleep restored me. But Malcolm volunteered for carpool duty anyway, and he took Jenny with him and the boys. "You're still wound too tight, love. Relax."

I didn't fight him. I did feel the aftereffects of having been wound so tight. So I turned on the morning news with the television on mute and reclined on the couch, enjoying the sound of the light rain pattering on the patio roof.

The doorbell rang.

Groaning, I rolled off the couch and checked the camera display on my phone. It was Viv. Curious, I hurried to open the door. "What's up? Don't you have work?"

"Not yet. We're still between jobs." Viv unwound her colorful scarf from around her neck and followed me back to the great room. "I came over with news about the Hubbards. Talk about weird, Hel."

I sat on the edge of the couch. "So they are in Witness Protection."

"I don't think so. But they're hiding something." Viv sounded intent, not at all as carefree as I was used to. "Based on that one time we stumbled on someone in Witness Security, I knew what signs would indicate the Hubbards were under government protection. I didn't see any of those. So after I eliminated that possibility, I went back to basics. Checked all their records from when they lived in Denver. And they're totally clean. *Too* clean."

"What does that mean?"

"It means," Viv said, "that either they have miraculously never had a single run-in with the law, not even a parking ticket, or someone scrubbed their records. It's like—well, whoever it was wanted to make them completely unremarkable, so there wouldn't be anything to raise suspicions if someone like the police, or like me, investigated them. But that kind of perfection is suspicious all by itself."

"I think I understand. But I still don't know what it means. Who would need to be that unremarkable?"

"I don't know. What I do know is that there are no records of them in Denver other than the official ones, like marriage certificates and driver's licenses. Anyone who grows up in a place—and there's also no record that they lived anywhere else—has things like school records or a job history or sometimes notices in the local paper. None of that exists."

I was starting to feel nervous. "What about Maddy's job? She said she worked as a chemist—there has to be a record of that."

"There is. And it matches exactly the story she told you. And

Bronson Hubbard was a dentist with a practice in Aurora, or actually a member of a practice, and the girls went to a private school in the same town. It all makes sense, except that I can't find evidence that they existed before about ten years ago." Viv bounced a couple of times on the couch cushion. "This is so cool!"

"How is it cool? I think it's creepy. It's like they were erased by someone not very competent. Weren't you telling me you read a book about someone who did that for a living?"

"That was fiction. I don't know if anyone really does that. Except I'm sure it wasn't the government, so maybe it *was* some professional who helped them start a new life. I *really* want to ask the Hubbards how they did it."

"You can't do that!" I exclaimed. "What if there's some sinister reason for it all, or they're being hunted by the Mob?"

"I won't. I just wish I could." Viv sighed. "I'm not done searching. I came to see if there was anything else you could tell me about the family that might be an angle."

"They've been really good at not letting any secrets out. I know Maddy always wears expensive jewelry regardless of her clothes. Maybe she has a store she shops at, or a designer she prefers."

"That's not a bad idea. If I could find that person—you know I'm good at getting people to talk about themselves, and it's just a short step from there to getting them to talk about others." Viv stretched and leaned back. "I will figure it out."

"That sounded more ominous than you probably meant," I said.

"Oh, I meant it that way. People who are keeping secrets will usually do anything to keep those secrets from seeing the light of day. Think about what you'd be willing to do to protect the oracles' secret, right? I think we need to know what the Hubbards are hiding. Anyone who's concealing their past this thoroughly isn't doing it to keep people from knowing they once had an unfortunate tattoo." She stood. "I need the toilet, and then you want to go for coffee? Get out of the house?"

"Sure." Then I remembered the Savants might still be a threat, and cursed. "I shouldn't. Not without letting Malcolm know. If anything happened—"

"I get it. The Savants really suck."

"I'll make coffee anyway. I need something hot on a day like this."

But I stayed in my seat after Viv went to the washroom and thought about what she had learned. If it was true that someone had altered the Hubbards' records, it had to have been before they moved to Denver, because that was the only thing that made sense given the details Viv had learned. They'd moved to Denver from somewhere else and someone had erased that previous location from their history and given them a new life in Colorado. Then they'd moved from Denver to Portland, and... what? Whatever had happened in their past, they were still worried about it even two moves later.

I felt a moment's worry that Viv's digging might expose the Hubbards, but it didn't last. Viv was careful and thorough, and she cleaned up her tracks both literally and figuratively. Then I felt guilty about spying on the Hubbards. My interest was mostly curiosity, and idle curiosity didn't entitle me to pry into their affairs. But that didn't last, either. Viv was right: if there was any possibility Maddy's secrets might be a danger to me—because I was keeping plenty of secrets myself—I needed to know.

About twenty minutes later, I heard the garage door open and the sound of the land yacht's engine. I stopped mid-sentence, listening. Viv said, "We could go—"

Without warning, I was hit by prophecy. Usually, a prophecy began with a swooping, rushing feeling like dropping out of the sky on birds' wings. This time, it hit me hard, like a paving stone wrapped in a pillow. The last thing I was aware of before the images overwhelmed my natural senses was the coffee mug falling from my suddenly nerveless hand.

Wherever I was, it was dark with billowing smoke, the air currents shifting wildly in the heat of an unseen fire. Then the smoke was gone, and I was standing atop a tall building, not one I recognized. My vision-self took a step forward and plummeted headfirst toward the invisible ground. Before I hit the ground, I found myself in a pit with a floor that moved, seething with the bodies of hundred of snakes that raised their heads and flicked the air with their tongues, searching for me.

Terror at these images gripped me, and I made myself take a mental step back. Danger. The prophecy warned of danger, but to whom?

As if that one sane thought were a trigger, the images shifted again, and I saw Talbott Academy, and Alastair, and dark figures moving in on the school, and Alastair again. Then I was back in my living room, and Viv was picking up the coffee mug and saying, "What a mess. Prophecies aren't exactly—"

"Alastair's in danger," I gasped, and scrambled past the great room furniture through the kitchen just as Malcolm came through the door holding Jenny. His smile fell away as he registered my distress.

"Helena," he began.

"Alastair's in danger," I repeated. "The school. We have to go."

Malcolm gripped my shoulder. "Take a breath. Viv?"

"I've got Jenny," Viv said. "Go."

Malcolm set Jenny down and rushed with me, not to the land yacht, but to the faster and more maneuverable Camaro. My heart was racing. The memory of those images of danger played over and over in my mind. "We have to hurry," I said.

"We are," Malcolm replied. "Call Jeremiah."

I'd forgotten in my panic that the boys weren't alone. With shaking hands, I fumbled my phone out of my pocket and found Jeremiah's number. I listened to the ringing and tried to calm my breathing. Jeremiah would get to Alastair before I could. At the moment, as grateful as I was for the prophecy's warning, I hated its imprecision. Why couldn't I have seen the threat in detail?

The call went to voice mail. I swore and tried again. Same result. I closed my eyes briefly and braced myself as the Camaro took a corner at speed. What speed, I didn't know and I didn't want to know. Malcolm was an excellent driver even before magic was involved. I was sure no law enforcement officer would see us, and even more sure we wouldn't have an accident.

My phone buzzed with an incoming text. Jeremiah. <Can't talk, will be overheard. Something wrong?>

I managed to text the basics of what I knew to Jeremiah, though with the motion of the speeding car, autocorrect was not my friend that day. After a pause, Jeremiah said, <Have 3 of us watching the school, no paper magi to give us cover going in. No other info?>

I ground my teeth in frustration. While Jeremiah was excellent at concealing himself outdoors, he wasn't a paper magus, master of illusions, and he wouldn't be able to get past the school's security measures without causing the kind of ruckus I wanted to avoid. <Hold on>, I texted, and lowered the phone to my lap. *What danger is Alastair in?* I asked myself.

This time, I felt the familiar swooping sensation before the prophecy presented me with—myself. My own face, staring back at me, but something was off about it. It took me a minute to realize the eyes were the wrong color; they were the hazel mine had been before becoming the oracle had turned them a strange blue-brown.

"I don't understand," I said aloud.

"Understand what?" Malcolm asked. "Hold onto something."

I grabbed what Malcolm had told the boys was the "oh crap" handle above the door and hung on as we swung through a tight arc going around a corner. "It says I'm the danger. That can't be true." Without another word, I focused on the question *What action will save Alastair?*

This time, my perspective was like a camera on one of those live cops shows, where the cameraman is running behind the cops as they chase someone. The "camera" jogged up the sidewalk to

Talbott Academy, went through the door—and the vision was over.

"Keep going," I said, then added, "I'm sorry, that was stupid. The prophecy says we have to find Alastair at school."

I glanced at my phone in my lap and saw Jeremiah had texted again. <Saw you go in, do you need backup?>

Confused, I read the message again. Then horror short-circuited every nerve in my body, numbing me briefly. "Malcolm," I said. "Someone who looks exactly like me just entered the school."

"What?"

"Jeremiah saw her. Me. Malcolm—"

"That's impossible," Malcolm said. "Every Warden has Viv's improved lenses for piercing illusions, even the most powerful adept ones. There's no way the Savants could have made an illusion Jeremiah couldn't see through."

"Then it wasn't an illusion. But Jeremiah wouldn't make a mistake like that." I grabbed my phone again and texted <It's not me, it's someone else, don't know how>. I sent that message, then hesitated. The only way Jeremiah could get into the school would be by breaking in and terrifying everyone else, and in the excitement and furor, my double might get away with anything.

<We can go in, give the word>, Jeremiah texted back.

I looked out the window at the streets and cars rushing past. Malcolm swerved smoothly around a Mercedes and accelerated along the streets with a hiss of tires on wet pavement. Quickly, I oriented myself. We were less than a mile from the school. <Watch for a Savant attack> I texted. <Don't go in. Will let you know soon>

"Try to stay calm, Helena," Malcolm said, making the turn onto the road in front of the school. "Alastair is an oracle. It will warn him."

"Are you sure of that?" I said, frightened by the hysterical edge to my voice. "What if the warning is just for me?"

"I'm sure. Alastair has never broken a bone, he's never been in an accident, he's never needed stitches except that one time, and that was a school fight. Every time, the oracle has warned him well before he was in actual danger."

"I swear I'm buying him a phone after this. I can't bear not knowing."

Malcolm skidded into the parking lot and yanked on the hand brake. The car shuddered and stalled out. I was already out of my seat and racing up the sidewalk with Malcolm right behind me.

The main door was heavy enough to require some exertion. It was enough to bring me to my senses. If "I" had come through the security door, someone might wonder why I was doing it again less than five minutes later. "Malcolm, stand in front of me so the camera sees you," I said, and positioned myself so I wasn't fully visible.

The door lock buzzed, and Malcolm pushed the door open. We both hurried through, not running. Malcolm put a hand on my arm, slowing me. "Whoever it was must have checked in at the office, or security would have stopped her."

"Let's find out. Stay here and watch, in case Alastair..." I wasn't sure what I hoped for, to end that sentence with.

I entered the office and summoned up a smile, but I was still breathing heavily and I was sure I looked like a madwoman. "Clarice, did I remember to sign in?" I panted.

Clarice, who'd been poised to greet me with her usual perky cheerfulness, looked confused. "Of course. About five minutes ago. You know we don't mind if you forget, it's just that it's policy—"

"It's a good policy." I grabbed the sign-in clipboard and scanned the list of names. My signature was at the bottom, along with a time four minutes earlier. It was definitely my signature, and the sight made my heart pound so hard I hoped a rib didn't crack. "Did Alastair come by here?" I asked, guessing wildly at what my double might have said.

"No," Clarice said, her confusion deepening. "Wasn't he in his classroom?"

"Thanks." I ran from the office before she could ask any more questions.

"Clarice thought it was me," I told Malcolm. "I came in and signed the clipboard, and I guess I told her I was going to find Alastair. Damn it, why did I have to be so friendly with the staff? They wouldn't let me roam free in the school if I wasn't me. Which I wasn't."

"Calm down," Malcolm said. "You're nearing hysteria. We need another prophecy to find out where the doppelganger went."

I nodded. The office had too good a view of the hall, and I might be conspicuous if I prophesied outside its windows. Instead, we crossed the hall to the bathrooms. As we did so, someone exited the men's room.

It was Alastair.

I gasped as he flung himself at me, sobbing. "Mom, I'm sorry!"

"You don't have to be sorry. Did you see a threat? You did the right thing."

"I saw you come in—saw you in a prophecy—only I knew it wasn't you. And the vision said Ms. Torres would be fooled. So I asked for the bathroom pass and then I ran." Alastair's voice shook, but the tears were subsiding. "Mom, it's all my fault. I shouldn't have kept secrets."

"What secrets? Alastair, if someone comes after you, that is not your fault."

Alastair shook his head violently. "It *is* my fault. I was scared you'd be mad, so I didn't say anything."

Malcolm put a gentle hand on Alastair's shoulder. "You know you can tell us anything, and even if we're upset, we won't yell at you. Now, what secret were you afraid to reveal?"

Alastair wiped his eyes and said, "I told Liv I'm an oracle."

CHAPTER FOURTEEN

"You—" I stopped myself before I could shout loud enough to draw Clarice's attention. More quietly, I said, "When was this?"

"The night they came for dinner." Alastair's tears began again. "I had a prophecy, a spontaneous one, when Liv and I were in my room, and I guess I looked sick or something, because she noticed and wanted to know what was wrong. And I panicked. I've never had a prophecy where someone saw me before, and I didn't know what to say." His final words were drowned out by sobs.

I hugged him close. "I understand. We haven't discussed what you should do under those circumstances, and it makes sense that you were surprised. It's all right."

"It's not all right!" Alastair exclaimed. "It's what you always say, we can't tell anyone or bad things will happen. And now someone is after me! What if Liv told her parents, and they told someone else, or—"

Malcolm put his arms around both of us. "We can't worry about that now. There's a Savant agent in the school somewhere, and we have to deal with that first." He looked at me. "Is Duncan in danger?"

"I don't know. The prophecy didn't include him. But we can't leave him here if someone is wandering around wearing my face."

"The Savant's here to kidnap me," Alastair said with a kind of wondering horror that made me sick.

"Alastair, nothing will happen to you," Malcolm said. "You need to wait in the office while I get Duncan, all right?"

I glanced past him, and my heart sank. "Crap. Clarice is watching us. Go to Duncan's classroom now and I'll distract her. Alastair, if I have to leave and come back, do *not* go with me unless I give the code word, understand?" The idea of Alastair walking voluntarily away with my double made me feel even sicker.

Alastair nodded. He'd stopped crying, but his face was a mess and he needed to blow his nose. I reached for my purse to hand him a tissue and realized I'd left it at home. Something to worry about later.

Malcolm was already gone. I hurriedly steered Alastair in the direction of the office, madly going over plausible excuses for both Malcolm and me to have come to the school at once to pull Alastair out of class and to get Duncan as well instead of letting Clarice send a runner with an early release note. By the time we reached the office, and Clarice was staring at me like I'd lost my mind, I'd come up with something not completely ridiculous. I hoped.

"I'm really sorry to disrupt things, Clarice," I said. "The boys had dental appointments this afternoon and I completely forgot until Mr. Campbell reminded me. He's gone to get Duncan—can I sign the boys out? Oh, and Alastair needs a tissue."

Clarice's familiar beaming smile was gone. "Ms. Campbell, you know we don't—"

"Thanks. Here, Alastair, blow your nose." I leaned away from Alastair and whispered to the woman, "He's afraid of the dentist. I'm hoping he'll outgrow this oppositional stage—so embarrassing, right?"

"Yes, but—"

"We really are in a terrible hurry, but I promise this won't happen again. I know how important school policy is." I smiled manically at Clarice, whose answering smile was weak and made her look five seconds away from calling the EMTs to take the crazy lady away.

The door opened, and I turned to see Duncan, his backpack slung over his shoulder. I silently swore. I hadn't thought about Alastair needing his backpack if I was pulling him out of school early. Hoping Clarice wouldn't notice, I said brightly, "Where's your father?"

"Dad said to say he's getting Alastair's homework," Duncan said. His hands were shaking, and he looked unnaturally pale.

I helped him sit in a chair next to Alastair and then leaned on the counter again. "It's been a long month and it's not even over yet," I said. "I know the boys are looking forward to Halloween. How about Alison?"

"Alison?" Clarice sounded as confused as if she didn't have a daughter named Alison. "Oh, well, she wants to have a Halloween party instead of trick or treating."

"They grow up so fast!" I exclaimed. "She's twelve now, right?"

Clarice was gradually relaxing. "Thirteen in November."

"So next year is her last year at Talbott. I hope that's not a difficult transition." My lips were babbling with no input from my brain now as I madly ran over possibilities for why Malcolm hadn't returned. Duncan looked like he knew, but I could hardly interrogate him in front of Clarice, and Clarice would definitely find it suspicious if I took the boys to wait in the hall instead of the office.

Nearly a minute later, through the big glass windows of the office that made it look like a fish tank, I saw Malcolm approaching. He was moving easily and didn't look injured, so maybe he hadn't found my double. That frightened me. Someone who looked just like me, but who wasn't under an illusion... the possible dangers she could pose were far too numerous.

Malcolm opened the door. He was carrying Alastair's backpack. "Sorry about the delay, but Ms. Torres had some instructions for Alastair," he said smoothly. "Let's go, boys."

Both Alastair and Duncan looked to me for confirmation. Their caution cheered me even as it made me angry at the need for it. "After your appointments, what about a visit to the *aquarium*," I said, and they relaxed.

Malcolm hurried us out the front door, his body shielding us, and I got the boys into the back seat of the Camaro while he stood beside me scanning the playing fields and the parking lot for threats. Finally, he said, "Let's go," and I strapped myself in and closed my eyes, releasing a little of the tension I'd been under.

When I opened my eyes finally, I said, "Aren't we going home?"

"We're going to the Gunther Node," Malcolm said grimly. "If Liv told her parents, and her parents are Savants—"

"Don't we have to assume that's true at this point?" I asked bitterly. "I was so sure... never mind. Anyway, I'm not sure how much 'if' there is about it."

"What matters is that Maddy and Bronson know where we live, and if Castellan sent someone after Alastair, he might think to send attackers to our house."

My heart pounded once so hard I thought it had stopped. "Jenny!"

"Viv is bringing her to the Gunther Node too, Helena, along with our emergency bags. It will be all right."

Alastair let out a choked sob. "This is all my fault!"

"Alastair," I said, then couldn't think what to tell him. It was sort of his fault, but he was nine and not ready to bear adult burdens. "Alastair, you made a mistake, but it's just bad luck that your mistake involved the Savants. You need to stop blaming yourself and decide how you're going to act going forward."

"Your mother and I should have considered the possibility of you needing to cover up a prophecy," Malcolm said. "I'm sorry we didn't go over a plan for that, Alastair. But Mom is right that it's time to move forward. We aren't angry with you, and we don't blame you."

Alastair nodded and wiped his sleeve across his eyes.

"Dad," Duncan said in a shaking voice, "did you kill that lady?"

I gasped. "What?"

"The woman pretending to be you attacked us outside Duncan's classroom," Malcolm said. "And no, Duncan, I didn't kill her. I subdued her, and when you ran to the office, I took her outside and handed her over to Jeremiah and the other two Wardens watching the school. I'm afraid the best I could do was a misdirection, so casual observers didn't see me hauling an unconscious woman across the playground, but if she had Savant friends, they might have seen her."

"They didn't stop you, though. So maybe there wasn't anyone else. Maybe it was just her."

"That's my hope, Helena. Duncan, you did very well in not panicking. Both you boys were brave the way I want you to be." Malcolm briefly gripped my hand. "Jeremiah will bring her to the Gunther Node for examination and questioning. We have got to find out how she managed her trick. She looked exactly like you, no illusion."

"I wonder what it means that her eyes were the wrong color," I said. "It's like the Savants were working from old images of me." Then I shuddered. "I can't bear to dwell on it anymore, but I can't pretend it didn't happen. That would be more dangerous."

"Worrying won't help," Malcolm pointed out. "And, since we know almost nothing, it also is a distraction. Unless you feel you should prophesy again."

"I'm too agitated for anything but a spontaneous prophecy," I said, "and I sort of hope I don't have one of those, either."

We fell into silence, without even the sound of the radio to fill the void. I made my mind go blank and counted cars, trying to guess the models with only a glimpse of the manufacturers' logos. I was terrible at guessing, but it calmed me.

When we made the turn onto the access road leading to the Gunther Node entrance, I saw another car ahead, a battered Lexus GX that looked like it was a refugee from a demolition derby. It was Viv's beloved car Clarence. Some of my tension eased. Viv was here, she had Jenny, and... well, we weren't exactly safe, but we were together, and that comforted me.

Viv parked a short distance away from the Camaro and lifted Jenny out of her car seat, shifting to avoid Night-Noon, who leaped out of the back seat and ran to greet the boys as if she hadn't seen them for weeks. It occurred to me we'd have trouble getting home, since even if there was a way to fit the car seat into the back of the Camaro, there were six of us to cram into the sports car. I tried to focus on how hopeful a thought it was that we'd be going home eventually.

Jenny ran to me, and I picked her up and hugged her. She struggled to free herself from my too-tight embrace. "Aunt Viv forgot the color game," she declared. "I felt scared, but it wasn't me. I want to color a square."

"I will remember, and you can color a square when we go home," I assured her.

"What happened, Hel?" Viv said. "Jeremiah made it sound like we were in danger of a direct missile strike."

Alastair grabbed my hand. When I looked down, his face was white and terrified. "Viv," I warned. Then I drew him in with my free arm and hugged him, too. "Don't be afraid of things we can't change," I whispered. Alastair nodded, but his grip on my hand didn't change.

To Viv, I said, "A Savant came after Alastair at the school. The oracle protected him, and Malcolm captured the Savant and turned her over to Jeremiah to bring her to the Gunther Node. But we don't know how much else the Savants know about us, so we're staying here for now."

Viv nodded. "What else can I do?" She handed over the backpacks and duffels that Malcolm called our "bug-out bags," packed with emergency essentials like changes of clothing and so forth for situations like this one.

"I'll call you when I know more. Tell Judy, will you? Jeremiah will know the details."

"Sure," Viv said, but she looked uncertain, and I could tell she wished there was more she could do.

We'd reached the painted circle of thorns that marked the teleportation entrance to the node. Alastair and Duncan huddled together with Night-Noon while Malcolm picked up the handset on the wall of the Gunther Node's airplane hangar to announce our presence. The boys looked so much like refugees, scared and clinging together, my heart ached. Jenny's face was pinched and white, and she looked on the verge of tears. She hadn't been present for the incident at the school, but she was clearly picking up on our fears, and I felt even sicker at the thought of the emotions we were inflicting on her.

The world blinked, and we were in the gardenia-scented transit hub. I'd never felt so grateful for its stark concrete dome and the way everyone passed us without paying us any attention. Some of my fear subsided.

I saw Lucia approaching and felt even better. She wore an expression of extreme annoyance that I doubted was directed at us. "Campbell. You're needed in Red 47. Davies, come with me."

Jenny flung herself at Lucia's legs. "We are so scared!" she declared, not sounding frightened at all. "There are bad men and Daddy is going to hurt them for scaring us."

"That's right, peanut," Lucia said. She picked Jenny up and tucked her under one arm like a football, making her giggle. "We are going to make sure those bad men don't try this again, ever. Now, how would you like to see your special room?"

"Lucia, I—"

"Don't thank me, Davies. This is what we're here for."

Malcolm held me for a moment. "We'll fix this," he said. "I told you Campbell Security has access to everything we need to make the Savants suffer. Don't be afraid."

"I'm not afraid for myself," I said, glancing at the boys.

Malcolm's jaw tightened, but he didn't say anything else, just kissed me and then ran toward the red-outlined opening.

Lucia strode off toward the purple door, prompting Night-Noon into a run. I prodded Alastair and Duncan into motion, and we hurried after her.

We rode the elevator down a level to the residential floor, which didn't look any different from the floor above: same cream-painted concrete walls, same highly-polished concrete floor, same warm LEDs lighting the walls and floor. But the doors were more widely spaced, and there were no colored lines painted on the floor, guiding visitors. Presumably once you made it this far, you knew where you were going.

The doors were numbered sequentially, starting with 01. Lucia stopped at one labeled 17 and turned the knob—no weird illusory overlays pointing at a hidden button, thankfully. She reached inside and flipped a switch, and lights came on, not incandescent bulbs or LEDs but natural sunlight like in the day care.

I marveled at the interior. Despite the lack of windows, I wouldn't have guessed the room was deep underground. It was furnished much the way my own home was, with comfortable cream-patterned couches and upholstered chairs surrounding a low coffee table, a television mounted on the wall, and a thick, plush carpet. A kitchenette half the size of my own kitchen occupied one corner of the room, with full-size appliances of stainless steel and a wide bar with four tall stools surrounding it.

The boys dropped their bags and ran off to explore what lay beyond the three doors. I set my and Jenny's bags down and took Jenny from Lucia. "I'm glad to be here. It's been an awful day."

"Get settled in. I may want you to talk to your doppelganger.

They ward-stepped her in about half an hour before you got here and Jeong and Chaswick and a couple of other bone magi have been studying her, trying to figure out how she managed her little stunt."

I shuddered. "I'm not sure I want to face her. It's such an eerie thought, a duplicate of me."

"If the bone magi can't work out what happened, we're going to need the oracle," Lucia pointed out. "Because there's no reason the Savants can't try this again. You think we need two of Campbell running around? Or two of me?"

In my exhaustion, that hadn't occurred to me. "All right. The kids will need to go to day care."

"Day care is closing in about an hour and a half. I'll send someone to sit with them." Lucia gripped my shoulder briefly. "It will be all right, Helena. My word on it."

When she was gone, I sat on a couch with Night-Noon next to me and listened to the boys argue over who got the top bunk. Jenny didn't scream, so I knew it wasn't a serious argument. We were safe, but we couldn't stay locked in the Gunther Node forever. I was so tired I wanted to curl up on whatever bed was available and sleep until the world made sense again.

Someone knocked on the door, and I let out a tiny shriek I immediately felt embarrassed about. I got up and opened the door a crack to see a couple of techs in black jumpsuits holding a pile of metal poles and a child-sized mattress. "Hi, Mrs. Campbell," the woman said. "We brought a bed for your little girl. There's only the bunk bed in these family units."

I backed away and opened the door wider. The two carried their burdens into the bedroom, making the boys stop shouting. I watched from the doorway as they assembled the bed with a minimum of fuss. Colorful jungle animals painted on one wall made the bedroom look cheery, as did the bright bedding on the bunk beds. The male tech opened the closet, revealing a pile of blankets and an extra pillow on a high shelf. He made the bed while his companion gathered up the tools they'd used. It all happened so swiftly my fuddled brain imagined I was watching a film played at double speed.

Finally, the techs said goodbye, and I watched Jenny put Mrs. Anderson to bed in the small bed. Alastair and Duncan had worked out their disagreement, since Duncan's bag was on the upper bunk. I left them to decide how to arrange their things and went to look at the other bedroom. It was bigger than the first and decorated in plum and mahogany and cream like an upscale hotel room. I sank into the chair in the corner and closed my eyes. Just a short nap...

I woke, startled, when Jenny tugged on my sleeve. "Mommy, I need a snack," she said.

I groaned and stood, checking my phone display. I'd slept for thirteen minutes and I didn't feel rested, just groggy. Bedtime couldn't get here fast enough.

The refrigerator was stocked lightly, apparently within the last few hours, because nothing was expired or smelly. I poured milk for the children and set out a package of Oreos. Not what I'd usually serve them only a couple of hours before dinner, but my exhaustion said it wouldn't hurt them to be indulged occasionally. I was still too overwrought to want food, but I got myself a glass of water and drank it down thirstily.

Another knock sounded at the door, and I opened it to find Julie Northrup from the day care standing there. She had a large tote slung over one shoulder and smiled at me pleasantly. "I hear you need a babysitter."

"Oh, Julie," I said, feeling guilty. "You can't possibly want—I mean, this is what you do all day."

"Yes, and that makes me ideal. It's all right, Helena. Let me do this for you." She walked past me to a chorus of "Miss Julie!"

I blinked away unexpected tears at this kindness. "Thank you," I said, discarding more protests as being potentially rude.

"I brought books and games, and in a while we'll go to the cafeteria for dinner," Julie told the kids. "Now, I think your mom needs a nap, so how about you finish your snack and we'll read together?"

I hugged Julie and hurried into the bedroom so the children wouldn't see me cry. I knew it had been an awful day, but I hadn't realized it had left me so emotionally fragile. The reminder that there were good people in the world, people who cared about helping others, felt so good, so reassuring, I sat on the bed and wept a few tears before wiping my eyes and lying down. I wasn't sleepy, at least I didn't think I was, but in only a few seconds, I was soundly asleep.

CHAPTER FIFTEEN

I slept soundly and woke to the ringing of my phone. Surprised that I had a signal down here—there were a lot of places in the Gunther Node that had no bars—I answered. "Lucia. I'm sorry, I fell asleep."

"It's all right. We didn't need you until now. Come to Red 47 when you're ready." She hung up as abruptly as always.

The kids and Julie were gone when I left the bedroom, and Night-Noon was curled up asleep on Jenny's small bed. I checked my phone and discovered it was after six. They'd probably gone to dinner. The thought made my stomach rumble, but I ignored it. Lucia's summons had to take precedence.

Red 47 was deeper inside the Gunther Node than anywhere else I'd been except for the holding cells. In fact, it was around the corner from the cells. I controlled a laugh that felt too close to hysteria at the thought of how well I knew the location of the holding cells despite my commitment to being law-abiding. Now was not the time to lose control.

A couple of Wardens in black fatigues stood outside Red 47, both armed with long steel knives as well as guns. They nodded politely to me, and one of them opened the door, though not very wide. I slipped inside, they shut the door, and I found myself behind a handful of bone magi in teal or maroon scrubs, all of whom glanced at me when I entered. Lucia's second in command Dave Henry, armed the way the Wardens had been, stood next to the door. He nodded, but he didn't say anything. His eyes moved constantly, scanning the room. I hesitated, then decided Lucia hadn't summoned me to stand around and pushed past the Wardens.

Cinderblock walls covered in thick gray paint gave the room a frighteningly institutional look, like a prison crossed with a fallout shelter. The concrete floor was rough rather than polished, and my feet scuffed along it like it wanted to hold me in place. The room was bare of furnishings except for a single metal chair that looked like a low-backed throne of iron at its center. Leather straps with gleaming metal buckles attached to the chair's thick arms and legs, restraining a woman who looked almost exactly like me.

It wasn't a perfect likeness of how I looked now. She wasn't wearing the same clothes I was—in fact, nothing she wore matched anything I owned, which relieved my mind of the fear that the Savants had somehow gotten into my closet. She was disheveled and her hair was coming down from her ponytail. Her hazel eyes were unfocused and passed over me without a hint of recognition.

Rick and a bone magus I didn't recognize stood on either side of the chair, with Lucia facing the woman and Malcolm at Lucia's side. The unknown magus's hand was wrapped around my double's forearm, skin to skin.

"Davies," Lucia said by way of greeting. "Our friend here isn't being as forthcoming as we'd like. I could use some assistance."

I surveyed the woman again, focusing on her face, which was relaxed and bore the hint of a smile. That had to be the result of the unknown bone magus's persuasion. I'd been the victim of it once and had hated how compliant it made me, encouraging me to be open so my enemies could extract information from me. At the moment, the thought of it being worked on her filled me with plea-sure. "What have you learned so far?"

"Her name is Betsy Daw, and she is a Savant operative," Malcolm said. "She hates elves and believes anything is justified if it means their destruction. And she's resisted saying anything else. She's well-trained, whatever else she may be."

"So you don't know how they made her look like me?"

"Every time we ask her a question related to Savant magic, she starts reciting nursery rhymes," the unknown magus said, her tone of voice frustrated. "Part of her training, probably. There's not much more I can do to make her willing to speak without killing her."

"All right," I said. I closed my eyes and let a question sink deep within me: *How did they make her look like me?*

Images flooded my mind, dizzying me. I saw the same masked and jump-suited people I'd seen when I prophesied about Craig Jessop, but now those images were overlain with photographs of me, candid shots taken on the street from a distance, and photographs of a woman I didn't know, overlapping each other until only my photo remained. With the images came a deep, wordless knowledge, and I felt sick again.

When the prophecy passed, I said, "They used adept magic to transform her. Correspondence magic. They had—they had pictures of me, and they altered her body until it resembled mine. But they couldn't—" In time I remembered the Savant woman might not know the details of my magic. "It wasn't perfect. They didn't get the eyes right. But it's a permanent transformation. They can't turn her back."

Lucia grimaced. "Betsy," she said in a soft voice I wouldn't have thought the acerbic Lucia capable of, "is this true?"

Betsy smiled lazily. "It's a sacrifice I've made before. Don't remember what I looked like in the beginning."

"You mean you've been transformed before," Lucia said.

Betsy nodded, her head flopping as if she was too weak to hold it up. "It's what I do."

"Why did you go after Alastair?" I demanded, unable to stop myself. "For leverage over me?"

Betsy smiled again, "Mary had a little lamb, its fleece was white as snow," she began.

Lucia let out a frustrated *pah* of breath. "And there she goes again," she said.

I looked closely at Betsy and saw a spark of cunning in her eyes that infuriated me. She was playing us, and she enjoyed it. I tried another question: *How do we get her to talk?*

More images whirled about me, and I caught my breath. As simple as that?—but I wasn't sure I could manage it. It wasn't like me at all. A memory struck, not a part of the vision, but of Alastair's tearful, frightened face, and my resolve hardened.

I blinked away the last of the vision. "Let her go," I told the bone magus. "I mean, not, let her go, but stop compelling her."

"Helena," Malcolm said. He looked concerned, like he didn't know what I could possibly do that he and Lucia and those bone magi could not.

I shook my head and made a quelling gesture. "Just wait." I hoped I was right. I hoped I had the nerve to carry out my plan.

The bone magus looked to Lucia. Lucia nodded. The bone magus removed her hand from Betsy's forearm and stepped back. Betsy's lazy smile and half-lidded eyes didn't change, and she went on reciting the nursery rhyme for about a minute. Then her voice trailed off, and she shifted her weight. Her arms flexed against the restraints. "Given up?" she asked in a mocking tone. The sappy smile was gone, and her expression was cold and hard and defiant.

Lucia glanced at me and raised one eyebrow. I took a deep breath, hoped it didn't look like nerves, and said, "How did Castellan know my son has magic?"

Betsy smiled. It was a nasty expression that said she felt she held all the cards. "You people are so noble. So convinced you're right. You're not willing to make the hard choices."

I stood my ground. "How did Castellan know my son has magic?"

Betsy grinned, and in a singsong voice said, "Peter, Peter, pumpkin eater, had a wife—"

Fury surged through me, and I rode the wave, lunging forward and slapping Betsy so hard her head snapped back. Before she could recover, before anyone could stop me, I grabbed her chin with my aching hand and made her look at me. "Think again," I snarled. "I warned Castellan what would happen if he made this personal. You came after *my child* and I am going to make you wish you'd never heard of the Savants."

Fear flashed across Betsy's face for the briefest second before she resumed her arrogant, confident expression. "Nice try," she said, "but—"

I squeezed her face, shutting her up. "Don't. Because I'm not done with you. You think I'm weak? Castellan doesn't know the half of what I'm capable of. Your body's malleable now, isn't it? That's your secret. Every transformation makes you better able to accept a new one. Which means you're primed and ready for me to turn you inside out and leave you a twisted mass of flesh."

Her eyes widened, and she tried to pull away from my hand. "You're bluffing."

"Am I?" I squeezed even harder, drawing an involuntary gasp from her. "I'm going to start with your eyes. Blind you so you'll never see what's coming. Then I'm going to turn your muscles to jelly, and when you can't support your body anymore, I'll make the skin slide off your bones so every nerve is exposed. And you'll be awake for all of it. You'll be trapped in this husk of a body, awake and aware, because they made you that way, didn't they? Made you capable of sustaining that kind of damage so you could endure the pain and trauma of your transformation into the ultimate assassin. I'm going to put that to the test. And whenever I feel you haven't suffered enough, I'll break one of your bones and watch it heal crooked."

I released her chin with such force her head rocked back again. "You get one chance. Keep me interested, and I'll leave you alone. Bore me, and, well, you can see just fine with only one eye, can't you? For now, anyway."

Betsy sucked in a breath. Her eyes were so wide the whites showed all around the irises. "My superior said my orders came from the top," she gasped. "Mr. Castellan sent word. Sent the pictures for my transformation, sent pictures of the boy, but I never spoke to Mr. Castellan directly, I swear it. I don't know how he found out the boy is an oracle. I don't know what an oracle is, even."

Lucia put a hand on my arm and gently moved me to the side. "What were your orders?"

"To capture the boy and bring him to Mr. Castellan. I wasn't going to hurt him. Mr. Castellan wants him unharmed." Betsy strained briefly against her bonds. "I don't know the details. I work more efficiently when I focus on my task. So they never tell me why a job needs doing, just that it does. Please. I swear—"

"What else did the Savants plan?" Lucia asked. "What other attacks?"

Betsy shook her head. "My division works alone. I only know Mr. Castellan wanted an oracle." She leaned forward as best she could, like that would convince Lucia of the truth, but her eyes were on me. "I wouldn't have hurt him. I swear to God I wouldn't have."

Lucia turned to me. "Well?"

I made myself look as hard and vicious as I could, though my anger was cooling off and a deeply-buried part of me was screaming about what I'd done. "It's enough. For now." I turned on my heel and walked out of the room.

Outside, I kept walking the few paces to the opposite wall and leaned against it, pillowing my head on my arms and sucking in great breaths of air. Distantly, I heard the Wardens who stood sentinel outside Red 47 asking if I was all right. Then Malcolm was there, putting an arm around my shoulders. "That was terrifying," he said, quietly, and the lack of condemnation and anger in his voice calmed me.

"For me, too," I said. "But I knew what I had to do. It's her greatest fear, being altered into something barely viable. I think that threat is how they keep those assassins in line. And there wasn't time or space to tell you so you could be the one to threaten her."

"I had no idea you were capable of anything like that."

"Well, I was sort of counting on her never having seen *The Princess Bride*." I drew in a final, shuddering breath. "It's possible, you know. A bone magus could totally do all those things I threatened. But we never would, would we?"

"You sounded like you didn't care. Mama Bear protecting her cubs."

"For a minute, I didn't. But it's not who I am." I wiped tears from my eyes and added, "I'm starving."

"I think there's lasagna for dinner," Malcolm said. "But first—" He drew me into his embrace and held me close. "Forgive me for not protecting you better."

"What are you talking about?"

"If I had gone on the attack when it was first possible, that incident wouldn't have happened. I'm so sorry, love. You shouldn't have had to endure that."

"Isn't that second-guessing yourself, though? You did what made sense at the time. And you're the one who always says you can't replay the past no matter what you learn in the future." I rested my cheek on his shoulder and breathed in the woody, masculine scent that was his alone. "I love that you want to protect us, but don't ever feel I blame you for failing when something bad happens. We're in this together."

"We are." Malcolm kissed me. "And it's time to plan again."

Malcolm and I joined the children in the cafeteria, where Julie was supervising their dinner. They barely acknowledged us, with the boys having reached the stage of playing with the remaining breadsticks and Julie being occupied with cleaning Jenny's messy face. Their distraction lifted my spirits slightly. I hoped it meant the boys had begun to recover from their ordeal.

I helped myself to lasagna and settled in to eat, feeling surprisingly hungry. "What now? I know we can't go home tonight."

"I have already set in motion the attack I referred to before, taking advantage of what Campbell Security learned about the Savants' organization. We will destroy key sites in a simultaneous assault—"

"Destroy?"

"Yes, destroy. Eliminate them so the Savants can't reap whatever benefits they provide. Killing personnel is not the goal of this first assault, if that's what worries you."

"I'm feeling bloodthirsty enough not to care. But I did wonder. I remember Castellan ordering the death of someone who'd failed him, and I think he doesn't care about his subordinates being killed. So I'm not sure that threat motivates him."

"That's the assessment we have from Cassie, who knows him better than we do. So we can afford to be compassionate, if that's the right word—to avoid excessive loss of life at this time. I can't swear that will always be the case." Malcolm was eating neatly but rapidly and had already nearly cleared his plate. "At any rate, our initial attack is intended to surprise and frighten Castellan. We'll strike, analyze his response, and strike again, this time at targets derived from his reaction."

"What can I do?"

Malcolm chuckled. "I don't suppose 'take a hot bath and relax' is an option?"

I swatted him lightly. "You know I won't be happy with that if I know you're out there—you're going on these raids, aren't you?"

"I am." Malcolm's smile vanished. "Finish eating, and then I have a few questions I want to put to the oracle. After that, I think the children could use some time with you. With both of us, but I can't stay."

"I agree. Promise you'll keep in touch? I don't care how late it is."

"I promise." Malcolm touched my face lightly. "Castellan is going to regret going after Alastair."

"What?" Alastair said, hearing his name.

"We're going to have a nice, quiet evening," I told him, "and tomorrow everyone stays home from school, all right?"

Duncan pumped his fist in the air and shouted, "Yeah!"

"But I have a project due," Alastair protested.

"It's only for a little while," I reassured him. "Besides, Kenny and Liv—" I stopped as Alastair's chin quivered. "Alastair, it's not your fault what adults do."

"I know. I just feel bad. I have some of the project stuff at the house."

"I'll have Ms. Torres pick it up, all right?" I pushed my tray aside and rose. "Julie, thank you again."

"It's my pleasure," Julie said, lightly pinching Jenny's cheek. "Let me know if you need anything else. Do you kids want to come to day care tomorrow?"

"Day care!" Jenny exclaimed. "I like stories!"

I felt Malcolm put his arm around my shoulders a moment before he kissed the top of my head. "Let's all go to our apartment now," he said, "and Mom is going to help me go after the Savants."

"Yeah!" Duncan shouted again. He seemed to have shaken off the effects of witnessing Malcolm's fight with Betsy Daw. "We're going to kick their ass!"

"Duncan, language," I exclaimed.

"I want to help, too," Alastair said.

"Not this time," Malcolm said. "You shouldn't be involved in this fight. It will be violent and possibly bloody, and you know how we feel about giving you time to grow up before witnessing such things."

"But I'm already involved, because it's because of me this happened," Alastair said, stubbornly. "I want to fix it."

Malcolm rested a hand on Alastair's shoulder, and I was struck by how alike they looked, both of them with their dark hair and set jaw and that fierce, brow-furrowed expression. "I understand. And you're right, when you make a mistake you should do what you can to repair it. This is not one of those times, Alastair. If I let you help, it would mean I'd failed in my job to protect you. You're going to have to sit this one out, I'm afraid, and I expect you to take that instruction seriously. Do you understand?"

Alastair nodded. "But it's not because I can't."

"It is most definitely not because you can't. You proved today that the oracle protects you, and that relieves my mind more than you can imagine." He squeezed Alastair's shoulder. "Come on. Lucia told me there's ice cream in the freezer."

Malcolm and I served ice cream to the children and then retreated to the bedroom, where I quickly gave him answers to three questions, none of which made sense to me. They all had military-sounding terms, so I hoped the oracle's prophecies would guide Campbell Security in kicking Savant ass.

After the third, Malcolm took me in his arms and held me close, stroking my hair. "This will be over soon," he said. "Castellan has no idea what he's roused."

"Won't he be suspicious if his agent disappears, or stops reporting?"

"I told you the attack was underway already. He hasn't had time to become suspicious. By the time he puts it together that Daw disappeared just as his sites were compromised, it won't matter what he suspects. And we want him to connect the dots, love. That is key to stopping him coming after you and the children again."

"I understand." I snuggled closer. "Are you going to join in the later attacks?"

"If I have to. It will depend on how things play out. I prefer to make my plans flexible. But don't worry. I'll be careful."

I kissed him. "I know. You always are."

Malcolm hugged and kissed each of the children, then kissed me a final time before leaving. To my surprise, I didn't feel the usual worry I remembered from the days Malcolm went on the hunt against monstrous invaders. Malcolm was sensible, and he would be careful.

We cleaned up the ice cream mess, and then I had them all get into their pajamas so we could watch a movie. I paid only half my attention to the brightly colored cartoon. The rest of me contemplated what might be happening. I considered prophesying to get a look at the attack, but decided against it. There wasn't anything I could do about what I saw, which was as likely to unsettle me as to reassure me, and I ought to pay attention to the children's needs.

But when the movie was over and the children were in bed, I realized I hadn't thought to provide for my own entertainment. I picked over the Gunther Node's private server, which had an extensive range of films and television shows, and discovered someone had laid in a supply of classic films, as if they'd known I was coming. I turned on *My Favorite Wife* and let it carry me off to sleep.

CHAPTER SIXTEEN

I woke, disoriented, to discover the movie was over, Night-Noon was sprawled uncomfortably across my chest and legs, and it was well after one a.m. Malcolm had left me a text an hour ago whose notification had for some reason not woken me: <First attacks complete, waiting on intel. Go to bed, back much later>

I staggered into the bedroom and changed into my night clothes. My short sleep had invigorated me, and although I climbed into bed as instructed, I was wide awake and desperately curious about what was going on. Finally, I set my phone on the bedside table and told myself to sleep. After some restless tossing, I managed to doze off again.

When I woke next, it was to unexpected daylight. Confused, I sat up in my unfamiliar bed and searched for a window. There wasn't a window, but actual sunlight radiated from where the walls met the ceiling, just like dawn creeping over a windowsill. Charmed, I rolled out of bed and went in search of the children.

Only Duncan was awake, watching television. It never stopped astonishing me how easily Duncan took to new technology. I'd needed five minutes just to figure out how to start my movie last night, but Duncan had taken only two seconds to learn how to access the entertainment server and find his favorite shows. When I entered the room, he quickly switched the TV off and pretended he hadn't been watching without permission. Normally Malcolm and I were strict about screen time, but this was such an extraordinary circumstance, I felt inclined to let Duncan indulge for once.

"Let's have breakfast, and then we'll talk about what to do today," I suggested.

Alastair slouched in. I noticed his pajamas were two inches too short at wrists and ankles. The contents of his bug-out bag needed changing now that he was growing again. "Can we have cereal?"

I felt a sudden and intense disinclination to cook. "Yes. Cereal is great. Why don't you two investigate the kitchen and see what's here?"

I went into the children's bedroom and roused Jenny, who stretched and yawned and said, "Mrs. Anderson is lonely. Jenny and Jenny didn't come with us."

Grateful that the real Jenny hadn't felt the need to throw a fit over her missing dolls, I said, "It's like a vacation. They'll all be together soon."

"Not soon," Jenny said.

That made me uneasy, but I picked her up and hugged her and said, "Time for cereal!"

Malcolm still hadn't arrived by the time we all finished eating, and I supervised dressing and brushing teeth and led everyone upstairs to day care. My twinge of guilt over what felt like fobbing them off on Julie and Frank mainly came from my knowledge that I didn't have anything to do that would justify me not taking care of my own kids. But with almost all our belongings being at the house, I had few resources for entertaining them, and they'd either go crazy with boredom or spend all day watching TV and get cranky that way.

Once I said goodbye to them, I found a place that got reception and called the school. There, I felt no guilt at all about lying about the boys being sick. I did text Maribel and Sabina with the truth, or an abbreviated version of the truth: Savants a danger, boys not ill.

After that, I texted Malcolm. <Progress?> I didn't want to be more pushy than that, in case he was in the middle of a fight. Again, I suppressed the desire to prophesy about Malcolm's condition or the status of the attacks, neither of which I could have done anything about, and trudged back to our apartment.

I was idly flicking through the list of classic movies when my phone rang. I snatched it up. "Malcolm?"

"Everything is well," Malcolm said. "The first assaults went off perfectly. I don't think I've seen so well-coordinated an attack as that in... ever, really."

I let out a sigh of relief. "I'm so glad. What happens now?"

"The second stage takes longer. We'll choose our future targets based on Castellan's responses—it's a complex tactical situation I personally find fascinating, like the best war games in the world." Malcolm hesitated, then added, "I'm afraid the boys can't go back to school for a while."

"That's a relief, actually. I was afraid you'd tell me we have to pull them out of Talbott entirely." I leaned back and propped my feet on the other armrest.

"That's still a possibility if this all goes wrong, but it's a last resort. For now, I think you should get them registered for a long-term absence."

"I have to go in to the school in person for that."

"It's safe. We've given the Savants so much to worry about I don't think their attention is on the school anymore. Are you doing all right?"

"Surprisingly, I'm bored. I'm sorry if that seems insufficiently concerned."

Malcolm laughed. "Understandable. I'll keep in touch. I love you."

"I love you, too."

Now that I had a task, I felt surprisingly cheerful, like I'd been released from confinement, though of course the Gunther Node wasn't a prison. I let Lucia know where I was going, just in case, and got another surprise: someone had brought the land yacht, and my purse with the key fob, to the Gunther Node last night. Released from confinement *and* with my own set of wheels. I reminded myself not to get overconfident and headed for the school.

The day was gray and overcast, but the lowering clouds couldn't kill my cheerful mood. The thought of what Michael Castellan must be going through now kept my spirits lifted. I liked imagining him in a frustrated rage as his well-hidden (he thought) military bases went up in flames, one by one. Occasionally I fantasized about facing him down and delivering a dramatic speech about not messing with my children that was completely unrealistic, because dramatic speeches weren't my thing. It was fun anyway.

I made a few stops before my final destination, first at home, to get Alastair's part of his group project, and then to the doctor's office to get Derrick, the children's pediatrician and a longtime friend, to write me a completely fake note for use at the school. Derrick was a Warden, a bone magus, and someone who'd been part of Malcolm's invader-fighting team ten years ago. He'd already heard from Malcolm and was prepared to help.

At the school, I spun another yarn for Clarice and then Mrs. Keith, the assistant principal in charge of students surnamed A-L: chickenpox, not sure where they got it, of course they were vaccinated, should warn the students in their classes. Here, this is the note from their doctor. Yes, it's terrible, and I feel just awful and hope no one else gets it.

I gave Maribel Torres Alastair's work and pretended I didn't see Liv staring at me. She was just an eight-year-old kid, but I was angry with her for being complicit in putting us in this situation. I tried to remind myself that she hadn't meant any harm, and that she probably didn't know anything about the Savants—though, was that really true, given that our children knew all about the Wardens, and magic, and their own oracular gifts? My cheerful mood faded.

When I left the school, the smell of rain lay heavy in the air, and I ducked my head against the cold wind that had sprung up. I was halfway down the sidewalk to the parking lot when someone came around the corner of a car and stopped ten feet from me.

It was Maddy Hubbard.

I froze. Maddy gazed at me without a hint of guilt on her features. I was sure I looked startled, at least, though I hoped my momentary fear wasn't evident. We neither of us moved for much longer than was natural. Finally, Maddy said, "Hi, Helena. How are you?"

"I'm fine," I said automatically. "How are you? How's Liv?"

"Fine," Maddy said. She still made no move to continue walking. "Looking forward to Halloween next week. She said she and Kenny and Alastair wanted to go trick-or-treating together. What do you think?"

It was the same banal blandness I was used to seeing in her. Without direction from my brain, my mouth said, "What did Liv tell you about Alastair?"

Maddy's brow furrowed slightly. "I don't know what you mean. Is something wrong?"

I stepped closer. Maybe this was stupid, but the sight of Liv in that classroom where Alastair should have been angered me. "Alastair's special. Liv told you how special, didn't she?"

"That sounds ominous," Maddy said, her lips quirking up on one side in a wry smile. "I hope you don't think—"

"Cut the crap," I said. "I just want a straight answer. What did Liv tell you, and what did you do about it?"

The smile vanished. "You don't know anything," Maddy said, and lunged at me.

It was an awkward lunge, and without thinking I sidestepped her, grabbed her arm, and wrenched it behind her back. She broke my grip with a twist of her wrist I recognized and spun to aim a punch at my stomach. I jumped back so the blow only grazed me. Our eyes locked. Maddy was breathing heavily, but she still looked dispassionate, like this encounter was nothing.

Then she turned and ran.

I darted after her. A little voice in my head was screaming at me to let her go, that there was nothing I could do if I caught her, but I was gaining on her and my body refused to stop.

Talbott Academy was on one of those streets that wasn't quite a major artery and wasn't a side street, but its playing fields abutted a quiet neighborhood of older houses, and the fence didn't completely enclose the fields. Maddy headed toward that neighborhood, bypassing the fence and bounding down the short incline to the next street. I had to slow to keep from tripping as I descended, and Maddy gained a few yards on me, but I leaped over the three steps at the bottom of the incline and put on speed.

Rain began to fall, and distantly, thunder rumbled. Maddy didn't slow, didn't waste time looking back to see how close I was. The surface beneath my feet became slick with water, but my running shoes gripped the concrete and kept me from falling. Little houses whose windows glowed with yellow light flashed past. I wildly wondered what their occupants thought of our strange race, one ordinary woman chasing another through the suburban streets. Dogs barked as we passed, one giving way to another as they defended their territory.

Then Maddy stumbled, and in the next moment I tackled her, bearing her to the ground. I barely felt the concrete scrape my wrists, because Maddy was fighting me, not with any science, just struggling and flailing at me. She got one arm free and managed to hit me a glancing blow across the side of my head, but despite being momentarily dizzied, I held onto her, getting one knee over her thighs to pin her legs.

Finally, I had her arms contained, and we stared at each other, panting. That little screaming voice had shut up, probably because it knew when a situation was futile. But it left me at a loss for words. Maddy remained silent as if daring me to speak first. Finally, the tension got to me, and I said, "What, Savants don't learn how to fight?"

Maddy licked her dry lips and said, "We're not the violent ones."

I stared at her. Then I laughed, though outrage wanted to turn it into a scream. "You've got to be kidding. I had to flee my home yesterday because your nonviolent friends want me and my children dead."

For just a moment, Maddy's impassivity cracked, and she looked surprised. Then she said, "That wasn't our intent."

"Really? What *was* your intent? Kidnapping Alastair? Is that supposed to make me feel better?"

Maddy shook her head. "You don't understand anything."

"Then start talking. Make me understand." I was becoming aware that I couldn't hold her forever, and that if I tried to call someone for help, she could probably break free. But the memory of how afraid Alastair had been made it impossible for me to let her go.

"Let me up first," Maddy said.

I pressed her harder into the ground, making her grimace. "Yeah, right. I can't believe I ever felt sorry for you."

"Why would you feel sorry for me?" Maddy looked puzzled.

"You were always so nervous, I thought you were on the run. In Witness Protection or something."

Maddy laughed, a short bark of a sound. "I was just crap at being a secret agent, always afraid you'd guess I was pumping you for information. I suppose that's better than you finding out the truth. I don't know what the agents who covered our tracks did, so for all I know that was the intention. Cover the truth with a plausible lie."

"I don't care. What did you tell Michael Castellan?"

Maddy's amusement evaporated. "Too much, and too little," she said. She squirmed, but only enough to get a hand on her necklace of red jasper beads and tug it away from where it was twisted close around her throat, choking her. "We were supposed to learn about you. About your plans to help Faerie take over this world."

"What?" I exclaimed. "That's not true."

"It doesn't matter. You're delusional, but your children are innocent. And when Mr. Castellan ordered us to bring Alastair to him, I told him I wasn't going to weaponize a child, no matter what his parents did." Maddy twisted the beads between her fingers. "That was five—no, four days ago. We haven't heard anything from him since."

"If you think that's going to impress me—"

"I don't care what you think. Your people are a danger to this world. The only way to protect humanity is by destroying Faerie." Maddy sounded utterly convinced of her words. "But I draw the line at hurting children."

Swiftly, she jerked on her necklace, snapping it so the jasper beads flew in every direction. In the next moment, her whole body jerked, and suddenly I was wrestling a dog, a big black Labrador that whimpered and whined and struggled to get free. I jerked upright, releasing its paws, and it rolled awkwardly to its feet and fled. Confused, I watched it go. Had I just witnessed Maddy turning herself into an animal?

Then I saw her. She was inside one of the fenced yards, climbing the back chain link fence and dropping into the neighbor's yard. I stared, bewildered, as she crossed the second yard, climbed another fence, and sped around a corner and out of sight.

I knelt to gather up some of the scattered stone beads. I'd been too preoccupied to pay any attention to her jewelry, but this was the least expensive thing I'd ever seen her wear, red rough-cut jasper beads the size of my thumbnail, set off with sterling silver rosettes. I rolled one of the beads between my fingers, then sniffed it. It didn't smell like anything, and I didn't think it was magical, but I was sure it had somehow helped Maddy make her escape. I tucked a handful of beads and some of the sterling silver spacers into my pocket and hurried back to the land yacht through the increasingly heavy rain.

Safely behind the wheel of the car, I assessed my condition. My hair was a wet mess, I'd scraped the insides of my wrists raw, the knees of my jeans were filthy from the wet concrete, and my damp sweater clung unpleasantly to my skin. I wanted nothing more than to go home and change, but I was still concerned about the possibility of Savant retaliation, so instead I put the car in gear and headed back to the Gunther Node, wishing I'd brought more than one change of clothes with me.

Maddy's behavior confused me. On the one hand, she'd sounded exactly like a Savant when she talked about elves and the destruction of Faerie. But I hadn't thought she was lying when she said she'd refused to hurt Alastair. Maybe that just meant I was gullible, but I wasn't in a mood to give her credit for any kind of good behavior, so I didn't think so. And she'd looked genuinely startled when I'd mentioned the possibility of Savants attacking my home. Almost as if she felt bad about her complicity.

I shook my head violently, chasing away my softhearted foolishness. Maddy and Bronson Hubbard were the enemy, and it didn't matter if Maddy didn't act evil. I called Malcolm and got his voice mail. "Malcolm, Maddy Hubbard admitted they're Savants," I said, weariness filling me to the bone. "She knows I know, so somebody should go to their house and pick them up before they flee. Or I guess Bronson might be at work. You know what I mean."

I spared a thought for Emma and Liv. What would happen to the girls if the Wardens captured Maddy and Bronson? Guilt, and a sharp pang I recognized as sympathy, struck me. If the Wardens did take the girls' parents into custody, something would have to be done for Emma and Liv, and if the Wardens handled it, that something would look a lot like kidnapping. I told myself not to worry about an event that might not happen, but that nagging feeling refused to go away.

CHAPTER SEVENTEEN

As I drove, I felt something dig into the crease of my thigh. I wiggled, and Maddy's beads shifted, reminding me of the other strange thing that had happened. After a moment's thought, I called Cassie.

She answered after three rings. "Helena, hi. Is something wrong?"

"I guess I never call just to chat, do I?" I said. "I have a question about adept magic." I decided not to go into detail about Maddy and Savants, because I'd forgotten what I'd already told Cassie about recent events.

"Sure. What do you want to know?"

"You told me teleportation of humans is impossible because humans can't be fooled into thinking the world is other than it is—did I get that right?"

"Yes. We can teleport objects and even some animals with virtually no limit, but not humans."

I rubbed the lumps in my pocket. They felt bumpy and rough beneath the fabric. "What about switching places with someone or something else? Is that not teleportation?"

"Ah. Well, yes and no. Adepts can swap the places of any two things within a certain range, say no more than half a mile. Mostly we only do it when things are within sight of one another. It's possible for an adept to swap herself with an object—not with another human—but it takes a lot of practice and usually requires something that acts as a fulcrum."

"A fulcrum is like the pivot point on a seesaw, isn't it? Is it the same in magic?"

"More or less. A magical fulcrum doesn't have to have physical existence, but when it does, it's something natural. A leaf, or a stick."

I awkwardly dug one of the beads out of my pocket. "Or a stone? Like a gemstone?"

"Sure, I guess. You sound like you have something specific in mind."

"I'm wondering what other uses adepts have for objects like that. I remember Marlin Dunfee used plants to make the golem that came after me. Is that typical?"

Cassie made a "hmm" sound. "That's just coincidence. A golem can be made of almost any material, not just organic matter. But a fulcrum—or, more specifically, a focus object that is turned into a fulcrum—has to have resonance with the natural world. I'm afraid I can't explain it better than that to a non-adept."

"It's okay, I get the gist. A focus object can do more than just act as a fulcrum."

"That's right. We use them for centering ourselves, and for amplifying certain magics. You want to tell me what this is about? Because I'm dying of curiosity." She sounded amused rather than impatient.

"I—" The thought of explaining everything that had led to my encounter with Maddy Hubbard wearied me further. "It's a long story, but basically I encountered a Savant who used semiprecious stones to work her magic."

Cassie hissed in surprise. "I didn't think there were any Savants who could work magic on that level. Most of them have killed too many times, and every death they inflict weakens their connection with magic until finally they can't use magic at all."

I sat up straighter. "You're right. I'd forgotten that." That meant Maddy couldn't have killed often, or maybe at all, which meant... probably nothing. There were lots of ways to commit evil that didn't take lives. But the thought niggled at me. "Well, this one could. She switched places with a dog to get away from me."

"You're all right, though?"

I touched my head and remembered I needed to brush my hair. "I'm fine. I hope we catch the Savant soon. It sounds like she could tell us a lot."

"Good luck," Cassie said, and we disconnected.

I considered Cassie's words as I drove. Again, the circumstance of Maddy being able to work magic despite being a Savant baffled me. I thought of all the times Alastair had been at her house, alone and unprotected, and I thought of all the chances she'd had to hurt or kidnap him. None of which she'd taken. I wasn't going to let my imagination run wild, supposing the Hubbards weren't our enemy, just because Maddy had behaved atypically for a Savant. But I did consider that one thing she'd said was true—I didn't understand them at all.

When I was inside the Gunther Node, I ran in search of Lucia. Malcolm hadn't called or texted back, and it occurred to me that if he was preoccupied with crushing Michael Castellan, he might not have seen my message about Maddy. Which meant if I wanted the Hubbards caught, I needed someone else's help.

Lucia called an invitation when I pounded on her office door. She was with Dave Henry and lowered the tablet they'd been looking at when I entered. "What's wrong?"

"Maddy Hubbard confirmed she's a Savant," I panted. "I called Malcolm, but he's not answering—"

"We'll handle it," Dave said. "Where is she now?"

I shook my head. "We fought, and she used Savant magic to escape."

Lucia rose. "We have Wardens watching the Hubbards' house. Henry, call them and tell them to take the Hubbards into custody if they show up. I—"

Her phone rang, and Lucia glanced at the display before answering. "What is it?"

She listened as the person spoke, then said, "That's fine. What else did she say, Torres?"

I gasped. Torres. Alastair's teacher Maribel Torres. "What's going on?" I demanded.

Lucia raised a finger to hush me. "Let me know if she returns." She set the phone down and said, "Torres says Maddy Hubbard just pulled Liv out of school. She said something about a dentist appointment, but Torres was suspicious and spied on her, and saw both the Hubbard girls leaving in a hurry. I think the Hubbards are making a run for it."

I swore under my breath. "If I'd been faster—"

"Don't worry about it, Davies. We'll find them. Though if you could prophesy about it, that would help."

Lucia's mildly acerbic tone made me blush. I was definitely under more stress than I'd realized. "Let me sit," I said, and took one of the chairs in front of Lucia's desk. Lucia and Dave staring at me made me self-conscious, so I closed my eyes and willed myself to know the Hubbards' current location.

The prophecy lifted me, swooping across the Portland landscape like I was a bird, something with big wings that could soar for hours without coming down. The cloud cover dimmed the sunlight, and rain fell in a gentle but unrelenting way across the city. I searched the roads below and saw a spot of bright sunlight, like a single ray had found a gap in the clouds, following the Banfield—or some car moving along the Banfield.

I found I had control over my view and dropped until I skimmed low above the roofs of the cars. Traffic was light at this hour, and even without the beam of sunlight I would have recognized Maddy's pearl-gray CR-V. I angled my invisible, immaterial body to look through the windows. Maddy was driving, with Bronson in the front seat and Liv and Emma sitting behind. All of them looked tense.

Gradually, the vision faded, and I blinked and said, "They're on the Banfield headed east. I don't know whether they intend to go north or south when they reach the 205."

"Which car?" Dave demanded. "The Trans-Am?"

"No, Maddy's car. It's a Honda CR-V."

"I know," Dave said, and hurried out of the office, putting his phone to his ear as he left.

I stared at Lucia, who was texting rapidly, not tapping the screen but swiping with her index finger as if drawing scribbles. "I can prophesy again in a minute, once they've reached the interchange," I said.

"That's fine," Lucia said absently, still texting.

I felt miffed that she'd encouraged me and now was treating my vision as unimportant. So I relaxed again and embraced the question *Where are the Hubbards going?*

Again, I had the bird's-eye view of Portland, hovering even higher over the city. From that height, the freeways looked like a drunken spider's web extending filaments in all directions. As I watched, the view became misty, not like it was fading, but as if it was turning into something else—specifically, a road map with numbered and lettered roads and cities, overlaying the real world like a translucent film. I was looking down at Happy Valley, near where my parents lived, but my vision was drawn not to their neighborhood, but to a sprawling building surrounded by hundreds of parked cars. The mall.

The vision dissolved, and I said, "They're going to Clackamas Town Center."

"Good. That's good," Lucia said, still absently.

Irritated, I burst out, "Aren't you going to do anything about it?"

"Of course." Lucia finally looked at me with her usual piercing gaze. "But we're also taking advantage of their absence to toss the Hubbards' house. And I'll send a couple of teams to intercept them at the mall. We'll catch them, Davies."

"The girls don't have anything to do with their parents being Savants," I said, feeling alarmed. "You can't be rough with them."

Lucia rolled her eyes. "I don't torment children, Davies." She stood, prompting me to rise as well. "I'll let you know when we have them. Go rest or something."

"I'm not tired."

"Then prophesy. But I need you out of the way while we handle this. If we bring the Hubbards in, I want to be as cautious as possible. I have no idea what kind of tricks they might play, and for all I know, getting into the Gunther Node was the plan, and threatening you was a means to an end." Lucia shepherded me out the door. "Read a book or something."

I scowled at her, but I couldn't think of a scathing retort.

I wandered back to the transit hub and then down to the apartment, where I threw myself on the couch and tried to prophesy. Half a dozen questions later, I was no more enlightened than before. Grumbling, I mentally went through my entertainment options. In the end, I decided against retrieving the kids from day care, since they'd probably be mad about it, and called Judy.

"Finally," Judy said. "Are you going to tell me what's going on? First you say you need me to pick Sophia up yesterday, then you say you don't need carpool today—were you planning to save it all up for girls' night, and kill me with impatience?"

"I'm sorry. Everything's been crazy. The Savants tried to kidnap Alastair yesterday, and we're... I guess we're in hiding at the Gunther Node."

Judy was silent.

"I would have told you—" I began.

"I'm not mad, just stunned," Judy said. "What made them

decide to go after Alastair now, given that they've known where to find him for a while now?"

I explained about the Savant kidnapper and Liv knowing Alastair was an oracle and Maddy claiming she'd refused to attack Alastair. Judy listened in typical silence, so different from Viv, who would have interrupted me for details a dozen times. "So, the Hubbards were supposed to investigate you because Castellan told them you're helping the elves destroy humanity," she finally said. "That's a flat-out lie. Why would Castellan lie to them about their mission?"

"I don't know. It still doesn't make sense. Maddy said Castellan ordered them to kidnap Alastair, and she refused. But she was still convinced I'm the bad guy. I don't know what to make of that."

"Lucia will pick them up, and you can ask."

I sighed. "Unless Lucia is right in her suspicions, and getting into the Gunther Node was what the Hubbards were really after. I don't know. I feel like we're asking all the wrong questions. And prophesying hasn't cleared any of it up. Every prophecy that isn't explicitly about their location is just a muddle of images."

"Which will probably make sense once it's too late to do anything about them," Judy said.

"Spoken like a rogue," I replied.

"You still don't know anything about roleplaying game classes, do you?" Judy said.

I tried to watch movies, but nothing kept my attention. Further prophecies about the Hubbards ran up against the oracle's lack of knowledge, which frustrated me not only because of their failure, but because it meant Lucia's teams hadn't caught them. I refused to feel inappropriate guilt. If the Hubbards had escaped, likely they weren't a threat to us anymore.

It finally occurred to me, some time in the middle of *His Girl*

Friday, that Maddy and Bronson had defied Castellan in refusing to kidnap Alastair. In all the chaos and confusion, I hadn't thought about what this meant. Surely Castellan wouldn't put up with that sort of defiance? And yet he'd frozen the Hubbards out instead, if Maddy had told the truth. They might be in danger from both sides, Wardens and Savants. In which case they really *weren't* a threat, at the least because they'd be too busy staying out of sight.

Even so, I hoped the Wardens investigating the Hubbards' house would learn something we could use. I still felt sick every time I remembered Alastair going to their house and how easy it would have been for Maddy and Bronson to take him to Castellan. I wasn't going to assume we were safe until I was certain of it.

Finally, tired of flipping between films and settling on none of them, I went upstairs to the day care. Only three other children, all of them very young, were still there, two of them playing with sorting-block puzzles, the third helping my children in one of their invented games, City. This involved building a city out of any and all available materials, blocks, books, dolls, cars, whatever. Alastair got up from the game with such eagerness I knew he hadn't been fully engaged.

"Is it time to go home?" he asked.

"I'm sorry, no. Dad is still gone, and I haven't heard what's happening with the Savants."

Alastair's face fell, and he said, "I'm really bored. I didn't bring enough books."

"We'll find something for you to do," I promised. Alastair was never happy unless he was doing something complicated enough to engage his attention fully.

"Look at the city!" Duncan exclaimed. "We never have enough things at home to build one this big."

"Yes, and I'm sorry to tell you that it's time to disassemble it," I said. "But I'll take some pictures so you can remember what a fun time you had."

The disassembly took much less time than I expected, and soon we were all on our way to the cafeteria for dinner. Mentioning Malcolm to the children had made me anxious about what he was doing. If he hadn't contacted me, it meant he was with the attackers, on a raid or whatever they called it. My concern for his safety warred with my concern over his success. I really wanted to get a phone call saying the Savants had been destroyed or at least prevented from attacking us ever again.

As we crossed the transit hub, Lucia emerged from the hall leading to her office, moving fast. She saw me and corrected her course, striding like she meant to conquer the ground under her feet. "Did you see anything?" she demanded as she neared.

Startled, I said, "I haven't had a prophecy—is it the Hubbards? Did they escape?"

Lucia waved that away. "It's the elves," she said. "They attacked a village in Ireland. There were no survivors."

CHAPTER EIGHTEEN

"But—" I instinctively clutched Jenny closer, enough that she protested and wiggled to get down.

"Shouldn't that be something the oracle would warn us about?" Lucia asked. I could tell she was trying hard not to make it an accusation.

"We don't get a lot of spontaneous prophecies about other people or events," I said. "Usually those have meaning to us, warnings about danger or events that will affect our immediate future. Even the spontaneous ones about others are still connected to us in some way. An elf attack—"

"Never mind," Lucia said. "It doesn't matter now. I have to move forward. The report came from Wardens at the Dailey Node, who said all the lights in Callann, the village, went out at the same time. The people they sent to investigate found human bodies but no elves."

Horrified, I said, "But that's going to be impossible to cover up. Isn't it?"

"Don't underestimate the Wardens, Davies," Lucia said. "If the elves had left survivors, then we'd have a problem. As it is, we'll make it look like a town-wide gas leak. That has its own problems, but it beats the authorities seeing a bunch of corpses with sword wounds."

"Their government will cover it up," Alastair said.

I stared blankly at him, surprised at his entrance into the conversation. Then I realized what he'd done. "Alastair, you are not to prophesy about this," I warned him.

He glared at me, and he looked so much like his father when Malcolm was intent on something difficult it momentarily took my breath away. "I can help."

"It's not your responsibility."

He looked even more stubborn. "Don't say I'm too young."

"Alastair, this is not—" I clamped my mouth shut on a terrible reply. Instead, I said to Lucia, "What can I do?"

"Nothing at the moment. We've got it covered. I wanted to know if you'd been warned."

"I wouldn't conceal that!"

Lucia shook her head. "I meant I wanted to know if there was anything else you'd seen that I needed to know about. But... yes. Either the oracle was warned and you didn't have time to tell anyone, or the oracle *wasn't* warned and we need to stop being complacent. You can't see everything, Davies."

She leaned over to address Alastair. He was getting taller, but he still looked like a child next to her—a defiant, scared child. "Listen to your mother," she said. "I'm never going to be so desperate that I'd abuse your gift. You're smart, and driven, and you care about helping others. Those traits are all going to help you as you grow. But there are things no child should have to see, and I expect you to use that brain of yours to know what they are. Understand?"

Alastair swallowed. "What about—"

"There's always going to be 'what about,'" Lucia said. "No exceptions. You get a spontaneous prophecy, fine. That's between you and your gift. But you are not to get involved otherwise. You want to help? That puts you under my jurisdiction. And I'm making it an order."

Alastair nodded. "I understand."

"Good. Come back in six years and we'll talk." Lucia straightened. "Go get dinner, Davies. I'll know more in an hour, and then I'll have some requests."

"I'll be ready."

I watched Lucia walk away, pretending not to hear Alastair controlling himself. I wasn't resentful of Lucia essentially disciplining my child, not when I felt she'd been more effective than I was. I needed Alastair to stay out of this as much as his oracular gift would let him. Her point about authority had hit Alastair more powerfully than anything I might have said about responsibility and duty, given that Alastair knew his impulses and mine were the same and that I sympathized with his desires. Finally, when Lucia had disappeared through the red door, I said, "Let's see what's for dinner."

Dinner was beef brisket and salad and slabs of Texas toast, with a choice of four types of cobbler for dessert. I spoke to Alastair casually about ordinary things, not referring to what had happened. He was smart enough to see Lucia's point, and proud enough to be embarrassed by her rebuke. He needed time to get over that rebuke.

We were eating cobbler when Malcolm walked through the door of the cafeteria. The children immediately abandoned their meals to rush their father, clamoring to tell him about their day. He absently hugged each of them and then gathered me into his arms for a kiss. "I'm sorry this took so long."

"I understand. Though I demand you tell me exactly what happened with the Savants as your penalty for being gone so long." He smelled like gunpowder and sweat and his clothes were filthy, but he didn't seem injured.

"Can you contain your impatience long enough for me to eat? I haven't had anything since morning."

"Of course. Duncan, stop jumping on your father. Let's all sit down and wait patiently." I was talking to myself as much as to them. I could contain my impatience, but I didn't enjoy doing so. It occurred to me that maybe Malcolm's story was inappropriate for the kids' young ears, but then I remembered how terrified Alastair and Duncan had been when Betsy Daw had infiltrated the school. They needed to know they were safe, and they deserved the details.

Malcolm filled his plate and returned to sit with us. "Our first attack went off perfectly, as I think I told you," he said, digging into his brisket like he really was starving. "We observed the Savants' reaction to the destruction of those sites. Just as we'd hoped, Castellan increased the Savants' military presence at certain other locations, telling us which were important. We went after those next."

"But he could have tricked you," Duncan said. "Maybe he only pretended. That's what Kerigon did in the game."

"That's a clever notion, Duncan, and you're right, that was possible," Malcolm said. "In this case, the way he moved his personnel told us he wasn't pretending. The secondary targets were bigger and more heavily defended, but we managed to destroy those, too."

I refrained from asking if people had died, Savants or Wardens. That might disturb the children, and it wasn't like I could do anything about those deaths. Instead, I asked, "Then what? More observation?"

"Then I sent Castellan a message, along with a list of our third-stage targets." Malcolm smiled at Duncan. "Those were a lie, sort of. They were all Savant installations, but they weren't the ones we intended to attack. The point was to show that we had him by the— that is, we had control, and we would go on attacking if he didn't back off."

"But what if he knows where the Wardens have bases?" Alastair asked. "Couldn't he retaliate?"

"We have six hundred and fifty more years of experience at staying hidden than the Savants or Astraeus Resources have, and it shows," Malcolm said. "It's true that Astraeus has money and influence, but their paramilitary power is focused on Savant activities worldwide, and locally, that means the Wardens have the upper hand. If anything, we're concerned about the Savants making a different kind of attack. Setting us up for an IRS audit, or exposing Campbell Security as a corrupt influencer of the government, that sort of thing. That is where we've put much of our defenses. The Savants won't find it easy to get at us."

"What did Castellan say?" I asked.

"He hasn't responded yet. I gave him twenty-four hours to think about it. If I haven't heard from him by then, we attack the tertiary targets and send another ultimatum."

"You could destroy them utterly," I said, and was horrified at myself, but not much.

"Astraeus is too big for that, and the Savants' operation is too widely spread. It's like a cancer that way—if you don't get every cell, it keeps coming back." Malcolm wiped his mouth with his napkin and took a long drink of water. "Even now, we don't know all their resources, or all the sites they control. The worst possibility is that Castellan is more devious than we believe, and he has an entire shadow organization within the Savants to protect against the possibility of someone doing what we've done."

"I wish I could prophesy about his intentions." The usual frustration I felt when thinking about Castellan surged through me.

"I know, but let's not worry about what we can't do, all right?" Malcolm's fork hovered over his peach cobbler, but he didn't take a bite. "For now, we have to act as if everything is as we've discovered, and at the same time take precautions as if it isn't."

"That's what Lucia is doing about the elves, I guess."

Malcolm, his mouth full of cobbler, made a questioning noise.

"Oh," I said, feeling uncomfortable. "You've probably been too busy... Malcolm, the elves have attacked. They killed everyone in a village called Callann, in Ireland."

Malcolm swallowed hastily. "Why didn't anyone tell me?" He

grimaced. "Because I was dealing with Savants. Now I'm reconsidering the thing about destroying the organization utterly. They waste our resources dealing with them when we should focus on the elves. What happened?"

"I don't know. Lucia didn't say much, and none of us had spontaneous prophecies about it."

"That seems odd. Why wouldn't you be warned of an elf incursion?"

I shrugged. "We don't see everything. The spontaneous prophecies are usually for our personal benefit. Which is good, because otherwise we'd never sleep for warnings about disasters around the world."

"Even so... no, never mind. You're right, you can't be expected to see everything."

Jenny grabbed Malcolm's arm. "The scary elf came," she whispered. "I don't like him. He hurts people."

"Jenny, when did you see the scary elf?" I demanded.

"Now. But I didn't scream. And I am scared but not him. I want to color a square!"

"And just like that, Jenny makes me a liar," I said lightly, trying to conceal my disquiet. "She sees elves all the time, and I know she's not old enough to ask for prophecies."

"She has the genetic difference. Maybe she's connected to the elves," Malcolm said.

"Then why don't I see them?"

"Good point. I have no other ideas." Malcolm finished eating and rose from the table. "I have to find Lucia and learn what happened in that village—"

"Callann," Alastair said.

"Callann. But I'll join you in the apartment soon. I need sleep." He kissed me and hurried away.

"Let's clear our trays, and then watch a movie," I suggested.

Once the kids were in their jammies and I'd started *How to Train*

Your Dragon, I settled in with the children gathered around, Jenny sprawled across my lap, Alastair and Duncan with Night-Noon lying between them. Poor cat, cooped up here when she was used to ranging free in the backyard. I hoped Castellan would cave and we could go home soon.

Though, was that safe? The Hubbards knew where we lived, and it was too much to hope they hadn't told Castellan. Even if Castellan was frightened out of sending more kidnappers or, shudder, assassins, that fear might not last. And then our home would be a trap rather than a haven.

The thought terrified me. I loved my home. It had been my refuge for more than ten years. I'd brought each of my babies home from the hospital to it. So many memories... the idea of losing it made me sick. And yet, after all, it was just a place. Home ought to be the people you loved, not the building you lived in.

Malcolm would probably say I should worry about that when it became an issue, but I couldn't live like that. I needed stability, and I got stability by planning for every outcome. So while the movie rolled on, and Jenny grew gradually heavier as she relaxed into sleep, I considered what we might do if we had to leave our house. Financing wasn't an issue; we could afford to buy a house outright. We'd need to live close to the school—unless that, too, needed to be abandoned.

That thought made me angry. I could just about cope with moving to a new house. Having the boys' education disrupted because Castellan might move against them again infuriated me. I wasn't sure why that was worse than upending our entire family. The boys leaving Talbott Academy felt more personal somehow, or maybe it was just my desire to protect them that made Castellan's attacks seem worse when they were against my children.

Alastair and Duncan were drooping by the time the movie ended, and Jenny was fast asleep. "Off to bed," I said, awkwardly rising with Jenny in my arms. She didn't wake all through me carrying her into the bedroom and settling her with Mrs. Anderson on her small bed. I made sure the night light was on—Duncan often woke around one a.m. and got up for a drink—and turned off the overhead light and shut the door.

When I turned around, I jumped. "Alastair! I thought you were in bed."

Alastair shook his head. "I don't think Lucia is right. I can help. I'm old enough."

I thought about that for a moment. Then I said, "Sit down, and we'll talk."

He sat on the couch across from me, so determined, so like his father. I controlled my first reaction, which was to remind him that Lucia had not given him a choice in this, and that she had a right to command his obedience. "Why do you want to help?" I finally asked.

"Because I have a gift. You help people all the time, and you let me do the augury requests. I don't see how this is different."

I paused again, searching for the right words. "Alastair," I said, "you know there are movies you're not allowed to see yet, and games you're not allowed to play. Why is that?"

Alastair shrugged. "Because I'm not old enough. But this is—"

"It's not different," I said. "Those movies and games are restricted not because of your age, but because you're not ready to process what they show. And when it comes to elves attacking our world, well, I've seen the havoc they cause. It's bloody and violent and as bad, maybe worse, as those things we won't let you watch. Worse, because with a movie, you know those are actors and special effects. If you see an elf cut someone's arm off, that's real. I assure you it's disturbing and terrible, even to me—and I've seen violence I hope you never witness."

He ducked his head. "I know. But if I can help, I can deal with it."

"What makes you so convinced you're essential to this fight, Alastair?" I demanded. "Are you saying everything will fall apart if you don't participate? Because that's what I'm hearing."

"I'm afraid of the elves," Alastair said in a voice nearly a whisper.

It was not the response I'd expected. "Afraid? How?"

"I saw them the night they came into our world the first time. When you were kidnapped." Alastair's narrow shoulders heaved as his breathing grew heavy. "There were only five of them, but they killed so many people. And if Dad goes after them, they might kill him, too. I want to stop them because I'm scared."

I knelt in front of him and took him in my arms. "I understand," I said. "You don't want to feel powerless."

Alastair nodded.

"I don't know how to fix that," I said, "except I think if I let you prophesy for Lucia about the elves and how to stop them, it would harm you in ways we can't imagine. That would be worse than being afraid."

"So what do I do?" Alastair cried. "I need—I have to help or I'll just go on being scared."

I hugged him tighter. "You and Dad need to have a talk. This is beyond what I know how to solve. I think he can give you a solution I can't. *My* solution is to ask for a prophecy about sending a nuclear weapon against Jenny's scary elf."

Alastair giggled. "I think I've seen him. The big one with the messy dark hair and the sword. He's the leader."

"I saw him in person. It was terrifying. I hate that Jenny keeps seeing him in vision." I shuddered, then released Alastair. "I don't know when your father will be back, so try to sleep, and I'll let him know what we talked about, okay? I love you, and I love that your reaction to fear is to face it head-on."

"I love you too, Mom." He wiped his sleeve across his eyes and went into the bedroom, closing the door behind him.

I sat back on the couch. I hoped that had been the right response. Alastair was going to be a force to reckon with someday, if we could help him survive to grow up.

After that conversation, I felt weary and in need of relaxation.

The apartment's bathroom had an enormous tub, and the draw of a hot bath enticed me. I started to get up, and a spontaneous prophecy swept over me, swooping me up until I felt like I was flying. I saw myself in a big, empty warehouse with white walls, one that smelled of diesel exhaust and damp. In one hand, I held my phone, and in the other, I held a sword. Not a real sword, but one made of millions of glowing golden letters that formed chains endlessly in motion. I recognized those chains; they were symbolic of the oracle's power.

My phone rang, an oddly echoing sound, and I came to myself to realize both the phone in vision and my real phone were ringing. The last vestiges of the vision filled me with the knowledge of who was calling. I pulled out my phone and without looking at the display answered it with, "What do you want, Castellan?"

CHAPTER NINETEEN

"Well, that was abrupt," Michael Castellan said. "I expected a politer response from you, Helena."

The disorientation from my vision combined with the rough night I'd had roused my irritation to anger. "You threatened me and my family, and you set spies on us. What the hell makes you think I'd be inclined to a polite conversation?"

Castellan chuckled. "All right, that's fair," he said, sounding not at all upset by my antagonism. "You're right, I haven't earned either your trust or your amity. It's a shame, really, because we ought to be on the same side."

"You know we're not." A thought occurred to me, one that would have frightened me if I weren't so angry. "How did you get this number? Maddy Hubbard?"

"I don't have your number. This call is made possible by a magical correspondence. So you don't need to be afraid that I can trace you to send someone after you—"

"You already tried that," I said. "We're squeezing your agent for everything she can tell us about your organization. Don't bother doing it again."

"Yes, I suppose your son warned you," Castellan said. "The young oracle."

"And *I* warned *you* what would happen if you made this personal." My heart was beating so fast it shook my body. "Stay away from us. If you try kidnapping him again, I swear I'll find a way to destroy you."

"I understand." He sounded so soothing it made me even madder. "I apologize. I really did mean only to talk to him, but I shouldn't have tried to take your child away from you, even though I wouldn't have hurt him. I promise I won't do that again."

"Good." His apology deflated me slightly, even though I didn't believe he meant it. "But you didn't call just to offer me an apology. What do you want?"

"To talk. Now that the elves have entered our world and killed humans, I hope you and your Warden friends realize that there's no more reason for us to be at odds. We both care about protecting our world from invasion and destruction."

He sounded so incredibly reasonable it roused my suspicions. "You care about taking Faerie's magic, not protecting our world. We don't have the same goals at all."

"I won't deny that was my original plan. The truth is, Helena, now that we've seen just how dangerous elves are, I've realized my goal is impossible. And I always wanted Faerie's magic to benefit mankind. That can hardly happen if humanity is destroyed." Now he sounded hurt, like I'd doubted his good nature, which of course I had. "I intend to turn my forces toward preventing the elves from killing more humans. I want to work with the Wardens toward that end."

There wasn't any point asking stupid questions about how he knew about the elf attack at Callann. "You can't seriously believe we'd trust you enough for a meeting. Not after the attacks we've made on your empire recently. More likely you want us where you can take your revenge."

"That was business, Helena, not personal, as you're so fond of making the distinction. We fought, and the Wardens triumphed—probably not as much as you believe, but you've made your point. I can accept my loss with good grace, as I said in my reply to the ultimatum I received. That was your husband, wasn't it? He's certainly got a dramatic way of proving his commitment to you." Castellan laughed. "I don't know how ethical it is, putting an entire organization's resources toward protecting his wife, but then, you're more than that to the Wardens, aren't you?"

I ignored the bait. "Then, if it's business, why are you talking to me? I'm not in charge of the Wardens."

"No, but, as I said, you matter to them. Tell me something, Helena—what exactly is your magic?"

"Like I'd give any information to you."

Castellan laughed again. "Your son is an oracle, and I wonder—are you an oracle as well?"

The memory of that golden sword hit me hard enough I lost my breath. "I am," I said when I regained my equilibrium. I wished I knew why it was safe to tell him that. I was sure he would use any information he gained as a weapon against us. But for whatever reason, this was something I did not need to conceal.

"That makes you a powerful resource—if you'll excuse me speaking of you as a thing just for a moment," Castellan said. "You can predict when and where elves will enter our world, know what attacks will be most effective against them—and that's just the benefits to our offensive. No wonder the Wardens were able to strike against me so efficiently."

I wasn't going to tell him that hadn't had anything to do with me. "I know what my powers are," I said irritably. "I don't need you to tell me."

"No, of course not. Forgive my excitement. But you see that I appreciate the magnitude of what you can do for the world. I want to join my forces to yours. I believe I have greater manpower, and my wealth—the wealth of Astraeus Resources—is enough that I can provide fighters, materiel, transportation. Working together, we have a chance."

"We don't—" I stopped before I could reject his offer outright. I didn't trust Castellan at all, but from what Malcolm had said, he was right about one thing: he did have resources surpassing the Wardens' in certain respects. And I knew virtually nothing about the plan for fighting the elves when they emerged into our world in greater force than they had at Callann. This was something I needed to pass on to Malcolm, or Lucia, or even Stirlaugson.

"You haven't done anything to make me trust you," I said. "This all sounds very noble, but it might just be you looking for a way to turn on us."

"That's a reasonable response, though of course I think you're being overly cautious. But I understand. How can I convince you?"

I wished with all my heart I was as suspicious as Judy, to come up with a good test of Castellan's true intentions. I wished even more prophesying about what he would do was possible. "You can't," I said. "But I'm not the one to make the decision. Call me back in three hours, and I'll tell you what the Wardens have decided."

"Fair enough," Castellan said, and the line went dead.

I sat gripping my phone like a lifeline. That whole conversation had been surreal. I didn't trust Castellan, and his offer of help was probably a trick. But I remembered five elves slaughtering men and women outside Seattle, and I imagined the streets of Callann littered with corpses. I didn't trust Castellan, but maybe the Wardens could make use of him anyway.

The door opened, and Malcolm entered, followed by Lucia. "What's wrong?" he immediately said. "You look like you've had bad news."

"Michael Castellan called me—no, it's all right, he said it wasn't a regular phone call and he doesn't know my number—"

"He was probably lying," Malcolm said. "I warned him what

would happen if he didn't back off." His phone was in his hand and he was texting rapidly.

"I think he was telling the truth about it being magic. Look, there's no history of a call at that time. And it doesn't matter. Malcolm, he wants the Wardens and the Savants to work together."

Malcolm stopped texting. "Again, he has to be lying. What he wants is to get revenge on us for the attacks we made."

"That's what I said. And I don't trust him. But I'm not the one who can make that decision, and suppose we need the Savants when the elves make a really big attack?" I rose from the couch. "They killed a lot of people in Callann, didn't they? And if the Wardens had been there to defend against the attack, many of them would have died, right?"

Malcolm hesitated, then nodded. "Elves are deadly and vicious fighters, and the fact that we're better prepared to kill them than we were on the slip near Seattle isn't much comfort."

"With the oracle's help, we have an advantage," Lucia said, "but it's limited by our knowledge of what to ask for. And now that the oracle is a person rather than a bookstore, I don't like putting the kind of pressure on you that might become necessary."

"Then maybe we need to figure out how to work with the Savants. I was going to ask you, Malcolm, what you thought about that decision. I want to know if I'm being overly trusting."

"I'm not sure. We did defeat the Savants soundly, so it's as likely Castellan sees the wisdom of not reopening hostilities as that he wants revenge." Malcolm's brow furrowed in thought. "Lucia?"

"It's worth investigating the possibility of an alliance of sorts," Lucia said. "With precautions. This could still be a trick. It depends on whether Castellan is more concerned about elves than he is about revenge or capturing an oracle for his personal use, and that's some-thing we can't know, given that you can't prophesy about his inten-tions." Her eyes narrowed in thought. "Do you have a way to reach Castellan with an answer?"

"I told him to call again in three hours. That's not too soon, is it?"

"Plenty of time to set up a meeting in our favor. I'll work out the details and give you our demands to relay." She still looked grim, but then she said, "It would be nice to only have one enemy to worry about," and I knew she was just thinking hard about the future.

"Did you have questions for the oracle?" I asked, remembering what she'd said before dinner.

"This takes precedence. I had a team track down the elves who destroyed Callann, and they learned the elves had retreated into Faerie through a slip that's disappeared. So at least we don't have to worry about a band of elves rampaging through Ireland."

"A slip that disappeared?" I had an image of a cut in reality sealing shut like a knife slicing through half-set Jell-O.

"It turns out that the slips made at thicker spots in the membrane between worlds resist being opened," Lucia said. "They close up after only a few hours. And Jeong tells me such a slip leaves a scar of sorts. Something that thickens the membrane and makes it more difficult or even impossible to open a slip there again. That means the elves who enter our world that way either have a time limit on getting back or are stuck here until they find something more accessible."

"Is that good, or bad?"

"So far, the elves seem to be returning through the slips they make, so in that respect, it's good for us. Means we don't have to worry about chasing them down. But if they ever decide they don't care about returning to Faerie, it could be a problem." Lucia shook her head. "It's not important now. I'll bring you our demands—I want to be here when Castellan calls. Talk to him myself."

The relief I felt at being able to pass this off to Lucia surprised me. I hadn't been afraid when I spoke to Castellan because anger had taken care of that. Now that my anger was past, I felt cold and worried. So many things could go wrong—but that was something to consider later.

When Lucia had gone, Malcolm held me tightly and whispered, "This will all be over soon, one way or another."

"Will it? Malcolm, you haven't said anything, but it seems to me we can't count on your deterrents to stop Castellan coming after us forever. However worried he is right now, suppose that feeling fades, or he changes his mind and decides attacking is worth the risk of Warden retaliation?"

Malcolm didn't say anything. Then he sighed and said, "I know. Everything I've done so far will only stop him attacking directly, and for a short time. He's determined and ruthless, and he'll find a back-handed way of getting at us. I've bought us a reprieve, but we need to consider other tactics."

"Like moving."

"Helena, I didn't want it to come to that, but—"

"It's all right. I realized what had to happen a few hours ago, and I'm coming to terms with it." To my horror, I started to cry. I didn't want to give Malcolm the wrong impression, or make him feel bad, like it was his fault we couldn't keep our house. My refuge. But it was late, and I was so tired—emotionally, if not physically. So I cried, and Malcolm held me, saying nothing.

When I got myself under control, I said, "Sorry about that. I really do understand."

"Understanding isn't the same as coming to terms with grief," Malcolm said. "I'm going to shower and change, and then we'll start making plans, all right? I know that helps you."

"It does," I said.

I reclined on the couch next to Night-Noon while Malcolm cleaned himself up. I felt empty now, devoid of emotion, and it was a surprisingly good feeling. It left me with the sense that, now that I was willing to leave most of my life behind, Castellan no longer had any power over me. I wasn't sure how true that feeling was, but I badly needed it.

An hour later, while Malcolm and I were busy making lists in preparation for moving, for relocating the boys to a new school, Lucia returned. She held one of her many tablets. "This is what we demand," she said, handing the tablet to me. "I've marked the things I've included that we're willing to compromise on."

"Should we compromise on anything?" I asked. "Doesn't that weaken our position?"

"We have to appear flexible, or Castellan will refuse to meet," Malcolm said. "Giving up on some points lets him feel he still has power."

"And those are all points we don't care about," Lucia said. "You're not to compromise on anything else, understand? We want to ensure your safety."

"*My* safety?"

"Lucia, is that wise?" Malcolm said.

"Given that you're the one he contacted, Davies, I doubt Castellan is willing to agree to any meeting you don't attend." Lucia frowned. "I don't like it, but I've done everything possible to protect you."

"And I will be there with you," Malcolm said. "If this is a trap, I will have to be prepared to shoot him if he threatens you."

"Mmm. I think he thinks it's cute that you're so attached to me."

"We'll see how cute he finds it when my gun is pointed at his head," Malcolm said.

THE SMELL OF DIESEL FUEL IN THE GIANT, EMPTY warehouse was stronger than it had been in my vision, strong and pervasive enough to make me feel ill. The damp chill of rain had seeped inside, the feeling clinging to my exposed face and hands, and

I wished I'd worn a heavier coat. I paced the warehouse's inside perimeter, trying to stay warm. The space was brightly lit, brighter than the dull gray evening outside, and its white walls reflected the light so there were no shadows anywhere. White girders high above supported the roof like the webs of some geometrically-inclined spider, one that spun steel instead of silk. It should have been completely innocuous. My knowledge of what was coming made it seem sinister.

The armed Wardens in their black fatigues didn't fidget or move around the way I was doing; they stood alert and ready to shoot. Their presence didn't relax me. I'd prophesied nearly a dozen times, trying to get a glimpse of the outcome of this meeting, and seen only masked figures in dark blue within and surrounding the warehouse. Never did my visions show them shooting, or engaging in hand-to-hand combat with the Wardens, but their stillness made them seem like creepy dolls, sinister like the warehouse.

Malcolm put a hand to his ear, touching his glass earbud. "Still no sign of advance troops. Castellan is keeping to the bargain."

"He's got ten minutes still. Why didn't he come early?"

"I imagine he doesn't want to spook us. If he's going to betray us, it will be after negotiations begin. That will be the best time for him to move his forces in for an attack." Malcolm didn't sound worried, but I was plenty tense enough for both of us.

A voice sounded in my ear. *"We control the territory for five miles in every direction,"* Lucia said. *"We'll know when he arrives. And there's no one in that area who isn't a Warden. No worries about a fire-fight alerting the local cops."*

I nodded, though she couldn't see me, and returned to pacing. I caught the eye of one of the Wardens, whose gaze swiftly shifted to something else. I probably should stand still, it was likely military procedure or something, but I couldn't stop myself.

Once more, I tried prophesying. Asking what Castellan, with his innate ability to foil prophecy, would do was pointless. *Where will the attack come from?* I thought. And just as before, I saw this warehouse filled with Wardens in black fatigues and Savants dressed in blue suits I thought might be flight suits, both groups armed with rifles, long-barreled or carbines, both groups facing one another. I didn't see myself anywhere in the vision, but that didn't mean anything. It was an image that told me nothing except that the Savants were prepared to kill.

I blinked away the last vestiges of the vision and walked to the warehouse door. It rolled on rails like a garage door, but it was three times the size of ours and looked like it weighed a ton. At the moment, it was open, and I could look out at the bare hillside and the dirt road, heavily rutted, that sloped down away from the warehouse. Dusk had fallen—Lucia might be confident of controlling the area, but she wasn't going to give up any advantage—and the air smelled of more rain incoming. Beams from big floodlights on either side of the door intersected right where the road met the warehouse and made a bright spot easily ten feet in diameter. The floodlights had magic on them, but I didn't know what the magic was or what it did. I hoped it was a trap of some kind, maybe something triggered by the presence of evil magic.

"*They're coming,*" Lucia said. "*A line of five Humvees. Everyone look alive.*"

I immediately retreated from the door and hurried back to Malcolm's side, a spot that put me clearly in view of the door. That was for my benefit as well as Castellan's; I wanted to be sure I saw any treachery he planned immediately. The Wardens all seemed to have gotten the same warning, because they came to attention in a way that made their earlier alertness seem like relaxation.

Then we waited.

After about a minute, I heard the rumble of large engines, a noise that gradually grew until it was a roar that drowned out all the other little nighttime noises. Flashes of headlights appeared, brightening and dimming like the vehicles were bouncing up a hillside. I didn't have a direct view of outdoors from where I stood, but I could tell the Humvees had stopped some distance from the door to let out their passengers. I clenched my fists once, then made them relax. I was definitely not going to show fear to these people.

The blue-jumpsuited figures I remembered from my vision streamed through the door, moving quickly but not running. They wore guns holstered at their sides, big ones I couldn't have managed myself, but no carbines or longer-barreled rifles as I'd seen in prophecy. My nervous anticipation ratcheted up a few notches at this deviation. I told myself it didn't matter. Fewer guns was good.

I counted as the Savants entered: twenty-four, just as agreed on, the same as the number of Wardens in the warehouse. Castellan would probably set more fighters to try to surround us, but Lucia hadn't thought that was a threat to be concerned about. "He'd be stupid not to," she'd said.

At the tail end of the group came Eris Reichert, dressed in dark gray fatigues with a pistol holstered at her side. She scanned the room before her gaze settled on me and she smiled her familiar, mocking smile.

"Where's your boss?" I said. I hadn't seen Eris here in vision, but she no longer frightened me.

Eris's smile broadened. "I'm assessing the situation, making sure you people didn't try anything. He'll come when I assure him there's no treachery."

"That wasn't the arrangement," I said.

"It's good sense. You set the terms, but Mr. Castellan isn't obliged to trust you any more than you trust him." Now Eris was scanning the ceiling. I didn't think there was any chance a bomb would be invisible against the white brilliance of the roof and girders, but I had to admit if I were Castellan, I'd be cautious, too.

Finally, Eris held a round black device to her lips. It was the size of an Oreo and looked like it was made of some space-age polymer. "It's secure," she said. "She's here."

I didn't hear a response, if there was one, but Eris put away her plastic Oreo and took up a parade rest stance. She was the only one who looked calm. The rest of the Savants shot glances at one another and at the Wardens, as fidgety as a bunch of teenage boys at their first school dance. I wanted to ask for instructions, but I didn't want to speak to Malcolm where they'd hear me, and I was afraid to touch the earbud for fear these nervous Savants might decide it was a weapon and shoot my head off.

I heard another engine, one higher-pitched than that of the Humvees, and watched the doorway, hoping for a sight of Castellan's car before he arrived, as if that would give me confidence. The engine roared louder, and by the sound of it the car was moving rapidly. The thought of Castellan speeding through the Wardens positioned to watch for an unexpected attack and driving straight into the warehouse unsettled me, and I was about to tap the earbud despite my fears when I heard Lucia shout, *"He's not stopping! Somebody grab that car!"*

In the next moment, a cherry-red Trans-Am with an elaborate bird painted on the hood, its wings spread wide, sped through the doorway, scattering Wardens and Savants alike before squealing to a halt in front of Malcolm and me. The passenger door flew open, and Maddy Hubbard leaned out. "Get in," she commanded. "Mr. Castellan's going to bomb this place to the ground in the next sixty seconds."

CHAPTER TWENTY

I opened my mouth to deny this outrageous claim and was struck so hard by prophecy I couldn't breathe. When I came to myself, I was stunned to find I was still standing. Then I shouted, "Get out! Now! There's a bomb incoming!" and dove for the Firebird.

Maddy leaned far forward so the seat folded out of the way. I clambered inside, followed by Malcolm, and Bronson put the car into reverse before Maddy had slammed the door fully shut. The last thing I saw was Eris, her face a mask of confusion and anger, shouting at her men to run.

We sped backwards out of the warehouse to the sound of bullets impacting on the Firebird. I couldn't tell if it was Savants, trying to kill me, or Wardens, trying to kill what looked like my abductors. A bullet cracked the windshield, and I shrieked and covered my mouth.

"It's all right," Maddy said. "They can't hurt the car so long as Bronson is driving. He knows it better than they do."

I started to ask what this meant and then froze. The crazy spiderweb of shattered glass left by the bullet, which I now noticed hadn't penetrated the windshield, flickered and then disappeared, leaving a perfect sheet of glass.

"How did that happen?" Malcolm asked.

"An ongoing connection between this car and its original state," Bronson muttered. "Can't talk. It's difficult." He braked and spun the wheel, turning us around to face downhill, and accelerated. There was a pop, and the car lurched. Bronson swore and to my surprise sped up. After a few seconds, the ride leveled out. "Tire," Bronson said, like it was no big deal.

I swiveled on the back seat to look behind us. Flashes of muzzle flare showed the fight was still going on, and figures made tiny by distance poured out of the warehouse, scattering in all directions. No explosion. The feeling that I'd made a horrible mistake despite my last vision crept over me. If I'd just cooperated in my own abduction—

The swift motion of a slim, dark shape streaking in from the east was all the warning I had to duck my head before the white light of an explosion turned the sky to midday brightness. A thunderous blast shook the ground, the car, and blew two of the Humvees off their wheels to impact against the others. Blinking away tears of pain, I stared at the shattered, burning remains of the warehouse. More small figures picked themselves up off the ground where the explosion had flung them. I was too stunned to be grateful that there had been survivors.

"That was close," Maddy said to Bronson. "Good driving. Everything okay back there?" she said, turning to me.

I realized people were shouting in my ear, chief among them Lucia, and without thinking I pulled the earbud out and tucked it into my coat pocket. "Why are you helping us?" I said. "Aren't you Savants?"

Maddy removed the rope of inch-wide amber nuggets from around her neck and snapped the string, holding both ends tightly so no beads rolled away. "We didn't know what else Savants do until

Mr. Castellan ordered us to kidnap Alastair," she said, sliding one chunk of amber off the strand and palming it. "I spent years working on a way to break down the barrier so we could stop elves from destroying our world. That's what we care about. Making this world safe for our children—for everyone's children."

"That's convenient," I said, though my last prophecy had told me something along those lines. I still wanted to hear what they had to say. "For all I know, you want me and my family dead as well." The gunfire had faded into the distance, and all I heard now was the roar of the engine, warring with the roar of blood in my ears.

"How did you know about the missile?" Malcolm demanded. "Is this a Savant trick, to have you apparently rescue us so we'll trust you? Don't think we don't still suspect you're lying."

"Then why did you get in this car?" Maddy shot back. "Helena's an oracle, right? How did you not know Mr. Castellan planned to level that warehouse with missiles just as soon as he knew for sure you were there?"

I said nothing. Feeling confident that they didn't mean me harm was a long way from trusting them with the secret of the oracle's weakness. Instead, I said, "I know you're on my side—"

"We're not on your side," Maddy said. "We're just not on Mr. Castellan's anymore."

"Then you can stop here and let us out," Malcolm said.

"I want to be far enough away from your people that they don't have a chance of coming after us," Bronson said. "Besides, they'll find out soon enough that this was only one of many strikes Mr. Castellan made tonight. Taking you out was only part of the plan."

"He would have killed two dozen of his own people at the warehouse, including Eris Reichert." I felt briefly numb. "He was willing to kill all those Savants just to get rid of me?"

"We didn't want to believe he was that ruthless, either." Maddy was still removing amber nuggets from the string and putting them in various pockets all over her trendy coat. "We've worked with his organization for years, and we had no idea the magnitude of what he had in mind for Faerie. And we certainly didn't realize there was this whole paramilitary operation going on behind the scenes."

"He tried to kill us after his assassin failed to kidnap Alastair," Bronson said. "We almost didn't survive, we were that clueless. It wasn't until Maddy encountered you at the school that we even found out about Alastair."

"I thought Liv told you!"

"Liv didn't say a word," Maddy said. "After I got away from you, we searched our house and found out it was bugged. Everywhere. Including all the bedrooms. That woke us up to reality. We were never anything but pawns."

"And that's why you ran," I said, "not because the Wardens were after you."

"Well, we didn't want either to capture us," Maddy said. "So we ran for our safe house—the one we'd prepared as a haven against Warden retaliation. We didn't think we'd have to use it against our own people. But that was when we learned Mr. Castellan's plan for tonight." She brandished one of the luminous amber beads at me. "I was listening in to hear how he intended to come after us, and instead got the details of what he meant for you. You must really have pissed him off."

"That was me," Malcolm said. "I organized a series of raids on key Savant properties that devastated his organization."

Maddy snorted an indelicate laugh. "Mr. Castellan believes it was Helena's oracular power that showed the Wardens where best to strike. I wish I could tell him the truth and see his head explode. He'd be furious to think he was just out-planned."

"He's had the only chance I'm willing to give him," Malcolm growled. "Helena, can you see where Castellan is right now?"

"I can try," I said. I leaned back, steadying myself against the movement of the car, and willed myself to know Castellan's current location. It was the only prophecy the oracle could give an answer to when it came to prophesying about the man, with his uncanny ability to defeat the oracular gift.

The rushing sensation of a prophecy swooped down on me, and I felt lifted into the air, into the darkening sky. I flew faster than a bird, over roads and fields and hills until I dove at a lone, darkened mansion perched on the top of a hill. Nothing moved behind its windows; no one walked around its perimeter. Yet I had the impression of a fortress, with barred doors and windows, guarding something important.

With that, I passed through a window in the upper story and sailed through empty, unlit, unfurnished rooms. There wasn't anyone there, but I was experienced enough with my gift to know that only meant it wasn't his primary residence—

—and with that, I rose up out of vision and gasped, "There's a house on a hill. He's there. I think it's his headquarters. But I didn't see anything to tell me where the house is, so give me a—"

"No need," Maddy said. "It's his house in the Cascades. We've been there. But it doesn't matter. Once he finds out his missile didn't kill you, he'll be on the move."

"He can't afford to stay, because I warned him what I would do if he broke the terms of our agreement," Malcolm said. "Helena—"

"I can't find out where he's going, remember?" I realized the car had come to a stop and Maddy and Bronson were staring at me over their seats. "And if he gets in a car, I can't go on prophesying his current location, over and over, without exhausting myself, possibly before he reaches his destination."

Malcolm swore and thumped the back of Maddy's seat. "If he leaves the country, it's going to be difficult to find him again."

I watched Bronson and Maddy exchange glances, familiar glances I'd shared with Malcolm many times. They were the kind that said the two were debating whether to reveal some secret. "You know where he's going," I said. "Tell me!"

"We have a guess," Bronson said. "There's an airfield about forty miles from the Cascades mansion. It's how he reaches the house if he's coming from anywhere but Seattle. A plane there will take him to Sea-Tac, where he's got a private jet. And *that* can take him pretty much anywhere in the world."

"Then we have to go," I said. "Now."

Bronson and Maddy exchanged glances again. "Don't you have Wardens you can send?" Maddy said. "Just two of you can't take on Mr. Castellan and all his goons."

"We can get there faster than the Wardens, and we have to stop him leaving." I leaned forward. "My children and I had to flee our home because of you. You owe us."

"We've got children to think of, too," Bronson said. "This isn't our fight."

"That's where you're wrong," Malcolm said. "Castellan deceived you just as he did us. More so, because he warped your devotion to a good cause to his own selfish ends. You wanted to protect the world from Faerie, but Castellan is willing to let elves roam this world, killing innocent humans, while he plays games with the Wardens. You can't tell me you don't want to see him stopped."

"Killing?" Maddy said.

"Didn't he tell you what happened in Ireland?" I said. "Elves sneaked through their own slip and massacred a village called Callann. Down to the smallest child."

"No," Bronson said. "We hadn't heard." He revved the engine once before putting the Firebird into gear and accelerating down the road. "The airfield is fifty miles away," he added, "but I'd back this car against Mr. Castellan's clunky Land Rover any day."

He didn't look like he was trying to hold the car together through force of will anymore, so I asked, "Is that how you rebuilt the car? Magic? Malcolm said you didn't act like someone who'd done the work."

Bronson grunted. "I made every system return to its original manufacturer's state, one by one. Much harder than fixing things by hand. But the goal was to achieve a perfect understanding of the car's self, in case of moments like these."

"You didn't anticipate a high-speed chase with gunfire, did you?" Malcolm asked.

"Not really, no." Bronson took the freeway onramp at speed. "But it's the things you don't anticipate that are the ones you want most to be prepared for."

I settled back in my seat. "You'd better tell Lucia what's going on, Malcolm." I put my earbud back into my ear, winced at the shouting, and removed it again.

Malcolm tapped his earbud once and grimaced. "Shut up," he said. "Lucia, what's the situation? Was anyone killed in the missile strike?"

I couldn't hear any voices, but Malcolm's tension dissipated slightly. "All right," he said. "We weren't kidnapped. The Hubbards brought word that Castellan intended treachery, which was where the warning came from—right, Helena couldn't have predicted Castellan's actions." He stopped talking for a moment, then added, "We know where he's going, and we are on the way there now."

"Whitmore Air Field," Bronson said over his shoulder.

"Castellan has a plane waiting at Whitmore Air Field," Malcolm repeated. His expression grew sour again. "With respect, while Campbell Security works closely with the Gunther Node, I am not your subordinate. And this is no longer a matter of official action. Castellan made this personal, and I intend him to suffer the consequences I promised."

I watched him closely as he spoke. He wore the hard, angry expression I had seen only rarely, and only once directed at me. It was the expression that said he was done being cooperative, and the time for compromise had passed. It did not bode well for Castellan. I'd never felt so grimly pleased to see him look that way.

Malcolm waited a much longer time before speaking again. I guessed Lucia was trying in vain to convince him to wait for backup.

"Those other attacks are irrelevant," he said. "Stopping Castellan before he leaves the country is our primary goal. He's proven the Savants aren't interested in a truce, or collaboration, or even détente. If we don't stop him, he will gain a foothold elsewhere, and the Savants will never stop being a problem for the Wardens. Send backup, yes, but we're not waiting." He tapped his earbud again and then removed it from his ear and tucked it away inside his coat pocket.

"What other attacks?" I demanded, dread rising up in me.

Malcolm didn't look at me. "The strike at the warehouse was one of many Castellan ordered, just as Bronson said. Simultaneous attacks on other important Warden sites. Not many, because our ability to conceal ourselves is better than the Savants could penetrate, but enough to be a distraction, particularly if you and I were killed."

My feeling of dread grew. "Malcolm, where did they strike?"

"Lucia wouldn't say. She claimed it would distract us, if we were, as she put it, 'hell-bent on killing ourselves and doing Castellan's work for him.' I'm just as happy not to know. The children are safe in the Gunther Node, and that's all I care about."

Images of my house in flames rose up before my eyes, and I almost asked *What is the condition of my house?* before realizing Lucia was right. If Castellan had bombed my house, that would be a hell of a distraction.

Maddy still held two amber nuggets in one hand and was idly juggling them between her fingers like David Bowie in *Labyrinth*. Impulsively, I asked, "How does it work? The stones, I mean."

Maddy looked over her shoulder at me. "Magic is thin on the ground here in our world. Some of it is locked up in natural objects, trees or grass or stones. Anyone who knows how can siphon the magic out of them and use it to boost a transformation, or teleportation—any kind of magical working, in fact. You nearly caught me at it that day in the classroom. I was mending one of the decorations with magic when you came in."

"I never guessed. You both kept your secret well."

Maddy laughed, a bitter, self-mocking sound. "I actually believed my superiors when they said my habit of using stones was a crutch. I suppose the truth was they'd killed too many people to be able to use magic at all, and they didn't want me asking questions about why they didn't do what I did."

Unexpected sympathy welled up inside me. "That must have been a terrible discovery, learning that your work was on behalf of someone evil. Were you actually a chemist?"

"Of course. My work on the barrier was related. I analyzed the barrier's components, looking for a way to chemically alter it so it could be dissolved. And then you got rid of it for us. At least, that's what we were told. That the Wardens wanted access to Faerie for its magic."

I laughed. "That's what the Savants want. Not us."

"I'm sure there are a lot of things we've been told that aren't true." Maddy sounded bitter again.

Malcolm said, "You wanted the best for humanity. That's nothing to be ashamed of. Castellan used that desire against you. He's the one who needs to feel guilty."

"He's utterly convinced that he's right," Bronson said. "The conversation we overheard left no room for misunderstanding. He wants elves out of the way not because they threaten our world, but because with Faerie's magic he can take over any organization, any government, and use it to benefit him."

"If not for the threat elves pose to humanity, we Wardens might have been willing to let Castellan attack them and see his organization decimated," Malcolm said. "But standing back for that purpose means not intervening when the elves come after humans as they did in Callann."

"So we were right about that," Bronson said. "Elves are dangerous, and they want humans destroyed."

"As far as we can tell," I said, and then wondered why I'd said that. My memory of Jenny's scary elf surfaced. There was no question he wanted humans eradicated. So why had I just given the elves the benefit of the doubt, even in a backhanded way?

"You think some elves might have a different view?" Maddy asked. "How is that possible? They hate us for poisoning them and their world."

"I don't know that any elves feel differently," I said. "I guess I'm saying we still know very little about them. They might want more than just destruction. Gabriel Roarke says they used to enthrall humans to do their will, and maybe that's still true. Maybe they want slaves as well as victims."

"Who's Gabriel Roarke?" Maddy asked.

"Oh." I considered the Hubbards' probable reaction to learning there was one good elf in the world and decided I didn't care. "He's an elf who was—"

"An elf?" Bronson exclaimed.

"He's not like modern elves. He was trapped in our world for a thousand years. And he's committed to protecting humanity." Malcolm spoke with a finality that suggested Bronson shouldn't have any more outbursts.

"An elf," Maddy said. "An elf opposed to other elves."

"They hate him as much as they hate us," I said, though it wasn't as if I'd heard them say that. Gabriel had said modern elves would see him as a traitor, and that was close enough.

We all fell silent then. I sat back where I couldn't see the speedometer, though from the shaking of the car I was sure we were going much faster than the speed limit. The moonless night cocooned the car in blackness, lit only by the lights of the dashboard and the headlights streaming out in front of us. We were still on the back roads, but soon enough we'd reach the freeway, and then... well, Maddy probably could work an illusion that would keep the speeding car from being seen, and Bronson drove like an Indy 500 speedster. We'd get there in time and, more importantly, in one piece.

Malcolm took my hand. "We'll stop him," he murmured.

"I know." I didn't say that I was sure Malcolm meant to stop Castellan permanently. Bronson and Maddy, as adepts, didn't take life because it affected their ability to do magic. I wasn't at all sure they would be on board with the kind of terminal justice Malcolm had in mind. In truth, years ago I would have shared that opinion. But Castellan had proven he was willing to kill me and Malcolm, he'd shown he wanted Alastair for his oracular gift, and I no longer felt like giving him the benefit of the doubt that he'd changed.

Bronson made the turn onto the freeway. I checked my phone for the time: not even eight p.m. That had all taken practically no time, though it had felt like forever. Traffic was light at that hour, but there were still enough cars on the road I expected we'd have to slow.

But Bronson said, "Hold onto something," and accelerated, a steady increase in speed until it felt like we were flying. I braced myself against the side of the car and gripped Malcolm's hand as Bronson weaved effortlessly between cars that ignored the dangerous lunatic bearing down on them. Strangely, I wasn't afraid. We would reach the airfield, and we would stop Castellan. Whatever it took.

CHAPTER TWENTY-ONE

W e stayed on the freeway for at least half an hour before taking an exit whose sign I didn't see and heading east. I wasn't sure how long it took before Bronson slowed and said, "We're getting close." Ahead, illuminated by a couple of small floodlights, was a pale blue sign that read, in big black letters, WHIT-MORE AIR FIELD. Below that was a second, smaller sign, this one dark green with white letters, that read *Private Property—No Tres-passing*.

"Now what?" I asked. "Is the car invisible?"

"I made it unmemorable," Maddy said. "It's too difficult to make something that moves invisible. And if Mr. Castellan has guards, they'll be alert enough to see past the misdirection."

"I'm sure there are guards," Malcolm said.

"Give me a moment, and I'll see what I can learn," I said. Without waiting for anyone's assent, I closed my eyes and willed a knowledge of the airfield's defenses. I was caught up immediately in vision, but I didn't fly over the area as I'd expected. Instead, I saw a drawing of the area, almost like a blueprint, with stark black lines on a white field. I examined it closely, committing it to memory as best I could before rising out of the vision.

"That's not enough," I said as soon as I recovered my equilibrium. "One more." This time, I focused on the question *Where is the weakest point in the defenses?*

Again, I saw the drawing, but this time, the lines pulsed with red light, brighter in some places than others. I made note of the places where the red light was dim and blinked away afterimages.

"There's a... I don't know what all the names are, but an enclosed airplane hangar, and a smaller building attached to it," I said. "Guards are posted around those buildings, and at the entrance to the airfield, where there's a little hut and one of those striped poles to block the road. The weak spot—hang on."

I dug my phone out of my pocket and popped the little stylus out, then opened a new note page on my phone. Swiftly I sketched a tiny copy of what the prophecy had revealed and tapped one side of the rough circle centered on the airplane hangar. "My prophecy says this is their weak point, but it wasn't specific as to why, so I don't know if the guards have limited line of sight, or if they're lazy, or what."

"I'll have to investigate," Malcolm said. "The rest of you, wait here."

"I'm not waiting," Bronson said. "Mr. Castellan tried to have us killed, and I want an explanation."

"An explanation?" Maddy said. "What could he say that would justify trying to kill our family? I want to make sure he can't try it again."

"Fine, but neither of you are combat trained," Malcolm said, "and I need to survey the area before we make our attack. This will end badly if you give our presence away."

"I said we couldn't make ourselves invisible," Maddy said. "But we have other ways of concealing ourselves. And it's going to be riskier if you go in twice. Better we stick together."

"*Don't* tell me to stay behind," I said. "That's the sort of thing that leads to me being captured and made into a hostage."

Malcolm sighed. "All right. But I expect every one of you to follow my orders. This is not a democracy. I have decades of experience in this kind of infiltration, and I know what to do."

"Just so you don't order us to do anything against our principles," Bronson said, which told me he'd been thinking about the kind of vengeance Malcolm might take.

"Follow, then," Malcolm said. "Helena, stay back a short distance. Not too far, but enough that if you're seen and we aren't, we can get the drop on any attackers."

I nodded. To my surprise, while my heart rate was elevated, my heart wasn't pounding the way it would if I were terrified. All the dangers we'd faced until now seemed to have made me incapable of fearing for the future.

Bronson pulled the car off the road and shut off the engine. As soon as Malcolm was out of the car, he stood still, his head tilted as if listening for a distant sound. Then he gestured, glancing once at me, before walking toward the still-unseen airfield. I let Maddy and Bronson go before me.

The night was still, with only the sound of a billion insects sending up a high-pitched whine in three-part disharmony. I felt horribly exposed despite the darkness, because we'd left the trees behind well before we reached the road leading to the airfield, and I was sure we were visible as dark blotches against the lighter landscape. At least I was wearing a dark green sweater beneath my brown coat instead of something white.

After about five minutes, the airfield's buildings became visible, well-lit by tall stadium lights that also illuminated some of the runway. The runway stretched out northward out of sight except for a couple of colored lights that weren't more than specks marking the course. Some cars were parked outside the smaller building, not in a parking lot but haphazardly, as if their drivers had just stopped wherever they felt like it. I saw a couple of armed guards in the same blue jumpsuits the Savants had worn to the warehouse ambush. They looked plenty alert, but I trusted my visions and was sure we were headed in the right direction.

I'd almost lost sight of Malcolm, not because I'd fallen behind but because he moved like a cat, when he slowed and came to a halt. "There," he whispered.

Ahead, a lone guard stood with his back to the airfield. He was armed with a carbine rifle like the ones I'd seen when I was preparing for the warehouse meeting, and he stood alertly surveying the grassy fields where we lurked. Then he yawned, and the muzzle of his carbine bobbed, and his stance didn't look quite so alert.

"I can take him out, but the others will notice his absence in just a few minutes," Malcolm said. "We'll have to be prepared to run."

"I have a better idea," Bronson said. "I can take his place."

"An illusion?" Malcolm said.

"It won't pass close scrutiny, but it will be good enough that no one will approach to investigate." Bronson turned to Maddy. "Can you see him clearly enough?"

"It would be easier if he was in full light, but yes." Maddy brought one of the amber beads out of her pocket. "Hold still."

I scanned the distance instead of watching Maddy—it wasn't as if I'd see anything different—searching for more guards who might notice the moment when Malcolm subdued our sleepy friend and Bronson took his place. There weren't any within sight. Based on my memory of the vision, I knew we were at the far northwestern edge of the patrolled area, close to the runway but not to the buildings, and I guessed this wasn't considered important enough to put a lot of manpower on. Castellan was going to regret that decision.

"Helena and Maddy, wait here," Malcolm said. I snapped my attention back to the others. Bronson, of course, looked exactly like himself still. Malcolm moved silently around to the north, while

Bronson took a few more steps toward the guard and then crouched. Maddy and I crouched as well.

In one swift motion, Malcolm appeared next to the guard and put him in an expert sleeper choke hold. The man jerked once and was unconscious in seconds. Bronson was moving before Malcolm lowered the guard to the ground. He picked up the carbine and stood at attention the way the guard had. Malcolm glanced around, then ran back to where Maddy and I waited.

"I don't think Castellan is here yet," he began, and the sound of an airplane engine cut through the tinnitus of the insect chorus, roaring in anticipation. We all stared at the airplane hangar. Its back was to us, but the sleek white shape of the plane was barely visible where it had been wheeled out onto the tarmac.

Malcolm swore under his breath. "Helena, how many men are we facing?"

I put a hand on his arm to steady myself and closed my eyes to prophesy. In less than a minute, I had an answer. "Ten guards—nine now we took care of that one—plus another four henchmen in Castellan's car. Another six or seven running the airfield. The pilot."

"I can't eliminate all of those without giving Castellan a chance to run for it. My guess is he will drive as close as he can to the plane and go directly to it rather than spend any time in the outbuildings." Malcolm was looking past me at the hangar as if he wished he could trick Castellan into entering.

"Bronson and I could create a powerful illusion that would occupy those men," Maddy said, "but it will alert Mr. Castellan, and he'll run for it. We'd lose our advantage."

"What about concealment?" I asked. "Make those guards unaware that anything is wrong."

"I—" Maddy looked pensive. "Yes. The perimeter guards, at least. But I'd have to be near the center."

"That takes care of eight guards," I told Malcolm. "And I don't think the airfield personnel are combatants. What do you think?"

"It works," Malcolm said. "Stay here and watch for my signal. Then run where I do." He ran silently back to Bronson. I saw his lips move, and Bronson nodded. Then Malcolm gestured in a "follow me" way, and I ran with Maddy after him.

Now I was afraid. As we drew closer to the outbuildings, the lights grew brighter, and soon we were running across bare earth and our footsteps sounded loud enough to echo, not quiet as they'd been on the grass. Every second I expected to hear shouts, or gunfire, or both. But no one noticed, and we reached the windowless wall of the hangar without difficulty. I glanced over my shoulder at Bronson, who was still playing perimeter guard. I hoped he was part of Malcolm's plan. I hoped he'd be willing to use that carbine if it became necessary.

The sound of the plane engine was deafening at this range. Malcolm didn't bother speaking. He gestured again and made his way along the wall in the direction I guessed the gate was. Maddy followed him, two amber beads clutched in her hand, and I brought up the rear.

We came around the corner and were suddenly in full sight of the road and the gate with its striped pole, about two hundred feet away. The abruptness sent a shock through me, numbing my hands and face for a second or two. Malcolm didn't act like it mattered that we were in plain sight, probably because there was no one to see us. He kept going, heading for the smaller of the buildings, so I followed. Again, no one shouted a warning. The two men posted at the gate were watching the distance, standing casually as if this was any other job.

I saw movement on the road just as two tiny circles of white light appeared. Headlights. Castellan's car was arriving. I ran faster, following Malcolm, but not outpacing Maddy. Malcolm entered the building just as I reached it, and I waited outside, concealed behind it, watching those two circles of light draw nearer.

I still couldn't hear anything except the airplane engine, so when

Maddy appeared in front of me, I clapped my hand over my mouth to hold back a startled squeak no one else could have heard either. Maddy pointed in the direction of the building and gestured to me to follow. With one last look up the road, I ran after her.

Inside, the half dozen men and women I'd seen in vision were standing well away from their computers, and one man was just removing his headset. Malcolm held them all at gunpoint. "We have no quarrel with you," he said, pitching his voice louder though the noise was quieter indoors. "Kick your phones over here, and stay well away from any communication equipment. If you try to contact Castellan, I will shoot."

There was a bustle as the airfield techs set phones on the ground and kicked them in Malcolm's direction. "Helena, pick them up," Malcolm said. I scurried around gathering phones and then, lacking any way to carry them, set them on a couple of chairs beneath the windows.

"Good," Malcolm said. "Now, lie facedown with your hands behind your heads."

I had no idea where Malcolm was going with this. I knew he wouldn't shoot innocents, or at least people who weren't actively shooting at him, and we had no way to tie them up. But it was clear he suspected they were loyal enough to Castellan to want to try to warn him of an ambush.

By now the crunch of tires on gravel was loud enough to be heard over the engine. Malcolm shifted position to stand between the open door and the nearest window. Maddy moved to the other side of the door. That left me standing there with no idea what to do and no time to prophesy. I backed away, skirting the people lying on the floor, and stood against the wall where I could see through one of the windows.

The headlights flashed directly through the windows for a moment, and then the car came to a halt and the engine turned off. From my position, I could see the extended rear of a matte-black

Land Rover and the driver's side rear door. Someone dressed in a blue flight suit got out of that door and walked around the rear of the car. I heard the sound of another door opening.

Someone screamed.

I jerked, startled. One of the women lying on the ground had raised her head and let out a shrill, terrified, wordless scream. I leaped forward and slapped her into silence, but it was too late. Gunshots sounded outside, and the car engine revved.

Malcolm raced from the building, his gun at the ready. I didn't dare go anywhere with all the gunfire—didn't know where Malcolm thought he was going, given that there was no cover anywhere except this building and the airplane hangar.

Tires squealed, and a spray of gravel rattled the corrugated steel walls of the building. Maddy, peering through the window, held her handful of amber beads close to her chest and closed her eyes. There was a thump, the sound of skidding, and the shrill sound of brakes grinding against the drum without pads.

Shouts and more screams filled the air as our captives got to their feet and stampeded out the back door. My first reaction was to stop them, which was stupid as I had no weapon. Then I remembered that if they were fleeing, they weren't likely to attack us. And none of them had made a move even to retrieve their phones, let alone come after Maddy or me. Still, I watched to make sure they all left.

More gunfire. I risked a glance through the window. The Land Rover had slewed to a halt some twenty feet away. At least, I assumed it was the same car. It now looked fifty very hard-used years old, its sleek paint job peeling and rusted, its tires bald, and one side of the windshield cracked. As I watched, the driver leaped out and fled. A shot came out of the darkness and shattered the remaining headlight, dimming the lights around the hangar and building.

Three guards positioned around the devastated Land Rover, concealed behind its open doors, fired shots in the direction I'd seen Malcolm run. They either weren't aware that Maddy and I were in the building, or Malcolm was giving them more trouble than they'd expected. I guessed both.

"This way," Maddy said, jerking her head at the back door. "We need to get behind them."

"And do what?" I exclaimed.

"I don't know, but I'm not going to sit here and do nothing." Maddy ran outside, and with a muttered curse, I followed her.

We edged around the building between the parked cars until we could look past the corner to see the firefight. I grabbed Maddy before she could go farther. "Malcolm might hit you by accident."

Maddy nodded. "Let me think about this."

The thug behind the driver's door jerked and fell as one of Malcolm's shots hit home. In the distance, shouts sounded, as if despite our precautions some of the guards had seen past Maddy's illusion. Frustrated, I backed away. I didn't know where Malcolm was, I didn't know if Bronson had joined the fight, and I had no idea if Maddy could work magic that would change the outcome of this fight.

But I did have a way to find out.

I leaned against the cold steel wall and closed my eyes. I couldn't find out what Castellan intended to do, but there were other options. I mentally ran over a few possibilities before settling on the question *How do we defeat Castellan?*

Images rose up before me, tangled flashes of sight. I recognized fragments of the scene I'd just witnessed with the car and the men huddled behind it. I saw myself within that scene several times over, taking different actions, exactly as if I had Castellan's ability to confuse the oracle and it was presenting me with various likely futures. I saw Malcolm wounded, Malcolm dead, Malcolm threatening Castellan, over and over and tangled with the images of me like a puzzle with only one solution. Then the solution came into focus, and I emerged from vision with a gasp.

What I'd seen was crazy enough I couldn't delay or I'd talk myself out of it. Without a word to Maddy, I hurried through the cluster of cars, looking for the mud-spattered blue Jeep. Its rear gate was open, its spare tire lying flat on the ground. I reached for the tire iron I'd seen in vision and hefted it. Then I ran back to the fight.

Maddy was focused on the gunfire, so she didn't see me make a scuttling, bent-over run for the rear of the Land Rover. I paused to catch my breath, then stood erect and in three long steps came up behind the thug hiding behind the rear passenger door. Without hesitation, I swung the tire iron, cracking him across the back of his knees, then against his right shoulder with all my strength.

The thug screamed. His gun fell from his hand, and he lurched forward against the door. I snatched up the gun, aimed it into the back seat compartment at Castellan, and said, "Call them off, or I shoot."

CHAPTER TWENTY-TWO

"You wouldn't—" Castellan began.

I squeezed the trigger. The sound of the shot was explosive this close. Castellan let out a pained gasp and grabbed his arm. Blood seeped between his fingers.

I switched my aim to point the gun at the man I'd hit with the tire iron. "Don't," I said coldly. "Face down, now." Moving slowly, the thug rolled onto his stomach and raised his hands to cup the back of his head. His right arm moved like it was still mostly numb from the blow.

With the gun aimed at Castellan again, I said, "Get out. And tell them to throw down their weapons. I'm not sure how many bullets are left in this thing, but I won't hesitate to use every one of them on you."

Castellan awkwardly climbed out. "Stop shooting!" he shouted. "Put down your weapons. Do it now!"

With a few final shots, the gunfire stopped. I kept my gaze and my gun trained on Castellan. After a moment or two, I heard Malcolm say, "That's enough, Helena."

"This is how it goes, Malcolm," I said, though my hands were starting to shake. "Don't worry."

"You can put the gun down, Ms. Campbell," Castellan said. "You've made your point." He looked pale in the floodlights, but he stood as calmly as if his arm wasn't still dripping blood.

"Have I?" I said. "I warned you. You had a choice—leave my family alone, or suffer the consequences of making this personal. This is where the choice you made leads. Do you really think I'm so stupid as to believe you'll ever leave us alone?"

"I don't have much choice, do I?" Castellan lowered his bloody hand to his side. "You've bested me, you and your Wardens. I can't afford to let you go on attacking my organization, which means I have to back down. You have my word I won't come after your family. Your children are safe from me."

"Like I said, I don't believe it." I changed my aim so the gun pointed at the center of his chest. He was two feet away. Even I, who hadn't practiced shooting in months, couldn't miss that target.

"Helena," Malcolm said, "you don't have to do this."

"I've killed in defense of my family before," I said.

"But not like this." Malcolm didn't reach for the gun. "Stand down."

"Don't bother," Castellan said, reaching behind himself.

Time slowed to a crawl. I saw everything that happened as if those moments were frozen in drops of clear amber resin, trickling past. Castellan pulling a gun from the back of his waistband. My gun wavering and then slowly arcing to the side as Malcolm shoved me out of the way and brought up his own pistol.

And Castellan's chest exploding in a burst of bright red blood.

I came to myself on hands and knees, the gun a few inches from my right hand. Malcolm crouched over me, resting one hand on my back. "Helena, are you hurt?"

I shook my head. "What happened?"

Malcolm rose and helped me to my feet. Bronson Hubbard stood a few feet away, looking stunned. He still held the carbine rifle aimed at Castellan's heart. "I didn't think, I just fired," he said distantly.

Castellan lay on his back, sprawled as if the gunshot had punched him. At that distance, maybe it had. His bloody lips moved in speech I was too far away to hear. I didn't try to listen. There was nothing he could say that I cared about.

Bronson suddenly convulsed like he'd been shot, though I hadn't heard gunfire. "He's dead," he announced. "I felt it. It's like..." He swallowed. "I don't have a comparison. But I can feel his death like a weight on me."

Maddy put an arm around his shoulders. She didn't say a word.

The distant sound of car engines came to me over the rising wind. "We have to get out of here," I said. "Suppose that's the police?"

Malcolm cast a glance over the blue-jumpsuited thugs. "We can't leave them in a position to give our descriptions to the authorities."

"I can take care of that," Maddy said.

A sudden prophecy stunned me with its brief clarity. "We won't need to," I said, and walked to meet the approaching cars.

Malcolm shouted my name and raced to my side, grabbing me and bringing me to a halt. "Are you crazy?" he said. "We can only cover up so much, and the more deaths, the harder it is."

"I told you that's unnecessary." I pointed at the car in the lead. "We just need to talk to her."

"Her? Her who?"

The dark red Nissan Pathfinder came to a halt a dozen yards away, and the doors opened. "Eris Reichert," I said.

Eris slammed the driver's side door shut and approached us. I was sure she wasn't unarmed, but she wasn't wielding a gun, and she waved at the men and women who emerged from the line of cars behind hers in a gesture that commanded them to stand down. "Where is he?" she demanded.

I pointed at Castellan's body. "There."

Eris took a few more steps and jerked to a stop. She stared at Castellan. A muscle in her jaw twitched. "Who took my revenge from me?" she grated.

"Does it matter?" I said, forestalling Bronson. There was still a chance Eris, violent as she was, might want to take her anger out on him. "This is what happens to those who attack me and my family, Eris. I don't think I need to say more, do I?"

Eris gave a little shake of her head. "And here I thought you were weak," she said, sounding almost admiring. "Castellan screwed up big time. I told him he should kill you when he had the chance, but he thought he could manipulate you."

"Don't even think about following his plan," Malcolm said coldly. "We are still in a position to raze Astraeus Resources, not just the Savants, to the ground."

"Not likely," Eris said. "We've got our fingers in a dozen pies. You may be good, but you'll never find all of them. But I take your point." She snapped her fingers, and a couple of the blue-jumpsuited men approached. "Get him on the plane. We'll arrange for a cover story for his death."

"Who will be in charge now he's gone?" I asked.

"Does it matter?" Eris repeated my words back to me with an evil grin. "There are a lot of us who shared Castellan's vision of conquering Faerie, and some of those are in a position to take over. I guess you'll find out eventually. But I'll warn you, we all still see you Wardens as an impediment. So don't think Castellan's obsession being over means the Savants aren't still your enemies."

"How generous," I said sarcastically.

"Call it my thanks to you for sparing me the work of killing Castellan myself." Eris looked briefly furious. "He dared consider me expendable. No loyalty in the world survives that."

Eris's thugs began shuffling around, some of them lifting Castellan's body, others running for the plane like they had to catch it, though despite its engine running it didn't look like it was going anywhere. Bronson threw the carbine rifle away, his expression still dully horrified. "Back to the car," he said.

"Oh, and Helena?" Eris called.

I half-turned to look at her. "What?"

"I still know where your sons go to school," Eris said with a mocking smile.

My hand clenched, and I wished I still had the gun. I wished I even had the tire iron. Anything to wipe that smirk off her face. "Not anymore," I said.

We returned to the Firebird, which was where we'd left it. Part of me had anticipated Eris doing something to it out of sheer spite. But it was completely unharmed. We all got in, and Bronson wheeled it around and headed back the way we'd come.

We didn't get far before we saw headlights. A lot of headlights, some of them bumping along off the side of the road, all of them moving fast. Malcolm tucked his earbud back into his ear and tapped it. "Lucia? Are you with that fleet of cars headed toward Whitmore Air Field?"

I leaned back and closed my eyes, listening to Malcolm's half of the conversation. "Castellan is dead. No. I don't know, but Eris Reichert took charge of the remaining Savants—no, I believe she will be preoccupied with filling the power vacuum within Astraeus. Just —all right." To Bronson, he said, "Stop the car, but I suggest you and Maddy stay inside. To avoid any misunderstandings."

I clambered out behind Malcolm and walked to where Lucia was getting down from the behind the wheel of a giant pickup truck whose tires were almost as tall as I was. "Well?" Lucia demanded. "Who killed him?"

"I will discuss everything that happened, but in private. Some things still need to be concealed," Malcolm said.

Lucia looked past him at the Firebird. "And you think you get to decide that?"

Malcolm stared her down coolly. Lucia glared at him. The

moment stretched on until, exasperated, I said, "It's complicated, Lucia, and like Malcolm said, he's not your subordinate. Couldn't you, I don't know, give him the benefit of the doubt?"

"You went haring off after a dangerous lunatic who—" Lucia's mouth clamped shut. "Never mind. Are you saying the Hubbards *aren't* Savants?"

"I don't know what they call themselves now, but they're not the enemy." I took a step that put me more directly between Lucia and the Firebird. "It's cold, and I don't want to argue. And they saved—"

The roar of the Firebird's engine took me by surprise. I spun around in time to see Bronson accelerating into the distance, away from the road. He was going fast for a car like that on rough ground. "No!"

Malcolm's hand closed on my arm. "It's all right, Helena," he said. "It's how it has to end."

"No, don't give chase," Lucia shouted, then repeated it into her earbud microphone. "Still want to say that's not the act of a guilty person?"

"You know it's not that simple," I retorted.

"I do. I was mostly kidding. Besides, what more could we learn from them?" Lucia shrugged. "They're better off gone. The Savants are a threat to them, even if we aren't."

"I know. It's—not important, you're right. Just tell me—what else did Castellan destroy?" Now that the urgency was gone, the fears I'd suppressed rose up and demanded my attention. "What's so potentially distracting you couldn't tell us?"

"It's not all bad news, though I don't want you freaking out," Lucia said. "They destroyed the access point to the Gunther Node—"

I gasped. "What?"

"I did tell you not to freak out, Davies. The access point is nowhere near the node itself. All that did was shut down movement in and out until we could create another transportation circle. Which should be completed by the end of the hour. It's no big deal. Just an annoyance. But with your children being inside, I was pretty sure you'd start imagining cave-ins or earthquakes, so I didn't say anything."

I controlled my breathing. "Okay. Sorry. You're right. Was there anything else?"

Lucia pinched her lips tight. "They hit the Board of Neutralities building. That, we couldn't do anything about. It's practically downtown, on the waterfront, and the explosion, as the news is calling it, rocked its neighbors and caused an almighty panic. But because of the mundane authorities taking over search and rescue, we can't get any of our people in place. And we don't know who was inside at the time. It wasn't late enough for the building to be totally empty."

"Ms. Stirlaugson," I breathed.

"Possibly. It doesn't look good. She and Erich Harrison aren't responding to calls, and I know he was in town this week." Lucia shook her head slowly. "We'll do what we can, but in this case, there's not much we can do except wait on search and rescue."

The idea of Stirlaugson being dead shook me. We weren't friends, but we'd been through a lot together, and I was used to her as a formidable force within the Wardens. "That's terrible."

"Well, it's not all," Lucia said.

"There's more?" I said. "What could be worse than that?"

THE AREA AROUND OUR HOUSE WAS STILL CORDONED OFF when we arrived, and fire trucks and police cars were parked haphazardly up and down the street, partially blocking traffic. I got out of Lucia's enormous truck and slipped as my foot nearly missed the step because I was staring at the charred, stinking ruin that had been my home. Neighbors milled around outside, avoiding the police and the firefighters. I heard someone say my name, probably Maria

Martinez, our babysitter Ysabel's mom, but everything was blurry and distant.

Malcolm put his arm around me, supporting me. "We could have been in there," he whispered. "Or Ysabel with the children. Hang on to that."

I nodded, but he, too, sounded like he was coming from very far away. I'd decorated that home. I'd raised every one of my children there. All those meals and parties and holidays, every time Malcolm and I had made love in our bedroom—all nothing but memory now.

"Excuse me," Malcolm was saying to a thin, wiry policewoman who looked like she was in charge of directing traffic around the catastrophe, "I'm Malcolm Campbell. This is our home. Can you tell me what happened, please?"

The policewoman looked briefly stunned. "You're the owner?"

"Yes. We've been away for a few days. Was there a fire?"

"A gas explosion—here, talk to the fire chief." She guided us to where a heavyset but athletic-looking middle-aged man was talking to a soot-stained firefighter. The firefighter had removed his helmet, and an inch-wide stripe of clean skin below his hairline that contrasted with his blackened face showed how fierce the fire had been.

Malcolm introduced himself, and the chief looked like he wished he could be anywhere else. "Witnesses heard an explosion around 6:20 this evening. The fire definitely started in the kitchen and spread from there. It burned hot and fast, and it took a while to contain it, but fortunately it didn't spread to your neighbors."

"I agree, that's very fortunate," Malcolm said. "And fortunate that no one was home."

The chief's expression changed. Now he looked relieved that Malcolm wasn't one of those entitled rich jerks who blamed everyone around him for unexpected catastrophes. "I'm sorry, sir. I know this is a terrible loss."

"It is, but as I said, I consider it fortunate that no one was hurt or killed." His arm around my shoulders tightened. "Was anything saved?"

"I'm afraid not." The chief focused on me for the first time. "Mrs. Campbell. I'm so sorry."

"Thanks," I murmured. "I think I need—" My knees wobbled, and Malcolm caught me before I could fall. "No, I'm fine, don't call an ambulance," I said. I hadn't seen the fire department medical truck, and I really didn't want to wait around here until an ambulance arrived.

"If you're sure," the chief said. I was sure he wanted me examined, but it wasn't as if I'd been rescued from a burning house. I was just emotionally devastated. That was all.

Malcolm helped me into Lucia's truck, then went back to discuss things with the fire chief. We were insured, so that was a thing to deal with, unless the insurers blamed us for the "gas explosion" and wouldn't pay out. But we'd already decided we couldn't come back here anyway, right? I remembered Eris's evil, leering smile and shuddered. There was no way I would put myself in her power even a little bit, and I didn't take chances with my family's lives.

Someone tapped on the glass, and I rolled down the window. "Hi, Mrs. Campbell," Ysabel said. "Are you all right?"

"I'm glad no one was hurt," I said automatically. Breaking down in front of the teenage babysitter was not something I wanted to do.

"Yeah. I mean, yeah. It's just—" Ysabel stepped closer and lowered her voice. "You won't think I'm crazy?"

I leaned down to hear her more clearly. "I don't think you're crazy. Why would I?"

"Because of what I saw." Ysabel cast a glance over her shoulder. "I saw something hit your house and blow it up. Not a gas leak like they said."

"You saw *what*?"

Ysabel blushed. "I told you you'd think I'm crazy."

"No, I don't, but... that's unlikely, don't you think? What was it?"

"I don't know. Not a meteorite, because those are faster—I've seen one, and it's gone almost before you see it. Like a bomb? Or a missile?" She shook her head. "I've been playing too many video games. I know it's my imagination."

I didn't know what to say. I didn't want to call Ysabel a liar or an over-imaginative teen, but I couldn't tell her the truth, because what good would that do? "I know my eyes play tricks on me sometimes," I finally said. "Maybe it was something else entirely. Space garbage—that falls out of the sky sometimes, right? Anyway, I don't think you're crazy, but it doesn't matter now what caused it, because my house is gone either way." I heard myself say those words, and my throat closed up. I blinked away tears and added, "And it's time to make a new start."

CHAPTER TWENTY-THREE

The following Saturday, I opened the door of our Gunther Node apartment and welcomed Loretta Deveaux in. Usually, Deveaux intimidated me by the sheer force of her presence. Now, having faced Castellan down and witnessed the smoldering rubble of my home, I felt nothing but relaxed at seeing her. Malcolm sat on the couch, watching Jenny carry on a conversation with Mrs. Anderson that ignored the rest of us.

"Thanks for letting me stop by," Deveaux said. "You've had a difficult week. I heard about your house. What a bastard."

"We couldn't have gone back regardless, so I'm choosing to think of it as pushing us into the future." I didn't say that I had crying jags in the middle of the night when I thought of everything we couldn't replace, like the children's Christmas ornaments or the old photos that hadn't been digitized.

"Very wise, though you'd be justified in being upset, anyway." Deveaux knelt beside Jenny. "Hi, Jenny. Is this your doll?"

Jenny nodded. "This is Mrs. Anderson. She misses Jenny and Jenny and Jenny. They are gone with the old house. Mrs. Anderson is going to a new house."

"And so are you," Deveaux agreed. "Did you color more squares for me?"

"Yes, and I always get check marks now!" Jenny exclaimed.

Deveaux glanced at me, and I nodded. "She's had perfect accuracy for the last six days."

"And I don't scream," Jenny went on. "It scares people. I don't want to be scared."

"I see," Deveaux said. "You mean that you feel it when your screams frighten others."

Jenny nodded. "Sometimes they are angry instead. But mostly it's scary."

This surprised me. I hadn't realized Jenny could tell when her screams of terror affected others. "Why would they be angry?"

"I don't know." Jenny shrugged and made Mrs. Anderson walk across the coffee table.

"You've heard children make those awful piercing shrieks in a store, apparently for no reason," Deveaux said with a grimace. "How often have you felt annoyed by them? Or angry at their parents' lack of discipline?"

"That... makes sense," I said.

"So, what does this mean?" Malcolm said. "She can tell the difference between her own emotions and others'. That doesn't stop her feeling those emotions, and it doesn't stop them affecting her. It just means she's learned not to show those effects."

Deveaux stood. "Jenny, I'm going to talk to your parents for a minute, and then I want to show you a new game, all right?" She steered us into the bedroom and pulled the door mostly shut. "Jenny learning to distinguish between her natural emotions and others' emotions is critical," she said in a voice not loud enough to reach Jenny. "It was something none of our test subjects ever managed. The inability to distinguish eventually drove each of them mad."

I drew in a startled breath. "Why didn't you tell us?"

"Because it would have negatively affected Jenny's development.

You would have felt anxiety every time she had to discern the difference, and she might have picked up on that and been unable to accurately make a distinction." Deveaux looked more serious than I'd ever seen her. "It might even have accelerated the madness."

Malcolm's hand closed firmly on my upper arm. "You said this wasn't an experiment."

"And I stand by that. But helping Jenny means following experimental protocols for not contaminating the process. I promised I wouldn't treat her like a test subject, and I won't, but she's just passed beyond anything we achieved in our telempathy program, and figuring out what to do next requires careful procedures." Deveaux glanced over her shoulder as if afraid Jenny was listening through the half-open door.

"We understand," I said. "What *do* we do next?"

Deveaux let out a deep breath. "The next step is to teach Jenny to put those external emotions at a distance from herself. Knowing they aren't her emotions is one thing, but the more powerful the emotion, the more likely it is that an external emotion will bleed into her own emotions."

"Meaning that she might feel someone else's anger, and it will make her angry," Malcolm said.

"Precisely. We want her to be in control of how she feels. Emotions are powerful things, Mr. and Ms. Campbell. They can alter our perceptions of a situation and make us behave irrationally. Start a fight over a perceived slur, or do something stupid out of love. Jenny will have enough problems dealing with her own emotions— just like everyone does—without the burden of being made to feel angry, or sad, or joyful by someone else."

"Are you sure she's ready for this?" I said. "She's only three, Dr. Deveaux. That seems like you expect greater maturity of her than is reasonable for that age."

"I don't anticipate her mastering this skill for a while, Ms. Campbell," Deveaux said. "But her youth is a benefit. Learning to isolate others' emotions from her own will become second nature, and by the time she reaches puberty, when hormonal changes mean increased emotional volatility, she won't have to think about doing it. Unlike the most recent experiment, speed is not the goal."

I decided not to challenge her on the word "experiment." My initial misgivings about Deveaux had faded over the weeks I'd seen her interact with Jenny.

"Let's talk to her again, and I'll give you all an assignment." Deveaux pushed the door open.

In the absence of parental supervision, Jenny had stopped bouncing Mrs. Anderson across the glass top of the coffee table and was now dressing her. "We have to leave our house because of the bad men," she was crooning to the doll. "The bad men chased us away. Now we will have a new house, and Mrs. Anderson will live in a castle, and there will be another Jenny and Jenny."

Again, my heart ached for the necessity of moving, and I blinked back tears. "Jenny, Dr. Deveaux has a new game for you, all right?"

"Can I still color squares?" Jenny asked.

"You're going to color something new," Deveaux said. She opened her clipboard and took out a pen. Folding the cover of the clipboard back, she removed a couple of sheets of paper that were written on with something I couldn't make out, revealing a fresh blank page. She knelt beside Jenny again and offered her the clipboard and pen. "Can you draw a fence for me?"

Jenny held the pen tightly and gazed at the page for a moment. Then she drew two horizontal lines mostly parallel to each other, spaced a hand's width apart. With careful deliberation, she drew more lines, vertical ones in pairs that joined at the top in a point. It was clearly a fence, if an old-fashioned one. I couldn't imagine why she'd chosen it, given that our old house was surrounded by a stone wall, and the only other fences she was familiar with were the vinyl one surrounding Judy and Mike's backyard and the chain link one surrounding the playing fields at Talbott Academy.

Deveaux said, "That's excellent, Jenny. It's a perfect fence. Now, I want you to remember how this looks, all right? And every time you feel an emotion that isn't yours, I want you to imagine this fence between you and the other person's feelings. It's okay if you still feel that emotion, but the fence will keep it from coming too close. Do you understand?"

Jenny nodded. "Can I color the fence?"

"Yes. Your mom or dad will draw another fence for you, and every time you imagine the fence, you get to color in one of the slats —these upright pieces." Deveaux ran a finger along one of the fence slats. "Any color you want."

"I will make a rainbow!" Jenny exclaimed.

"You do that." Deveaux retrieved her pen and clipboard and rose to face us. "You two should encourage Jenny to talk about her empathic events. We want her to feel comfortable with her ability. Not that I believe you've been negative about it, or tried to suppress it, but I hope you'll see this as a blessing and not a curse."

"I'm beginning to think that's possible," Malcolm said.

MONDAY WAS HALLOWEEN. I THOUGHT ABOUT TAKING the kids trick or treating in our own neighborhood, one last goodbye. Sure, the Savants knew our old address, but I guessed they were far too busy with internal politics to care about harassing us. In the end, though, I didn't think I could bear seeing that burned-out husk again, so we drove to Judy's neighborhood instead as had been the original plan.

The Savants hadn't contacted anyone associated with the Wardens since Castellan's death, more evidence that they were preoccupied with their power struggle. I hoped Eris Reichert didn't end up in power, though that seemed an unlikely hope, given how she'd been Castellan's main henchwoman. I remembered our last encounter and involuntarily shuddered at the memory of her cruel smile.

"It's pretty cold tonight," Judy said, seeing me shiver. "I wonder how long the kids will endure the weather for the sake of tons of free candy?"

"Longer than I want to, based on past years," Viv said. Her slim, tall frame was bundled up more heavily against the cold than even I thought necessary, but Viv liked to claim she was part lizard and would bask in whatever heat was available.

We strolled along the sidewalk, watching Alastair and Kenny lead our little pack of costumed candy-grabbers. I'd been surprised to see Alastair insist that the older children keep an eye on Jenny and not outrun her, and more surprised that no one had argued. Maybe he was growing up faster than I'd realized. I wondered if Lucia realized her offhanded comment about Alastair coming back in six years was something he'd hold her to.

Jenny came running up in her daffodil costume to display her plastic pumpkin bucket half full of candy. "I got another peanut butter cup!"

"Wow, that's a lot of those. Mommy might need to test it to make sure it's good," I said. I was a firm believer in the Mom Halloween candy tax.

"Okay!" She ran off after Duncan, dressed in his Kerigon costume, and offered her hand to Sophia to hold. Sophia wore a Princess Aurora dress that was part blue and part pink over warm leggings and a thermal underwear shirt with long sleeves.

"Remember doing this when we were kids?" Viv asked. "There was that one year we were old enough to go by ourselves, the last year before we gave it up as being too juvenile."

"We each had a pillowcase full of candy," I mused. "I can't remember what costume I wore, but I remember the pillowcase."

"It's funny how some traditions stay the same over years and years." Judy flipped up her coat collar to warm her neck. "Though I remember there was one house that served hot apple cider when I was young. They wouldn't do that now."

"I've been thinking about traditions more, after everything that's happened," I said. "New ones, old ones. Things we can maintain versus ones we have to give up."

"That's depressing talk, Hel," Viv said. "You're alive. Focus on that. Too many people died for you not to take that seriously."

"I can't believe Ms. Stirlaugson is gone," Judy said. "Father says they're not sure how to reorganize the Board, without her and Erich Harrison. Its influence was waning anyway."

"I didn't think that was true," I exclaimed. "Not after how she and Lucia were always at odds over jurisdiction."

"That was mostly because of Ms. Stirlaugson holding things together." Judy stopped at the corner and waited for the kids to join us. "On the other hand, not everyone is thrilled at the possibility of Lucia picking up the reins of power."

"Yeah, but no one else can do it as well as she does," Viv said. "Like that Rebecca Greenough in London. She talks a good game, but she's all talk."

"I don't like her, so I'm just as happy for her not to take over." I tucked my hands under my arms. My gloves weren't as effective as I'd hoped. "Kids, how about we make this the last three houses?"

A chorus of groans rose up from the five children. "C'mon, Mom, our buckets aren't full!" Alastair protested. He was dressed as either Wilbur or Orville Wright—I couldn't tell the difference, but Alastair got testy about being misidentified—and looked the warmest of the five in his fleece-lined bomber jacket and leather cap with goggles.

I surveyed their eager faces and sighed. "All right. Up this side of the street and back down the other, and then it's back to Aunt Judy's house for hot chocolate and candy exchanges, all right?"

They all shouted for joy and took off, with Alastair at the back tugging Jenny along with him. "That's so sweet how he looks out for his little sister," I said.

Viv snorted. "You didn't hear what he told the others about why Jenny was important. Apparently having an adorable toddler along increases the likelihood of them getting extra candy."

I gasped. Then I laughed. "I guess he's still a kid, after all."

We strolled along after the children, keeping them in sight. More parents walked ahead of us in both directions. I smiled automatically at an approaching couple. Then my smile froze. "It's Maddy and Bronson," I whispered.

Viv and Judy immediately turned their heads, surveying the street. "I don't see them," Judy said.

"It's an illusion," Viv said, and whipped her bag off her shoulder to dig through it for her illusion-piercing lenses.

I stopped her with a hand on her arm. "It's fine. Let me talk to them. I'll be right back." I walked forward to where the two had stopped and were watching me closely.

"I thought you were long gone," I said when I neared them.

Both of them startled. "You can see beyond our illusion?" Maddy exclaimed.

"The oracular gift isn't my only ability," I said. "But it doesn't matter now, does it? What are you doing here?"

"We have to go on the run for real this time," Bronson said, "but we couldn't abandon everything without making our lives more difficult. So we took advantage of the Savants' distraction to wind up our affairs here."

"And we figured, why not give Liv a chance to say goodbye?" Maddy added. "We knew the trick-or-treating plan and took a chance on it still being on."

I looked past them to where Liv, dressed almost exactly as Alastair was, was comparing the contents of her bucket to Alastair's. Tears came to my eyes unexpectedly, and I blinked them away. "I'm glad," I managed.

"We saw what's left of your house," Maddy said. "I guess we're not the only ones uprooting. I'm sorry. If we'd been more suspicious of Mr. Castellan—"

"He'd have gone on sending people until he found one with no scruples," I said. "I don't blame you, and Castellan is dead. Thank you, Bronson. I don't understand how killing affects adepts, but I know it hurt you."

"It was the right thing to do," Bronson said. "But I'll never forget."

"Can you still work magic?" I asked impulsively, not sure if it was an insensitive question. But they *had* indirectly blown up my house, so I figured I was due some insensitive prodding.

"I can, but the complicated stuff is harder." Bronson didn't sound offended by my nosiness. "If my overall abilities are weaker, it won't be something I notice until I'm right up at the edge of what I can do. But I'm not going to be careless."

"You aren't in the habit of shooting people," Maddy said. "I don't think it's an issue."

"I was about to ask where you'll go next, but that's none of my business," I said.

"We don't know how the current Savant leadership, whatever it is, feels about us. So we intend to disappear thoroughly. More thoroughly than whatever Mr. Castellan's people did to hide our histories before." Maddy smiled. "Who knows? Maybe someday it won't matter anymore who knows about us, and we'll see you again."

"Good luck." I glanced at Liv again. "And I hope things work out for your daughters. Alastair will miss Liv."

"And she'll miss him. But you never know. They could end up at the same university, in the same engineering course..." Bronson smiled. "Good luck to you, too, Helena."

I watched them as they joined Liv and the other children, heard the protests, saw the Hubbards and Liv walk away in the opposite direction. Then I strolled up to the tiny group and said, "Everything all right?"

"We wanted Liv to stay, but her parents said no," Alastair said. "She's moving away like we are. Now it's just Kenny at Talbott Academy."

"You'll stay in touch," I said, not caring that this was possibly a security breach. I couldn't bear the thought of Alastair losing both his close friends at once. "And it's getting late. You'd better move if you want to finish this street before Aunt Viv freezes solid!"

The five children raced off, shouting. How easily the pains of childhood could be overridden, even if only for a moment. I was sure Alastair would remember Liv for a long time.

I became aware of Viv and Judy flanking me. "What did that look like?" I asked.

"Like you were chatting with an unmemorable couple who didn't look anything like the Hubbards," Judy said. "What did they say?"

"Just... goodbye. Hopes for the future. It's maybe too much to ask that the Savants stop hunting them, even though I think it was Castellan who considered them traitors. But they have to worry about their family's safety, just like I do." I could barely see the Hubbards at the end of the street. They turned the corner, and were gone.

The three of us walked in silence, keeping within earshot of the racing children as they reached that same corner. Then we crossed the street as they did. Judy rubbed her arms. "I'm definitely too old to be the mother of an active six-year-old."

"You're forty. That's, like, the new twenty-five," Viv objected

"Well, nights like this it feels like the new fifty."

"Hot chocolate," I murmured. "With marshmallows."

I took another step, and a prophecy lifted me up, rushing through me like a hot wind that banished every trace of the freezing October night. The immaterial wind lifted me off my feet and carried me aloft, through a cloudbank that felt and smelled like cotton candy and to the top of a tall peak. Snow covered the mountain, but I still didn't feel cold.

A flicker of flame burned the cotton candy clouds away, and I looked down from my height at broad plains of yellow grass, blowing wildly. And there, below me, was the city emerging from the mountainside that I'd seen before. The elf city.

As if my recognition was a trigger, the wind swept me away so I was flying or falling or gliding toward the city and its new-penny copper gates. As I slowed and hovered before the gates, they opened, and hundreds of elves surged forward, their terrifyingly undead features making them seem like a zombie horde.

I was normally a total chicken when it came to horror movies. Now, though, I stood my ground, unafraid and even a little angry. I raised a hand to halt their progress, and to my surprise, the wave of elves stopped.

The elf at the head of the wave stared at me. He looked old, though that might have been his tangled white hair, so different from any of the other elves'. Then he raised his hand in mimicry of mine—

—and in another breath, the vision dissolved, and the children were clamoring around me, with Jenny crying. "Wait," I said, trying to regain my composure. "What happened? Is Jenny hurt?"

"I fell down," Jenny wept, "and my candy spilled. I saw the—"

"She saw something scary, some costume," Alastair said, his eyes wide. He jerked his head in Kenny's direction.

I got the hint. "Jenny, did they help you gather up your candy? How about you stay with me. You've got so much—look, your pumpkin is nearly full! Alastair, how many houses left?"

"Just four," Alastair said, with a pleading look that clearly said *please do not make us stop just because Jenny had a prophecy that scared her.*

"You all go finish, and meet us here," I said. I picked Jenny up and said, "Are you hurt?"

"I saw the scary elf," Jenny said. "And he saw me and he was going to get me!"

"That is not going to happen," I said. "He can't get you."

"But they can see us," Jenny whimpered.

I remembered my own vision and closed my eyes to banish the memory. "I know, and we'll figure something out. You were very brave."

"I put a fence between us, but I think he can break it," Jenny said. "But Daddy will stop him."

"He will, don't worry." To Judy and Viv, I said, "That was a coincidence. I saw elves, too, and I know they saw me."

"That can't be good," Judy said. "Even if they can't reach you physically, how sure are you you're protected in vision?"

"Not sure at all." I stroked Jenny's thick blonde hair. "But I'm serious about figuring something out. I'm sure I can prophesy a solution."

"Or prophesy a way to use the link against them," Viv said, sounding unusually serious.

"Against them?" I exclaimed.

"It's war, Helena," Viv said. "Callann was a declaration of war. And in war, you do whatever it takes to win."

I didn't know why her words chilled me more deeply than the night air. Obviously the oracle would be needed to fight this enemy, just the way it had been during the Long War. But I had been thinking of a similar kind of help, prophecies about where to attack or where to counter the elves' incursions. Viv's statement had sounded more like a call to arms.

Jenny wiggled in my arms, and I set her down and took her hand. "You're right, Viv," I said slowly. "I intend to do whatever it takes to win."

ACKNOWLEDGMENTS

This book took a lot of work and existed in two completely different forms before settling into what you've just read. Thanks for helping me figure out what story I wanted to tell go to Jacob Proffitt and Jana Brown. More thanks for enthusiastic proofreading go to Teleri Proffitt. All mistakes remain my own.

About the Author

Melissa McShane is the author of many other fantasy novels, including the Warmaster LitRPG series, beginning with *Warmaster 1: Dungeon Spiteful; Burning Bright,* first in The Extraordinaries series; and *The Book of Secrets,* first book in The Last Oracle series.

While her home remains in the Western US, she currently lives in Kerala, India, with her husband and two rambunctious Persian kittens. She wrote reviews and critical essays for many years before turning to fiction, which is much more fun than anyone ought to be allowed to have. You can visit her at her website **www.melissamc shanewrites.com** for more information on other books and upcoming releases.

For news on upcoming releases, bonus material, and other fun stuff (including kitten pictures), sign up for Melissa's newsletter at **www.melissamcshanewrites.com/contact-me-2/join-my-mail-ing-list/**

If you enjoyed this book, please consider leaving a review at your favorite online bookseller!

ALSO BY MELISSA MCSHANE

THE LIVING ORACLE
Hidden Realm

Hidden Enemy

Hidden Pursuit

WARMASTER
Warmaster 1: Dungeon Spiteful

Warmaster 2: Winter's Peril

Warmaster 3: Gamboling Coil

Warmaster 4: Sorrowvale

Warmaster 5: The Glory Games (coming 2024)

THE BOOKS OF THE DARK GODDESS
Silver and Shadow

Missing by Moonlight

Shades of the Past

Path of the Paladin

Bright Moon Deception (coming 2024)

THE EXTRAORDINARIES
Burning Bright

Wondering Sight

Abounding Might

Whispering Twilight

Voyager of the Crown

Tales of the Crown

COMPANY OF STRANGERS

Company of Strangers

Stone of Inheritance

Mortal Rites

Shifting Loyalties

Sands of Memory

Call of Wizardry

THE DRAGONS OF MOTHER STONE

Spark the Fire

Faith in Flames

Ember in Shadow

Skies Will Burn

THE CONVERGENCE TRILOGY

The Summoned Mage

The Wandering Mage

The Unconquered Mage

THE BOOKS OF DALANINE

The Smoke-Scented Girl

The God-Touched Man

Emissary

Warts and All: The Deluxe Expanded Edition

The View from Castle Always

Winter Across Worlds: A Holiday Collection